Printed in Great Britain
by Amazon

24618328R00169

Cover illustration by 2V Studios

ISBN 978-1-7393893-2-1

www.sophietoovey.com

To teachers everywhere,
and the National Education Union,
who have fought for better workload, pay and conditions for us since 1870.
My PPA and pension are forever in your debt.

'What is this life if, full of care,
We have no time to stand and stare.'

William Henry Davies

1

THE END

I type the final words with a flourish, then shout,

'Yes!'

Pressing play on my music app, Gloria Gaynor kicks in, so I leap to my feet and attempt to victory-dance around my bar stool. Sixty-eight thousand words of faeries, castles and assassins: DONE, baby! My dance move repertoire is limited and I end up playing invisible maracas around my ears. Then I fist pump the lampshade and the lightbulb swings precariously, dust motes swirling through the air.

'Go!' I cry dramatically, pointing at my yellowing, off-white door.

I'm about to add in a wiggle of my hips for effect, moving my arm out to the side and pointing to the beat, but I nearly knock my laptop over and hastily shunt it further into the rickety table. It's served me for ten years and a loud sneeze might cause it to restart. Danger averted, I grab my phone and snap a picture of my document screen, sending it to my Whatsapp VIPs. Katie, my sister, responds first.

Katie: Well done. Too bad you didn't come with us. Look at the view!

She sends me a photo of our family tent, pitched a little lopsided as usual, with a random dog in the foreground. She's a bit obsessed with dogs. I remember the last time we went camping, she kept fussing over the dog from our neighbour's tent, and every time I saw it, it was peeing against our windbreak. There have been many August bank holidays where the weather definitely wasn't as good as this, but it's typical that the heatwave is the one I opt out from. The feeling of Missing Out acts like a stealthy pinprick to my balloon of success; it starts to deflate and I hurry to repair the damage.

I finished my first draft.

Yes, I've not gone anywhere all summer, and my flat is still in need of replastering/redecorating/demolishing and rebuilding, but I've achieved my goal and now there is a young adult fantasy novel that previously existed only in my head.

Maybe if I'd gone camping, it would have rained anyway.

My phone lights up: this time it's the WC girls' group. It's short for Whidlock County girls, but yes, we chose a toilet door sign for our icon just to be cool. Over time the group has dwindled to just me, Deena and Clare, the two friends I've held onto from school. They're both in London now, something I try not to feel jealous about.

Deena: Yes! You did it. Well done Cassandra xx

Deena's always joking that I'm like Jane Austen's wannabe sister. It's useful having friends who did A Level English just so they appreciate period dramas.

Clare: Fantastic achievement Jen. Can't wait to read it! Xx

I smile and put my phone down on the table. The cursor on the laptop blinks at me, like it can't quite believe it either. This is the first time I've finished a complete draft.

I look out of my dingy flat window to see the bright blue sky. I'll be back in work tomorrow when the new school term starts, and then it'll probably rain for six weeks' straight.

I head outside for a walk in the not-so-scenic streets, determined to get at least a bit more vitamin D before the autumn kicks in. If there was a heat map of the world showing where I've made the most steps, Whidlock would look like an inferno contained in a postage stamp, because I've pretty much lived here my whole life.

It's weird when you're in a place which hasn't changed, but you've grown up and become someone else… Or at least, some modified version of yourself. It means that everywhere you walk, you tread on the off-cuts of your past, and then you realise they're still part of the fabric of your life.

When I see the salon where my mum used to work, I can still smell the sulphuric, throat-clogging mousse, and feel the silky cover-up garment she would whip around me and fasten at the back of my neck.

'Remember, I'm the only person allowed to touch your hair,' she would say, wearing her own hair in her naturally tight curls and refusing me every time I asked for her to relax or straighten mine. She would style my afro curls but she told me to take pride in my hair, rather than wishing it was different.

For a bleak moment, I wonder if my mum would have been proud of me now. What would she have said about my first draft? As an artist, she would have understood the uphill struggle of getting to this ending. If she had read it, would she see herself in the ethereal mother who disappears?

There's no point thinking thoughts like this. Time to focus on happier things. I grin, remembering my cardboard cylinder package that arrived this morning. It makes going back to school tomorrow bearable – just.

Whidlock County is a 1960s concrete monstrosity that brands itself as a *high school,* when in reality it's a comp with more holes in the roof than the local golf course. It smells of bleach (the aggressive kind that chokes up your throat) and is somehow designed so that the smallest amount of natural light can filter through the grubby windows, making the harsh tube lighting a necessity. It makes my flat look half-decent, the way that a moped makes a three-wheeled car look preferable. (In England, a roof is essential for any transportation device, because no one likes drowning. Besides that, you need an engine with more power than a clogged-up Hoover.)

There are barely any cars in the car park; I always like to arrive early on the first day of term. I walk on autopilot through the quiet corridors. I could probably do this blindfolded. I was a pupil here, and now I'm a teacher.

My classroom is narrow with enough desks for fifteen students, so around half the usual size. There's a door at either end –the heavy type that swings open and crashes against the wall on the other side– and the walls are painted the same orange as Fanta. Between the draught and tiny radiators, the room always stays about five degrees colder than anywhere else. Yes, it actually used to be a corridor, but when your school has no money, desperate times call for desperate measures.

I open my tube package, and pull out the Magic Bullet for all my life problems.

It's the perfect cat poster. Cute striped kitten with added 80s neon headband, arms stretched above its head, jumping off the ground with the word 'Believe' emblazoned across the top. It embodies my positive-thinking philosophy and will goad my boss, Geoff. He says he's a realist; I say he's the dwarf whose name rhymes with 'Dumpy'. I unroll the shiny paper and smooth it into position on the wall, pressing my fingers over the lumps of Blu-tack. My classroom walls are jam-packed, but I'm giving this new addition a prime spot.

This is how I cope as a young teacher in a struggling school: cat posters. And enough tea and biscuits to outdo even my grandparents' church, which had a monthly delivery of fifteen kilos of custard creams. Given that they were a fairly small, tight community, that's a high ratio of packets per head, and for a biscuit which I personally feel has been long over-rated.

The door opens. Thinking it must be Geoff, I immediately spin around, waving jazz hands with a gleeful grin.

'Ta da!'

It isn't Geoff.

Standing well over six feet in an immaculate suit, blue pinstripe shirt and tie, a man stands in the doorway, with the shocked look of someone who's just walked in on the dinner ladies' fundraiser performance of *Chicago*. He's pale; perhaps the shock has blanched him. I quickly lower my arms and attempt to recalibrate. I haven't seen a good-looking guy on site since the fire brigade visited last term, due to the mischievous (that's Whidlock code for *delinquent*) Year 7s who used bunsen burners to melt a laminated wall chart of the Periodic table.

'Sorry, I thought you were Geoff.'

I give what I hope is an endearing smile (side note– my smile is often cited as one of my best features, thanks to several years of braces torture), but he doesn't return it. Instead, his grey eyes flicker from the cat poster to each of the other walls of my classroom. I've built up five years of colourful displays which I think work with the bright backdrop quite well. I think that's lost on him, though, judging by the way he's assessing them in a three-second inclination of his head.

'Is this a *classroom*?'

He's got dark hair and the sort of lean frame that makes him look athletic, like a runner. New recruit for the PE department? PE teachers don't wear suits though.

I blink.

'Yes. I'm Jen. I teach English.'

Ordinarily I would hold out my hand, but he's looking at me as if I said I teach Martian. It's as if he's walked out of an Armani advert –dark hair, clean shaven, chiselled jaw. Maybe I've overdosed on caffeine and I'm hallucinating. English teachers have very over-active imaginations. But as the minutes pass, he's still staring at me, and I become more self-conscious of my skinny jeans and heart print patterned T-shirt. I wonder if I even look like a teacher to him; I probably look like I'm on the way to a gig. I could probably still pass for a student. He could be anywhere between 25 and 35. It feels slightly incongruous that he's in Whidlock County, where most kids' families are on state benefits and where staff appearances divide neatly into two categories: too frayed to care or already mid-nervous breakdown. I'm not sure which I fall into.

'Jen… What is that short for? Jenny or Jennifer?' he leans forward slightly, looming about a foot taller than me. Hair included.

Feeling slightly annoyed with the level of scrutiny this stranger is subjecting me to, I shift backwards a little.

'Jennifer.'

No one calls me that.

'I thought this was a corridor.'

He's looking left and right as if he's about to cross a road.

'Actually, it was once… I used to have a locker here when I was a student.'

'You were a student here?' his eyes lock onto me again. His unflinching stare pins me like a lopsided cat poster to the wall.

'Yes, funny, isn't it?'

He still isn't smiling. It's the first day of the school year, and we've just had six weeks off, and there are no kids in school because it's a training day. If you can't smile at this point, then you must be VERY hard to please.

'And your name is...?' I finally ask.

'Michael.'

'Not Mike or Mikey then?' I attempt a joke.

He raises an eyebrow.

'No.'

'Mickey?'

He straightens his shoulders and brushes imaginary dust from the front of his suit. 'I was looking for Geoff. Do you know that clock is wrong?'

I follow his gaze to where the clock is frozen at six thirty.

'I need to change the battery.' I mentally add this to my to-do list. 'I'm not looking forward to setting my alarm tomorrow!'

'I hate getting up late,' he says bluntly. Ouch. 'You can get more done in the morning when no one's around. What time do they open the building?'

Colin, the caretaker who lives in a house at the edge of the site, seems to be here at all hours, his keys jangling on his belt. He's always carrying materials to burn in his incinerator in the backyard. His philosophy: get there before the Year 7s. The eco committee has slowly started introducing more recycling, but Whidlock's carbon footprint rivals New York.

'Seven thirty I think.'

'It's cold in here.'

Wow, this guy is a machine gun. He makes Geoff look like the Believe kitten.

'Yes, it is a bit of an ice box. I've got my booster heater for the winter.' I nudge my toe towards my rickety oil radiator; I don't make contact or it will fall over. He wrinkles his nose.

'How do I get to Geoff's room?'

I can see him assessing the different doorways at either end of my classroom. His gaze is quick, analytical, like it could slice me in two. It's true that it's probably the quickest way to the department through my room, but I don't want him to think he can march through when I'm teaching.

'Well, I don't mind if you want to go through here today. You can go out through the other door. But usually you'd have to go round the long way, outside,' I nod towards the window, which is covered in grime, and then a protective security grille. Beyond that, you can just about see the path leading to the main entrance of the block, which has a corrugated roof so that the rain gushes off and creates an ideally-placed fountain for Year 8 boys to stand under and soak themselves on a wet day.

'Right.'

I keep meaning to clean that window. Or mention it to the janitor. Ah, well. I give it one last appraisal, then turn back to find that Michael is striding towards the door and is gone before I can say anything else. I'm not sure what just happened, but I feel the heat of my cheeks with my palms. Maybe he's another emissary from Inspire to Achieve, the private company who are responsible for making sure our school doesn't get shut down. Hopefully he'll find Geoff, my Head of Department, ask a few pointless questions, then disappear and leave us to get on with the real work here. These suited professionals look polished, but are about as much use as a fire drill during your free lesson when it comes to turning a failing school around. I just want to do my job, in my corridor-converted-classroom that makes you feel like you've been Tangoed, because it's all I've got.

I guess I was hoping that by this stage in my life I would have bought my own place and found a guy who was not either intensely obsessive or basically indifferent to me. Oh, and published a novel.

Given that I rent a bedsit and the last date I went on was over a year ago, I'm not doing too well on these life goals. But I have spent many hours creating colourful, vibrant displays – it's the artistic gene I inherited from my mum.

I wonder how many hours of my life I've spent in this room.

A depressing amount.

Last year was probably the second worst year of my life. No, make it the *third* worst. In first place: the year my mum died. In second place: the year before she died, when she left us to go to Jamaica. Then last year, I moved into the bedsit, my school was put on the 'red list', and the Head decided it was time to retire. So that's in third place in my rank order of Worst Years Ever.

It's no wonder I haven't been on a date; my own family probably needs to ID-check me against my passport because I've been buried under mounds of paperwork. So much of the 'support' visits and check-ups just sap all the joy out of teaching. When I look at my display boards with my favourite book covers, fanning out like a rainbow, it lifts my spirits. And the cat poster… Perfect.

By this time next year, I will have saved enough for a deposit on a house with a garden. Maybe I'll get a real cat. Neither intensely obsessive, nor basically indifferent. Just someone for company. And I will have redrafted my story so that it's ready to send out into the world.

I've got this. Believe.

2

I retrieve my Little Miss Sunshine mug from its secret hiding place in the filing cabinet (side note– we teachers are the worst for 'borrowing' things, and never giving them back. Then normalising our behaviour. Then justifying it. And now, even as an English teacher, I'm not even sure I could give you anything close to a dictionary definition of 'theft'). The cabinets in the staffroom are never opened by any of us, so it's a good bonus storage space which I'm borrowing. I grab a teabag and fill the cup while others bustle around, stocking up the fridge with cartons of milk and lunch boxes, some of which probably have padlocks on. It's always lovely to see everyone again and catch up after six weeks of holidays, lie-ins, day trips, and trying to avoid thinking about school in any way, shape or form.

'Jen!'

My best friend Steph, pushing the staff training smart-casual dress code to the limit with flip flops and a bright pink sundress, squishes me in a warm hug as I try to put my tea down to avoid it spilling everywhere.

'Steph, I loved all your photos. I'm so jealous.'

She looks fantastic, as always, with her shining brown eyes and pixie haircut. Her rich brown skin exudes sunshine. She evaluates me with a frown.

'Jen, you've got to start travelling more. You should have come with me!'

I stir my teabag round the mug. I'd decided that I needed to save and write, not spend a load of cash on expensive flights, but now I'm wondering if I made the right choice. The school year's starting again and summer's the best opportunity to travel.

'Maybe next year.'

Something else to add to my list. Ignoring the niggle of self-doubt, I grab my small bottle of (labelled) milk from the fridge, already crowded enough that moving one thing makes the whole shelf wobble.

'How's your writing?'

At least I have good news on that.

'I finished my first draft.' I can't help the smug smile. I've been talking about my story to Steph for months.

'Awesome! When am I going to see it on Amazon?'

I roll my eyes.

'When you've set me up a crowdfunder and made a generous donation.'

It would be great if someone decided to foot the bill so that my Alice in Wonderland mash-up with an assassin who falls in love with her target could be enjoyed by more people than just me.

'Quick! The new head's about to make a speech!' Sue from the Maths department hisses at us through the doorway.

'Can't even finish a conversation, let alone a novel,' I moan, dumping the tea bag in the bin and hurrying into the seating area.

'Good morning everyone,' the crisp tones of Janet Patchell, deputy head, cut through the murmuring chatter. She's wearing her familiar blue two-piece suit. 'I'd like to hand over to our new head, David Clark.'

'Thank you, Janet.'

I look at his familiar snake-oil-salesman smile and try not to frown too severely. It's been eight years but he hasn't changed a bit. He's impossibly young to be a Head; he's barely ten years older than me and there's something desperately teenage about his dark hair, waxed into position, clean shaven jaw and smooth cheeks. It suddenly feels like I am seventeen again, sitting in the History classroom, with the wet-behind-the-ears teacher-training version of David Clark shuffling his papers and reading out my notes on the French Revolution. Same smarmy hair, probably a cheaper brand of wax than his executive Head salary would afford him now.

I remember he played us some clips from the History channel and I could tell he'd never studied the topic, because he kept getting the dates mixed up and forgetting one of the three core values (liberty, equality, *fraternity*, come on David, this is on the pub quiz syllabus, never mind the Bachelor's degree). There was actually a fourth value: death. I wrote about it in an essay, which I found photocopied as a handout a few years later. He'd been using it with all his GCSE classes.

Only instead of my name at the top, it was his.

Now he's here to save my school. And he's packing double the wax.

'Whidlock County is a school that's always been close to my heart. I came here as a pupil, and in my first teaching post, before I moved to Cassley High. When I heard that the school was struggling and in danger of closing, I knew it was time for me to give something back.'

My eyes roll before I can even stop them. And they're twitching for a few more laps, held back only by some extreme mental discipline that Derren Brown would be proud of. It would have been great if he had just done his job properly when he was here as a teacher ten years ago, rather than painting himself as the saviour now.

'I've been sent here by our regional consortium, Inspire to Achieve, along with a few of my hand-picked leading practitioners: Joseph Vermont, to work in the Maths department, and Michael Chase, to work in the English department.'

I was right: Michael is another sharp-suited professional sent by the consultants, who earn more than three average staff put together. Only this time, he's going to be in the same department as me.

Joseph and Michael step forward to flank David. The three of them together look like they're posing for a Gillette commercial. I wouldn't be surprised if they all had matching cufflinks with the 'Inspire to Achieve' logo branded on them. I stifle a snort, making a slight sound. Michael stares at me and I look away quickly. Those razor eyes look like they could read minds. I need to keep my imagination on a tighter leash.

'We are here to raise standards,' David continues, in a tone that initially sounds collaborative, but which rapidly solidifies into the kind of top-down collaboration constructed from reinforced concrete. Tyranny. 'We all know a new approach is necessary. I might make decisions that you don't like, but I ask for you to keep an open mind. After all, we all want the same thing.'

I catch Steph's eye. She raises an eyebrow.

When the motivational –at times threatening– address is over, I stumble my way forwards, thinking it's best to get the first meeting over with. I mean, it might be awkward, but I need to be friendly and hopefully we can put the past behind us. He was a newly qualified teacher; he must have improved, otherwise he wouldn't be a super-executive head being paid an eye-watering salary.

David is talking in a low voice with Michael when I approach, smiling in what I hope is a 'let's make a fresh start' expression. When he notices me, a flash of recognition changes his face, and he stiffens, standing taller. My smile falters.

'Just wanted to say hello,' I say quickly, hoping to cover over the awkwardness.

'How welcoming,' he says, extending a hand. 'What's your name?'

Now I've had my share of bumping into ex-students unexpectedly, even just in the last two years, when they look totally different to their sixteen-year-old self. Girls perhaps can transform the most radically, with hair colour and style, weight loss or gain, and the power of make-up. But I'm not a transformer. I find photos of myself in school and I look almost exactly the same now– plus I was one of a small minority of Black and bi-racial kids. I also think it's fair to say that I wasn't a wallflower. I was on every committee that the school could possibly invent (allotment committee, Fairtrade committee, the committees-approval committee). I'm also the one whose mum died, which seems to be another of my distinguishing features.

No, he remembers me. Short of him presenting a medical certificate certifying amnesia (and caused by something even more violent than sustained application of hair wax) I know he's lying through his shiny teeth.

I blink as I take his slippery, lukewarm hand. His grip is just slightly tighter than comfortable.

'This is Jennifer,' Michael breaks in. 'She's in my department.'

Like he owns it. I turn my frown upon him and withdraw my hand from David's grip.

'What was your surname? I don't think I caught it,' Michael adds.

'Baker,' I say with a meaningful stare at David, who still gives me a politely-bemused-I-don't-know-you look in return. 'You taught me. A Level History: the French Revolution module. Liberty, equality, fraternity and death.'

I know he read out my essay enough to probably have memorised it, so I'm not buying his act one bit.

'Oh really?' he gives a tone of fake surprise. 'How strange. I can't remember you at all.'

I give a bark of laughter.

'I suppose you must have taught so many students over the years,' I say, with an understanding smile. 'It's funny, I can't actually remember what you *taught* me. Just that you were my teacher.'

I walk away and feel both of them glaring at my back.

When all of the boring or terrifying presentations have been given by various members of Senior Management (safeguarding, trips, pastoral care structure, behavioural policy), and we've eaten our free lunch (chicken curry), it's finally time to sit down in the department with a cup of tea, packet of biscuits, and chat about what we're actually meant to be teaching when the kids come in tomorrow.

Geoff heads up the table, with his usual checked shirt and jeans: standard first day back. He's got one of those awful clinical grey diaries and scrawls in it using a black rollerball pen. Next to him is Judy, looking majestically unfazed as usual with her black and pink silk scarf and dyed black hair. She's in her early sixties, and she's part time. Liz is sat two seats away from anyone else, her hair ironed flat and her fake nails tapping the desk impatiently. She's been the second in Department for years and is quite happy doing as little as possible and disappearing when the bell goes. Michael sits, his back poker straight, and a black organiser open in front of him. Using an expensive silver pen, he forms his letters precisely without loops and flair. His page is neater than a printed handout, and if it were a font, it would be Times New Roman. Whereas my scrawl looks more intelligent than Comic Sans, but only just. I pull out my flower-patterned diary and fish in my bag for a pen, then remember I stuck it under my headband earlier. I pull out the biro and click it, trying to look ready to make notes. Out of the corner of my eye, I see Michael roll his eyes.

'Welcome back, everyone,' Geoff begins. There's a slight hesitancy in his voice. 'I'd like to welcome Michael into the department.'

He gives a curt nod, his pen hovering over the page impatiently.

'I've got copies of your finalised timetables,' Geoff passes round sheets of paper, the black grids just waiting to be colour coded. Where are my highlighters? 'We had to make a few changes…'

I cast my eye over the class codes. Geoff had already spoken to me in the summer about which classes I was taking: the usual Year 7, 8 and 9, and my exam classes. I'm excited about piloting a small group of Year 10 students from the Additional Learning Needs (ALN) register, students I mentored last year. Then I notice a code I don't recognise.

'What's 11 B?' I ask.

At the same time, Michael says,

'What's 10 F?'

I look at him.

'That's my mentor group. It must be a mistake, you're not supposed to have them.'

'11 B is my group: I asked for a group of boys who are borderline D to C grade.'

We both look at Geoff, who coughs awkwardly.

'Well, there was a bit of a clash, and so we had to do a few swaps here and there.'

'Who's in the boys' group?' I ask immediately.

With a flip of his organiser, Michael begins reading out a list of the worst behaved boys in the school. I groan.

'What's this mentor group?' he asks.

'It's a nurturing environment for students with ALN.'

Michael's nostrils flare slightly.

'Let's discuss timetables later,' Geoff intervenes hurriedly, before Michael can kick up a fuss. 'We need to look at the curriculum.'

Geoff goes through the different topics for the term and the schemes of work, while Liz looks out of the window and I start doodling in my notebook. It's all quite familiar to me now. I'm trying not to let the thought of an all-boy class terrify me. Especially one that makes Goldie Lookin Chain seem like prep schoolers.

'Anyone want to share any resources that might help us kick off the new term with a bang?' Geoff's voice breaks into my thoughts.

My brain's still in summer mode. I struggle to locate my 'archive' file in my memory.

'I've got something,' Michael jumps up and puts a USB stick from his keyring into the computer. He opens the folder to reveal hundreds of folders, all meticulously labelled. My jaw nearly drops. How can anyone be that organised?

He opens up a PowerPoint, and there's a 3x3 grid with letters in each square.

'It's called Bell Time.'

It's basically the game Boggle, rebranded to be a teacher's starter when you don't know what else to do at the beginning of the lesson while Riley is still kicking a football around the yard but keen bean Ben is sitting waiting for the lesson to start.

'Students make as many words as they can from the letters. I run a competition and see who's got the highest number by the end of the week. Boys love it.'

He looks at me pointedly when he says this, as if he wants to give me some tips.

'Thanks, Michael, that's great,' Geoff says. He's still holding something back. He takes a deep breath. 'Well, there's something I need to tell you all… As you know, last year I was temporarily seconded to the Senior Leadership team when Janet was promoted to Deputy. David has negotiated with the governors to create a permanent Assistant Head position, and he very much wants to give this role to me, which I didn't expect.'

'That's really exciting Geoff,' I smile. He has been a seriously great boss, I am not surprised at all that David wants him on leadership.

'Thanks Jen,' he says. 'I'm just a bit sad to be less involved with the department.'

'What do you mean?'

'I can't do the Head of Department role and this Senior responsibility at the same time. Whilst I was seconded, I've been doing both– but it'll be a relief to just focus on the one job and do it properly. I've still got to go through the formality of an interview for the position, and they may get other applicants, but I wanted to tell you now to give you a heads up. David wants to appoint a new HoD and I expect he'll want to work closely with you, Liz, to help to manage the transition.'

Liz's face turns a shade of deep purple. I think she's forgotten to breathe.

'We've got a few weeks before it all takes effect,' Geoff continues. 'So let's focus on starting the term as we mean to go on!'

I exchange a worried look with Judy. Liz helping to 'manage the transition'? That would involve her actually doing something besides chain-smoking and eating Haribo. The sooner they can recruit someone, the better.

Then I catch a glimpse of Michael's face. He's not surprised to hear any of this, and he's underlining a note in his diary with a smug smile. My eyes narrow and I highlight my timetable with the same force I would use to restrain Year 9 from leaving early on a Tuesday afternoon. The positivity of the cat poster is already a distant memory, and I've been here less than twenty-four hours. This does not bode well.

3

It's chaos in the photocopying room the next morning.

I dash around, spilling my tea, and gather up all of the sheets, grids and target stickers I need. Bundling everything into my classroom, I nearly collide with Michael, who is walking straight through.

'Watch out!' I sway unsteadily, like a cartoon character suffering from an encounter with Taz from Looney Tunes.

'Sorry.' He manages to dodge around me and continues towards the door.

'You need to go round the long way next time,' I call after him. I'm sensing I've lost this battle before it's even begun.

I prepare all of my PowerPoints and check the clock on the wall. Then remember that I forgot to change the battery.

The bell rings.

It's standard fare with my form of Year 7s. They are pretty terrified and practically need help to pick up a pen. It takes nearly the whole of the extended registration time to get them to write their names on their homework diaries. There's just enough time to run a quick icebreaker game before break.

'Vote with your feet,' I explain, ushering them all to stand. 'Cookies or cake?'

I point to the two opposite walls and smile as the kids giggle and stampede to their wall of choice. Cake wins.

'The bell is about to go,' I announce, and on cue, the blaring klaxon sounds. 'Time for break, everyone.'

They shuffle out, just as Michael's head pokes round the other door. He sniffs the air, making a face.

'Smells like you've got a herd of animals in here.'

'Just Year 7s.'

He strides forward and knocks the wall, grimacing.

'I don't think much of the walls here. I hope your lessons aren't as noisy as that.'

I raise an eyebrow, crossing my arms in front of me. You want a showdown, cowboy? I'm ready.

'Lessons are about learning. No one learns in silence anymore.'

'So does that mean you've got some fun and games planned for your classes today? Maybe you should set up a dressing up box in your reading corner.'

He gives a sharp, dismissive nod to my area with bookshelves and two beanbags, and crosses his arms as well. Is he mimicking me? Or is this subconscious mirroring? I'm too busy psycho-analysing to give a witty retort.

'Maybe you should write 'Copyright Boggle' on your Bell Time PowerPoint.'

It's not a great comeback, and he knows it. With one raised eyebrow, he suddenly relaxes his arms and leans against the doorpost. His grey eyes stare at me intently, and I find my own arms lowering to an odd choirgirl pose with one hand crossed over the other. If I look down now I fully expect to see my old school tie and a pleated skirt instead of my own corduroy dress.

'Perhaps we should chat through some strategies for the all-boys' group,' he says, finally breaking the silence. 'I don't think your primary school resources are going to work on them.'

The insolence!

'I'm sure they'll be fine,' I say, with false confidence, turning away so I can't see him roll his eyes at me.

In reality, by the time it comes to meeting the group, my palms are sweaty and I'm checking the corridor, waiting for their imminent arrival. I haven't taught any of these individuals before, least of all as one testosterone-fuelled mass. I've had plenty of run-ins with them while being on yard duty though.

They bundle into the classroom and seem to fill it immediately, even though they are half the size of a normal class. Perhaps it's all the rugby kit bags. I take a look at my 'get-to-know-you' activity and make a quick decision to hand out their exercise books instead. All they have to do is write their name and mine, but there's a constant squall of noise as I write my name on the whiteboard for them to copy, and take the register.

'Tyler?' I call, looking around the room, reflecting that if this was a GP surgery, I'd get my hand bitten off every time I called someone's name. Sadly it's the afternoon graveyard slot and no one wants to be here. When I manage to make eye contact with one of them, they shrug and look out of the window.

It turns out that Tyler's the only one not here. I briskly introduce the first task: writing out what you want to do when you leave school, then sticking this in the front of your book as a reminder of your ambitions when it's Friday afternoon and you don't want to do any work. Or, judging by the slumping over the desks, any lesson at any time of day.

I circulate and see what the boys are writing: most of them want to go to college, which is heartening. I'm feeling quite pleased at the focus they're showing, despite the continued buzz of conversation, when the door opens and a tall, leaning boy saunters in.

'Tyler?' I address him, trying to keep my voice 'curious and neutral', as the behaviour handbook suggests. 'Why are you late?'

His hair is long and chaotic, over his eyes, and he's thin and spindly. His voice is surprisingly confident when he answers me.

'I was with Mr Myers.'

The Head of Year. He knows I can't argue with that. He finds a seat, smirking. The other boys quieten down, and it seems rather ironic that they give *him* such a respectful silence.

'We were just writing down our ambitions for when we leave school.'

I place a handout on the desk in front of him.

'Play Black Ops.'

The boys snigger. He obviously thinks he's hilarious.

'I meant something that you're *not* doing already.'

He looks more sullen now. I definitely lost the 'curious' and the 'neutral' is slipping into 'open lecture zone'.

'I'm sure most of you realise that passing English is going to be really important to get to where you want to go. I want all of you to have the opportunity to pursue the qualifications you need, and a 'C' grade will open doors for you to do that.'

I sense this class is going to need a lot of pep talks to get them through the next nine months until their exams.

As they're leaving at the end of the lesson, I notice Tyler talking in a low voice with another boy before going through the door. I tidy up, picking up various abandoned plastic bottles and shreds of paper on the floor, and I find a white business card on the floor with enigmatic text:

BEN

663344

I turn it over to look at the back: nothing. Who would bother to print a business card with only a first name and a phone number? Odd. I slip the card into my desk drawer, and when I turn back to clean the board, Michael's suddenly appeared, perching on the edge of one of the desks and surveying the room with darting eyes. I stifle a gasp.

'I didn't hear you come in.'

'So, how was my boys' group?' he says, scrutinising my face and completely ignoring my shock at seeing him apparate like Harry Potter.

I roll my eyes. Does he expect me to fall apart after just one lesson with them?

'Fine. Tyler is a bit challenging.'

He nods as though this is exactly what he expected, even though it's his first day in this school and I've been here for five years.

'I know it must be hard for you, as a female teacher…'

I give him my death stare and for once he shuts up.

'I thought I should ask you what you want me to do with your group tomorrow.'

I look at him suspiciously. He doesn't seem the co-operative type.

'Well, you could do the spelling diagnostic if you like? Then perhaps read something with them, an extract maybe?' Curious and neutral all over again. Who said behaviour management was just for kids?

He's still staring at me and I try to relax my face out of its frown.

'Any text in particular?'

'What do you like?' I imagine him reading Jason Bourne thrillers.

'Cormac McCarthy?'

Ugh, so depressing.

'No.'

'George Orwell?'

I make a face.

'Try something more middle-grade.'

'The Boy in the Striped Pyjamas?'

Grim but good.

'Sure.'

I turn away to stack some books onto the shelf, expecting him to disappear, but he doesn't.

'What did you think of Geoff's announcement yesterday?'

'About being promoted?' I bend over to retrieve some pens and glue sticks. 'I'm pleased for him.'

'Liz didn't seem very happy.'

I open my mouth, then close it again, straightening up. His eyes glow like a tiger's, ready to pounce. We hold each other's gaze.

'I know I'm new, but it won't take me long to find out what the lay of the land is, so you might as well just tell me.'

'Tell you what?' I stall.

'OK, I'll say it for you. She's been in that job for years and she doesn't lift a finger. Am I right?'

I turn away and busy myself with the clutter on my desk.

'Clearly I am,' he mutters to himself.

'Look, you can't just come in here…'

'And what? Don't you realise this school is on the verge of being shut down? That's what we're being paid to do, to come in and identify the dead weight.'

'Well I hate to think what you're going to say about me, then,' I challenge him.

His eyes glint.

'You obviously make a lot of effort,' he says carefully, while I wait for the axe to fall. 'I don't know how good you are, though.'

'I don't know how good you are, either.'

'You'll see,' he says immediately. 'I'll make sure of that. I take my job very seriously.'

'So do I.'

There is a pause while I put some rubbish in the bin.

'You really need to fix that clock.'

4

'I think he sounds majorly uptight,' my sister Katie pronounces as we scour through the sale rack on Saturday morning.

'That's an understatement.'

I sweep aside boring white tops and then I find it: a bright yellow shirt with pineapple print.

'And this is the opposite!' I hold it up in front of my T-shirt. 'What say you?'

'It's definitely on the zany side,' Katie rolls her eyes. 'But you're an English teacher; you can get away with it.'

'As long as I wear a silk scarf,' I add, mentally noting to check the accessories section.

'I can't believe the Head blanked you like that,' she says. It's sweet the way she always fights my corner. 'You should call him out on it.'

'I did try,' I shrug. 'It just makes me so angry that he's being paid some super salary to be a super executive whatsit and yet I've never seen him actually do anything good.'

'I wish I had more money,' Katie gives her usual moan as we queue for the checkout.

'This is your final year. You will earn more money than me in a depressingly short amount of time.'

'Well I've had to suffer a lot of indignities with farm animals to get this far.'

I consider Katie being a fully qualified vet. I hope she finds a job nearby. I don't know how Dad would take it if she moved across the country somewhere.

'Don't you ever think about finding a job that pays better?' she asks suddenly.

I frown.

'Money isn't everything.'

'No, but it helps. When are you going to move out of that horrible flat?'

'When I've saved enough.'

'You could save more if you lived with Dad, so that's not an argument,' Katie eyes me for my reaction. I give her an I-don't-want-to-talk-about-it look. 'I honestly couldn't bring myself to live in your flat, even if someone paid me!'

'Then it's a good thing it's me and not you.'

She's going back to uni tomorrow, and gives me a tight hug at the bus stop.

'Please… go and see Dad. Or at least call him,' she says, with her best puppy expression. She knows I can't resist it.

'I'll try,' I promise with a sigh.

When I get off the bus with my shopping bags and face the immediate heat, salt and swell in the air outside the chip shop, I plough on and up the steps to my one-bed flat next door.

'Been shopping, eh?' Sam the serial smoker offers his redundant comment in my wake.

'Yeah,' I call back over my shoulder.

Inside, the flat reminds me of Katie's student accommodation: wannabe shabby chic that's just shabby. I chose some patterned baby-blue curtains and matching cushion covers, but the grime of decades without proper cleaning gives everything a mangy, yellowed hue. Every surface has a sticky residue I can't get rid of. The stainless steel extractor in the kitchen is anything but stainless: I can see the drips of fat and grease clinging to the underside of the hood. One day I'll set the time aside to properly clean with bleach, boiling water, liquid nitrogen... It's fine. It's functional.

'Sam! Get your arse back in here.'

I can hear Gerry's dulcet tones through the wall as if it were made of tissue paper.

At least it's quiet in the mornings.

As I get ready for work on Monday, I am ready to start a new week. Pineapple shirt: check. Obligatory black silk scarf: check. I hesitate between black trousers (safe but boring) and a slightly edgy black pinafore dress. I choose the dress. I even find some pineapple earrings to complete the look. Perfect.

Just before I leave, I remember to scrawl a note to myself on the fridge: call Dad.

I get into the staffroom and head straight for the kitchen. Typical: Michael's in there. He's manoeuvring some gigantic coffee machine.

'Hi,' I say, finding a space to make my tea and awkwardly trying to get past him when I need the milk.

He's distracted by the machine, finally notices that he's in the way, and then moves to one side.

'What the–' he says, staring straight at me in horror.

'What's wrong?' I look over my shoulder, expecting to see some huge spider on the wall.

'Nothing, I just… wasn't expecting to see something that *neon*,' he nods towards my shirt with a wince, 'at this time on a Monday morning.'

I shut the fridge door a little harder than necessary.

'Just trying to bring a little sunshine into your grey and dreary business-suited life.'

I pick up my cup and sail off dramatically. Grey and dreary: good. Sounds intellectual. Business-suited life? Not so much. Oh well.

'So, on the agenda for this week,' Geoff opens the department meeting, frowning at an Excel spreadsheet with tiny size eight font writing. 'Raising standards.'

'What is that?' Judy pokes at the sheet playfully.

'The Head wants us to follow a standard agenda now for our meetings.'

'The Head needs to use a larger font,' I chip in, and Judy starts giggling.

'Why is the only thing they care about numbers?' Liz says. 'We're teachers, not statisticians.'

'Well, I'd like to raise something,' Michael says. Something about the glint in his eye makes me lower my mug. 'I taught the mentor group for the first time the other day. I have to say it seems a waste of resources having a class with only seven students. None of them seem to have any likelihood of passing. If we're going to have such a focused class, we could at least make it for the key marginals.'

No one speaks. I think I should probably count to ten before I say anything, but I don't make it past three.

'What? The mentor group isn't about getting good grades. It's about helping those students find a safe place in an overwhelming environment.'

'I get that they have needs,' Michael says. 'I mean, one kid couldn't even spell his name right.'

'Connor,' we say his name at the same time.

'We're not going to make any timetabling changes now,' Geoff intervenes hastily. 'It would give Natalie a heart attack.'

Natalie lives in one of the secret corridors of the school, and spends her time creating the timetable or sorting out exam papers.

'Now the Head wants to audit the department as he prepares to start the recruitment process for a new HoD,' Geoff continues. 'Liz, he wants all the Key Stage 3 schemes of work submitted to him by Friday. On Friday he will also give us a list of Year 11 key pupils and he wants us to give their books in for scrutiny.'

'Wait a minute!' Liz starts pulling faces and holding up one hand. 'ALL the Key Stage 3 schemes of work? And books? We've only just started the term.'

'Presumably the schemes of work are all in place, you just need to collect the information together for David to look over,' Michael says this deadpan, but I know what he's doing.

Liz starts ranting at Geoff while Judy and I exchange glances. Michael starts making notes in that infuriating planner of his. Then the door opens and David Clark himself walks in.

Liz falls immediately silent. Geoff looks nervous. Michael looks smug.

'Just thought I'd pop in,' David says, his voice smooth as always. 'Please, do continue.'

The silence rings. I look on the table for inspiration and I see a promo pack from the nearest theatre. I clear my throat.

'We were just discussing running a potential trip,' I pick up the leaflet, hoping it's something vaguely respectable and not Kinky Boots.

'Oh, what's the play?' David asks mildly.

I scan the listings: Chitty Chitty Bang Bang, Agatha Christie, 60s Night… Oh let there be something!

'Blood Brothers,' Michael answers.

I look down and see that he's right. How did he know that?

'It's on the syllabus,' Judy chimes in helpfully.

'Who were you thinking of taking?' David asks.

'My mentor group,' I say, as if it's obvious. Michael's eyes narrow. 'I can drive the minibus, keep costs low.'

'We can share the driving,' Michael gives me a hard stare.

We?

'Excellent,' David says. 'Cultural enrichment, learning outside the classroom... Just what we need.'

The bell rings for registration and the meeting is over.

5

'So, you're a qualified minibus driver?' Michael says casually when we meet at the sink, making end-of-the-day drinks.

'Yes,' I say, crushing my tea bag with a little more force than necessary. 'You?'

He gives a curt nod.

'But I bet you haven't done the County certificate,' I say, with more than a little self-satisfaction.

'What is that?' he looks riled. Perfect.

'County policy,' I say, grabbing my milk and sloshing it about. 'Not only do you need to have a category D licence, you also need to get the county's very own certificate in order to drive a minibus for an educational institution in this local authority.'

'How do I get this certificate?' he snaps, pressing buttons on his coffee machine.

'Jan in the office will book you in for a course. They usually occur every six months or so.'

'Six months?' he repeats, his eyebrows shooting up in disbelief. 'Why is everything here so inefficient? No wonder all the schools are struggling.'

'We are not struggling.' I slam the fridge door shut. 'We are just underfunded.'

'You're not underfunded, you're just throwing money away by having people in positions who don't do their job.'

We glare at each other. I feel I ought to defend Liz but to even name her would be to incriminate her as one of those people.

'So I'm in the passenger seat then,' he says, finally.

'I don't see why you invited yourself at all.'

'You can't go by yourself. You need a 2:14 ratio.'

What, has he memorised the staff handbook already? All seventy-four boring pages?

'Well there's only seven in the group,' I counter.

'That's why we're going to invite my Year 11 boys' group as well.'

Seriously?

'We can't fit all of them on the bus!'

'They won't all want to come, but we can offer seven places: first come, first served,' he says, taking a sip of his coffee. He has a plain white mug– no pattern, nothing.

'You've got this all figured out nicely, haven't you?'

'Well, be honest, you had no idea it was even on at the theatre!' he scoffs.

'And you did?'

'Does it matter? I'm not the one being all self-righteous about who deserves to go on this trip or not.'

I take a scalding hot gulp of tea, trying not to choke.

'Look, I don't mind booking the tickets…' he begins.

'I'll do it!' I wave my hand dramatically. 'It's my trip, and if you want to gate-crash, then fine, but I'm running it.'

He raises an eyebrow coolly.

'Okay. As long as you're happy with that.'

I stomp off to my room, spilling half my tea as I go.

My anger fades considerably when I see my mentor group's reaction the day I give out trip letters.

'We're going on a trip?' Connor clutches it as if it's a golden ticket. 'No one ever takes us on trips.'

'Do we get to miss school?'

'It's a matinee,' I explain. 'We leave at twelve and get back at six.'

'Is it just our class?' Lacey asks.

'Well, not exactly,' I falter. 'We need to fill the minibus, so Mr Chase is inviting some of his Year 11 class to come as well.'

'Who's in that class?'

I start to list some names.

'Jayden, Ollie, Tyler…'

The kids start to wince.

'But look, whoever comes, you all need to be there, because we're going to have a great time.'

I say it to convince myself more than them.

The term rolls on, and I'm swamped with marking, planning, emails, and now trip admin to top it all off. When it gets to ten pm, I make myself stop working, but I can't face even opening my story document, given that I've spent all evening on the laptop anyway. The days get shorter and when it rains (almost every day), the heavy cloud blocks any sunlight so that it feels permanently dark. Geoff gets his promotion and disappears more and more into the corridors of Senior Team, and Liz disappears too…

'She's gone on the sick,' Judy tells me, showing me a text message covertly: It's all too much and I can't cope. 'That's exactly what they wanted.'

'What, you mean they wanted her to cave?'

'They're putting the advert out,' Judy says. 'They wanted her well and truly out of the way. No prizes for guessing who's going to get it.'

'Who?' I ask.

Judy indicates her head towards Michael, who is packing his reams of photocopying and organising the handouts by class with Post-its in a large copy box.

'Surely there'll be other candidates,' I hiss.

'I doubt it,' Judy shakes her head. 'You've seen the news reports. Who wants to come to a school that might be shut down in a year or two? This is a failing school, Jen. Most people are applying for jobs elsewhere, desperate to leave.'

'Are you?' I panic. If I lose Judy…

'Don't be silly,' she waves her hand, gold bangles on her wrist. 'I'm retiring in a year anyway.'

'So soon? I thought you had five years to go.'

'I chatted with Bill and we decided to cut loose earlier,' she shrugs. 'Look around you, Jen. Everyone is stressed out to the max. It isn't worth it.'

'If Michael becomes Head of Department, he'll change everything.'

I think about my mentor group, and our Friday story sessions, where I read to them from my latest young adult library book. Best part of the day.

'You can try and fight the system,' Judy says, 'but you'll just get exhausted. Let the new Head appoint his guy and you just carry on being awesome.'

'How can I if he shuts down my favourite class in the name of Dickensian utilitarianism?'

'Well you can always apply for it,' she says in a cavalier manner. 'The worst that can happen is that you don't get it. You've got nothing to lose.'

But the more I think about it, the more I realise I do.

Scenario 1: I don't apply for the job. Michael gets it uncontested. Michael is unbearable. Michael cancels my mentor group and ruins the school. Michael becomes my boss. I run away and join the circus.

Scenario 2: I apply for the job. I have to work for hours to come up with all the brilliant, innovative things I have done in the last five years. I get a token gesture interview and I have to teach an all-singing, all-dancing lesson in front of someone scary. Then I get grilled by David Clark who is currently pretending that he doesn't remember who I am. Michael gets the job. Michael is unbearable. And so revert to Scenario 1…

The fact is, I'm not sure I have the energy for Scenario 2, especially given that the outcome seems cemented in David Clark's hair wax. I'm struggling to stay afloat with the normal workload of being a plebeian teacher. I can't even handle Michael's Year 11 boys' group, though I am not going to admit that to him.

Initially, they seemed okay. They weren't very quiet, and they weren't very quick to do anything, but they weren't out of control. Now I'm not so sure.

Some of them have been rocking up to the lesson fifteen or twenty minutes late. I mean, I have no idea where they've been and I can't leave the class to look for them. All I can do is phone the office and report that they're not in the lesson. Jan writes their names down on a piece of paper and then who knows what happens next.

I know they find English completely boring and it's the last thing they want to do after lunch as the last lesson of the day. The scheme of work Michael's asked me to use with them, to complement what he's doing, involves a lot of writing practice. I don't mind writing tasks, but they just seem to have no ideas to write about. A typical task might be 'Write a letter to your headteacher with your views on school uniform.' I stand there looking at a class where half of them are lounging around in hoodies, and some of them are wearing skinny jeans.

'Ollie, take the hoodie off please,' I say brusquely. 'You look like you're about to go bowling rather than sit in an English lesson.'

None of them shout open defiance, but they keep their hoodies on and wait for me to give up asking. I can either turn into a hen-pecking nag, and basically waste the entire lesson trying to fight battles about uniform, or I can selectively ignore it and try to move on. I pick the latter.

'What is positive about school uniforms?' I ask, my board pen poised.

Tumbleweed.

'Tyler?'

He shrugs.

'Costs too much,' Jayden says.

'That's a disadvantage,' I say as I write it down, although I find it ironic given how much Superdry hoodies and Nike trainers cost, all of which I see exhibited on a regular basis.

'It's restrictive,' now Tyler decides to speak up.

Soon we have a lot of points on the board for why school uniform is the bane of their lives. I turn and see them all, still lounging back in their chairs, their exercise books open but the pages still blank.

'Come on, you need to write this down,' I say.

'Haven't got a pen,' Tyler smirks.

I sigh and open my desk drawer. Every week I'm getting through a bag of biros.

'You're going to struggle in school without a pen,' I say as I hand it over.

With a lot of chivvying, it takes about ten minutes to get them to write down what's on the board, and I have to circulate the room constantly. It feels like as soon as I move away, they are off-task again.

'I'm giving you this sheet with some useful connectives and persuasive phrases,' I say, dishing out A4 handouts. 'I'd like you to choose five and then write five full sentences, each with a different reason why the Head should get rid of school uniform, seeing as you're all so passionate about this.'

Passionate is definitely an exaggeration, but maybe if I say it, it'll come true.

I give them five minutes of writing time, but there are a lot of conversations going on and not a lot of pens on paper.

'Time is nearly up,' I say, with my giant countdown on the board. 'Three, two, one.'

The klaxon sounds and I stand at the board, waiting. Tyler is passing a bag of sweets under the desk to Ollie, then a pen sails through the air and hits Jayden, who grabs it and prepares to throw it back.

'No throwing in this class!' I say. 'I'm still waiting.'

Then Michael comes through the door –probably to use my room as a corridor again– and they all instantly fall quiet and straighten up in their seats.

'Hoodie. Off. Now.'

Ollie scowls, but takes it off.

'I hope this class is behaving,' Michael says, surveying the room with beady eyes.

'We're just about to write some sentences about school uniform,' I say brightly.

'Appropriate.'

He walks through and out of the other door. Taking advantage of the silence, I launch into the next task. Once the lesson is over and I look through their books, I feel the sinking frustration that they've barely written a quarter of what I asked them. They are chronically lazy, disengaged, and they seem to have decided that my lessons are pointless and they don't need to do any work. I mark the books in red pen and write comments like 'You need to write more in the time given.' But realistically, I can't use many effective consequences on them for not doing the work. If I ask them to see me for detention, they will forget, because I only teach them once a week. If I ask them to take their book home to finish off, I'll never see it again. With all these book scrutinies that David seems keen on, I can't risk that. I flick through Tyler's book. Messy dates and titles, etched underneath with a line of pen but no ruler, half empty pages. I hope his name doesn't come up on the dreaded list.

I am not winning with this class.

I sigh and reflect that if I was six foot tall, a bloke who played rugby, then I would be able to walk in and they'd all go quiet for me. But instead I'm five foot five, I still get ID-ed, and I can't be the sergeant major that Michael seems to be. Every time I sneak a look into his classroom, the kids are all silently scribing essays in their pristine books. I can't compete with that.

The WC girls voice moral support on the group chat.

Clare: You're a great teacher, Jen. Don't let this new guy get to you.

Deena: Why don't you come down on the train this Saturday? We can have a laugh and you can chill out for a bit.

I reply: Sorry, I've got a list of students and I have to hand in their books for scrutiny on Monday. Maybe another time.

David's regime is well and truly underway. We have visits from outside agencies; 'learning walks' where random senior leaders stroll into the classroom, pick up a few books at random, and then scribble onto a clipboard and walk out again. The book scrutinies begin in earnest: a list of names is emailed to staff on a weekly basis and we have to submit these books for examination to check that we are marking them and giving feedback, and that the students have improved their work too. When I arrive in the morning, I walk past Michael's room and see him marking, marking, marking at his desk. Every day when I leave, I'm struggling with a box of books, precariously balanced with my other bags.

'You are a health and safety liability,' Michael tells me, intercepting me one day as I shuffle down the concrete steps without being able to see past the mountain of sheer bulk of paperwork/exercise books/all-the-rubbish I am holding. He takes the marking box from me easily, as if it was a pillow.

'Is it one of your hobbies to read the school's policies from 1991?' I snap back. 'You need to get out more.'

'You clearly don't have much social life if you're taking all this home.'

He's right, darn it.

'Well, at least my books will be *immaculate*,' I exaggerate.

He gives a snort.

'I'm sure they will rival the Art department, with all that colouring-in you've been doing.'

My cheeks flare. He's referring to the goals sheet, which I used with the boys' group, but I also used it with the mentor group and got them to decorate it so they could feel invested and proud, and make a positive start to their exercise book (which will then be filled up with red pen as I underline their spelling mistakes).

'I don't need to justify myself to you,' I say with dignity. 'You're not an inspector.'

'You'll have a new Head of Department soon,' he replies. 'Just saying what it looks like as an outsider.'

We've reached the bottom of the steps and we're facing each other. He's still holding the box.

'Maybe if you didn't use my classroom as a corridor, you wouldn't keep disturbing my lessons and making my classes lose focus,' I accuse. 'How would you like it if I kept walking into your lessons?'

'You're welcome anytime,' he says without missing a beat. 'Isn't that encouraged for creating a professional learning community?'

Every time he says things like this, I always feel so inferior, so under-qualified. Is this the effect he wants? I've been here for five years and he doesn't look much older than me.

'How long have you been teaching?' I ask.

'Eight years.'

I do the Maths– if he did teacher training after uni, he's probably about 29. Three years older than me.

'It is part of my role of being here, as a leading practitioner,' he adds.

He's unbearable. Why has no one told him this yet?

'What about you?' he asks suddenly. 'What are your ambitions?'

Right now: to punch him in the face. But I don't say that.

'Well…' I hesitate. I want to sound cool, calm and confident, but 'get out of my flat before its ceiling collapses on me and kills me in my sleep' doesn't quite have the same effect.

'Do you want to go for the HoD job?'

Ah, so this is what this is all about. He probably followed me here just so we could have this supposedly spontaneous conversation.

'Do you?' I feel it's better to put off answering. Curious… not very neutral.

'Yes,' he says simply. 'You?'

'I'm thinking about it,' I try to sound vague, which isn't difficult, given my uncertainty about pretty much everything we're talking about.

'Sometimes I wonder why you chose secondary when you seem more geared towards primary.'

He doesn't speak with any malice, but his point is clear: he doesn't think I'm good enough to teach older students. I should be running painting sessions with the nursery.

'I like working with a mix of students,' I say, trying to keep my cool. 'Can I have my box back?'

'I haven't offended you, have I?' he says, not relinquishing the box. 'Let me carry these to your car.'

'I don't need you to do that.'

I try to take the box and he pulls it out of my reach.

'You need to accept my apology first.'

'You didn't apologise.'

'I'm sorry,' he says, looking at me with those piercing grey eyes, the colour of storm clouds. They're strangely hypnotic, glowing with energy. It has to be said, they don't convey 'sorry'-ness at all.

'I don't believe you.'

'What, do you want me to write a sonnet about it?' he sounds annoyed.

'An Ode would be better. More lines.'

'People say *I'm* difficult to work with…'

'Yes, because you go around judging everyone.'

Just at that moment, David passes by to walk up the steps. He pauses.

'Great books, Michael, SLT were really impressed.'

He continues to walk, ignoring me completely. I stare after him, a mixture of embarrassment and hatred pouring flames of heat into my cheeks. Michael has the grace to look uncomfortable.

'Shall I carry these to your car, then?'

'I said no, thank you.' I snatch the box and, catching him by surprise, I am successful this time.

I huff as I walk off, not giving him a chance to respond, and hate the fact that my arms begin to ache within minutes. Stupid weak arms. I need to start weightlifting.

But it's worth it, to save telling him I don't have a car.

6

By the time I burst through my flat door, I drop everything I'm holding in an untidy heap on the floor before my arms can give way completely. I had to stop at various points to rest the box on the crumbly, graffitied wall which marks off the car park. I pick up the mail: boring bank and bill letters. I cast them aside and kick off my shoes.

My flat doesn't really have a hallway; you open the door straight into the living area. I hang my coat up on the peg and survey the usual mess. My desk is piled high with papers, stationery and empty tea cups. There's an obstacle course of shoes and hair styling appliances to get through to sit on the sofa. The cramped kitchenette is foggy with grease and needs a deep clean, but I keep putting it off. I look at the clock. I should really go for a run, or walk, or something, to do some exercise before it gets dark. I notice my scrawled note to myself on the fridge: phone Dad. I look at the box of marking and groan.

Multi-tasking is the way forward. I grab my coat off the peg and lock the flat door behind me, then scuttle down the stairs with my phone to my ear, dialling Dad's number.

'Hello?'

His voice is soft and familiar, and makes me think of peppermints and the smell of rain on his old coat. When was the last time I called him?

'Hi Dad, it's me.'

'Jen,' he says, and I picture him walking to his favourite armchair and easing himself into it. 'How are you?'

'I'm alright,' I say brightly. 'Too much marking but nothing new there.'

'Katie said that new Head is trying to make his mark.'

'Yes, he's only been here five minutes and he brings in a new policy every day,' I joke, but it's close to the truth.

'Change for change's sake,' Dad comments. He's not wrong there. 'When are you next coming over? Sunday lunch? I thought I'd cook a proper roast dinner.'

I gulp.

'Maybe,' I say. 'I need to see how the weekend pans out.'

I don't tend to make plans for the weekend. They usually go something like this: Friday night – take pain killers and go to bed early with a stress headache; Saturday – mooch about and mark books; Sunday – plan lessons for the week ahead. Steph's invited me out to drinks a few times but she lives in the city, and I just don't have the energy for the bus journey.

I finish the conversation with Dad –and my brief walk around the uneven pavements of the town– and return to my flat to heat up some macaroni cheese. I think of Dad's Sunday roast with a twist in my stomach – part physical hunger, and part emotional.

The thing with teaching is that it consumes you. And though I know I really should go to Dad and sort things out, I just don't have the head space to deal with it right now. I can't iron out this rift without talking about Mum, and that's always the sticking point. He idolises her and won't hear a word said against her; I can't forgive her for leaving us and then dropping herself back into our lives right before she died, like Chernobyl. We're still reeling from the impact, and I can't wash the toxicity away.

My thumb hovers over the dating app that I haven't used since Ryan. Should it be another of my life goals this year to find a boyfriend? It seems more hassle than it's worth. Ryan still lived with his parents, and wafted around, happily avoiding any adult responsibility. I didn't move out of my home so I could then become responsible for a man-child. We had dinner a few times, but when he kept pushing to come back to my flat, I pulled back. I mean, I suppose I could put it as one of my criteria: *Would Like To Meet— a guy who doesn't live with his parents.* But then I feel like a hypocrite, given that I only recently moved out, myself.

When your mum dies and you have a younger sister who needs you, and your dad disappears into his shed, then you don't have much choice but to stay.

Things are different now: Katie's at uni, Dad's obviously started cooking again… Maybe I could call in for a cuppa at the weekend.

I post on the WC girls group chat: Michael told me today he's applying for the HoD job (no surprise there). He asked me if I'm going to apply.

Deena: He's worried you're a threat. You should definitely apply.

Me: Seriously? He's so good it feels like a waste of effort to try.

Deena: Terrible attitude. Stop being down on yourself. You could do that job better than him!

Me: You've never even met him!

Clare: If you don't apply, you might regret it later. Plus, if he gets the job, then your chance is gone for the next few years — in that role, at least.

Me: I never thought of myself as HoD material.

Deena: You've got to put yourself forward. No one else will do it for you. Even if you don't get it, it says to the Head that you're ambitious, that he can't ignore you.

Me: He'll probably still try, tho.

My box of marking is waiting, but I put it off a little longer by scrolling through self-publishing advice on my writing group page. I didn't realise how much cost was involved. You can make your own cover and do everything on a shoestring budget, but it probably won't sell very well. If I want to do it properly, I need money for a professional designer, editing services, marketing… My head aches as I consider my savings account, earmarked for a deposit. How am I going to put aside money for my book as well?

I quickly check my work emails, and there's a link posted to the job advert that's gone out for the Head of Department role. I click to view it, and my eyes widen. I had no idea the HoD role came with such a hefty salary. If I was on that kind of money, I could buy the house, cat, and self-publishing package of my dreams! It might make this time in my grubby flat all worthwhile. Motivation renewed, I toss my phone to one side and pick up the first book to mark.

At least the balance between Michael and me is somewhat redressed in our department meeting the next day after school. Geoff is still heading up the meetings, and feeds back to us from the senior team.

'Great work on the books, everyone,' he says. 'I am proud to say our department has been recognised for our outstanding practice in our marking and feedback. Jen and Michael, you were both mentioned by name in the senior leadership meeting.'

I blush and feel gratified that all the late nights and painstaking annotation of books have paid off, whilst still feeling annoyed that David singled out Michael and blanked me.

'With Liz's continued, er, absence, we are going to need to make sure the key stage 3 schemes of work are in place. David wanted them a few weeks ago.'

'I can go over the Year 9 persuasive writing scheme,' Michael says.

Something else to go on his application form, no doubt.

'I'll do the Year 8 travel writing unit,' I hear myself volunteer. It's almost an out-of-body experience.

'Great,' Geoff looks surprised at how easy that was. 'I can brush up the Year 7 one and we'll be sorted. Next item: the trip.'

Michael raises his eyebrows at me: a challenge.

'I've distributed letters and money has started coming in,' I say. 'I think we'll fill all the spaces.'

'I was thinking we should run some kind of workshop to prepare the students before we go,' Michael says. 'I'd be happy to come up with something.'

'I was going to do that with my mentor group anyway,' I say, and I know it sounds petty, but this is what he reduces me to.

'How about you both work on it together?' Geoff says.

Michael and I eye one another across the table, like cats before they snarl and pounce.

'I suppose Jen could learn from my experience,' he says, with a glint in his eye. So now he knows he's been teaching for three more years than me, it's another thing he's going to hold over my head.

'I suppose *you* could pick up some pointers from *my* experience teaching students with additional learning needs,' I retort.

'I would love that.' His face doesn't agree.

'Excellent,' says Geoff.

When I walk into my classroom the following morning, Michael is sitting on a table, waiting for me.

'I've come up with a lesson plan.' He brandishes some papers. 'If you could just check through it…'

'Good morning Michael,' I say dryly, taking my coat off and sinking into my chair. 'I thought we were meant to plan this together, you know – *collaboration*?'

'Well, I know you're busy and–'

I hold out my hand and he gives me the plan. I skim through it.

'I don't like the starter,' I say. 'The mentor group won't cope with it. I think we should go for something more discussion-based.'

'Like what?'

'How about: what superstitions can you think of? Do you believe in any superstitions? We'll have to give them some examples, like walking under ladders, breaking mirrors. Ooh, what about some pictures, and they have to guess what the superstition is?'

'Could work,' he says, a little reluctantly.

I type my login details into my laptop.

'I like the writing task,' I continue, pointing at the relevant section. 'Have you drafted a handout yet?'

'Second page,' he says.

I shuffle the papers. It's fairly minimal with Times New Roman font.

'We'll have to change the font for starters.'

'Not Comic Sans. Promise me.'

'Kids like it. They can *read* it.'

'It just looks so amateur.'

'Well, no one's going to be knocking on your door for design anytime soon,' I retort.

'Thanks for your feedback,' he says sarcastically. 'So you don't like the starter, and you hate the handout... Yet when I merely commented that you seem suited for Primary, I have to apologise to you. How does that work?'

'I said I liked the writing task,' I repeat, my voice rising. 'You asked for feedback, and I gave it. I didn't ask you for career advice.'

'So have you decided about the HoD job?'

'It's really none of your business.'

His fingers twitch impatiently, and his eyes are glittering at me again. Brushed steel. We stare at each other for a long minute.

'When shall we teach this?' he indicates at the lesson plan. 'Pick a lesson and I'll ask for cover.'

'As long as I'm coming to your lesson too,' I refuse to enter some kind of patronising mentor-mentee dialogue.

'Sounds very *collaborative*,' Michael replies. 'Great.'

7

Michael teaches the boys' group in the morning, and as I sit at the back of the class, I reflect on how much better their concentration is at this time of day. I watch the starter task go down well, and I feel some sense of satisfaction in this. But mostly, I feel a mixture of envy and frustration.

Michael's commanding presence captures my attention, and he has the class eating out of his hand. He merely stands at the front, looming his six-foot-odd height next to the board, and a respectful silence ripples across the room. He eyeballs any student who's fidgeting or murmuring or off task, and they stop. He speaks with confidence and certainty, and demands to be heard. As I watch him speak, I notice the air of precision he exudes. Every word he says is carefully chosen. He asks specific questions to individual students. The same fastidious effort he puts into his sharp suits and shiny shoes is echoed in the finalised lesson plan, itemised to two minute timing blocks. The kind of exactness I would love to nail down, but I always seem to end up flustered by doing the register, answering questions, and the bell takes me by surprise every lesson.

I also don't want to admit how good he looks. He's even more of the catalogue poster guy than I first thought. Seeing him up there, in his element, with his eyes full of intensity… It's horrendously attractive.

I don't know why I am even thinking this. I must be *really* desperate.

I try to distract myself by looking out of the window. The oak trees that line the edge of the yard are turning yellow, and the ground is covered with the first autumn leaves. I remember sitting on the worn-out bench with Jamie, my first boyfriend, when we were in Year 11, our faces glued together. My stomach curls to think of it now.

I notice Tyler saunter in through the gate, a welcome distraction from my flashback. At least it's not just my lesson he's late for.

'Miss Baker.'

Michael's voice snaps me back to the present.

'Yes?'

'I just asked you whether you have any superstitious beliefs,' Michael says, a smile playing around his lips. He knows I wasn't paying attention, and he's caught me out like a naughty kid.

'Does history repeat itself?' I blurt the first thing that comes into my head.

His eyes flicker. I've surprised both of us with my answer. He inclines his head, staring at me for a long moment. I wonder if he can see the images in my mind: the school bench with Jamie, my mum boarding a plane to Jamaica…

'Perhaps that question is linked to the concept of inevitability,' Michael finally speaks. 'Is it inevitable that twins separated at birth will discover the truth? Or is it just their choices that determine their path?'

The lesson ends and the students file out. I try to escape but Michael blocks the doorway.

'I'd love to know what you were thinking about,' he speaks with a higher intensity than usual, his voice low and purring.

'I thought we were giving feedback tomorrow?' I stall, looking down at my scrawly notes, flustered.

'I don't mean about the lesson,' he says, and it feels like he's leaning closer.

Is he *flirting* with me?

'I have to go,' I avoid his gaze, because it's burning my cheeks up.

He steps aside, and I hurry away without a backwards glance.

When Michael comes to see my lesson with the mentor group, it feels like the room is barely big enough to fit him. He's squashed into a chair in the corner that looks comically inadequate for him. I try to calm the nervous flutterings by walking around the classroom, squeezing in between the desks, and it feels like there's chaos ready to break loose similar to pasta boiling over in a saucepan.

When you're observed, as much as you try to ignore the observer, you find yourself speaking in a higher pitch, sounding like a holiday rep.

'Okay, everyone, who can guess the superstition represented by the picture?'

I want to be oblivious to Michael scribbling notes on his clipboard every time I say something, instead of trying to immediately analyse if it's positive or negative, something I've done or something I've failed to do.

As students put their hands up and offer answers, I find myself relaxing more into the lesson. This is what I do. I know these pupils. I'm really starting to enjoy it when the door opens and Rose enters, avoiding eye contact.

I've taught Rose for several years now. She's actually quite bright to be in the mentor group, but she often gets kicked out of mainstream lessons for misbehaviour, so she's ended up almost permanently in this group. She's unfailingly honest, which I really like, but it does rub staff up the wrong way, especially as she has no filter.

'Nice to see you, Rose,' I say quietly. It's enough to get some eye contact from her and show her that I've noticed she's late. I'll mark it on the register and talk to her at the end of the lesson.

Michael raises his eyebrows and writes on the clipboard.

The lesson continues and they're onto the writing task. I move around from desk to desk to help the students, and Michael does the same, careful to avoid being in the same area as me. I can hear him joking with Connor about bad luck and I feel heartened: maybe he's going to see the value of this group, of small-group teaching.

Then I notice that Rose's head is down, and her hands are under the desk– she must be on her phone. Just before I can open my mouth, Michael is next to her and holding out his hand expectantly.

'Phone,' he commands.

Rose looks up in horror.

'I'll put it in my bag,' she says.

'No, you know the rules. Hand it over.'

This is going to be a car crash. I can see her expression as she looks up at him, the resolution forming on her face.

'No.'

He pauses for a beat.

'Perhaps you'd like to go to your Head of Year's office, then.'

'Fine.'

She stands, hoisting her bag onto her shoulder.

'I hate this school,' she mutters, and then stalks off.

Great.

The rest of the lesson passes without further hitches, and when the bell rings, I dismiss the class and wipe the sweat from my brow. Even in the coldest room in the school, an observation still makes me sweat. Michael has to teach now, so he mercifully disappears, and I have a free period for planning, so I can collapse in a heap.

I sigh and then remember: Rose.

I make my way to Matt Myers' office, and find Rose sitting outside.

'Have you seen Mr Myers?' I ask. She shakes her head.

I pull up a chair beside her.

'How are you doing? Is there anything bothering you?'

She shakes her head, but she's still avoiding eye contact.

'Are you feeling okay today?'

She shakes her head.

'What's wrong?'

'Period,' she says, mumbling so that I almost don't catch it.

'Oh.' I remember that she's on the list of students who receive free school meals. 'Do you have enough pads or tampons?'

She shakes her head again.

'I can get you some from Mrs Blake,' I explain. 'What about food? Have you had breakfast?'

'No.'

'Come on, then, I'll see what I can do.'

I take Rose back to my room and get her a sanitary pack from Poppy Blake, a pastoral officer, and forage in the staff room to make some toast. By the time I send her on to her next lesson, I've got about ten minutes of my free lesson left.

I go back to the staff room and put the kettle on. While my tea is brewing, I email the safeguarding officer, Menna, to let her know about the situation.

It sometimes feels like this job will kill me.

I'm thinking these happy thoughts, sipping my tea, when Michael bursts into my room, with the dreaded clipboard.

'Time for feedback?'

I look at him, and my eyes must still be glazed over, because he gives a slight frown.

'Are you okay?'

I blink and put my mug down. Snap out of it, Jen!

'I'm fine,' I gesture for him to sit down.

'What did you think of my lesson?' he asks directly, sitting opposite me on top of a desk.

No small talk with Michael.

'It was very good,' I answer truthfully. 'I enjoyed the pace, the questioning… You had the class's full attention.'

He nods, eager for something else.

'What would you change?' he presses.

I take another sip of tea.

'I think you should get the pupils talking to each other more. You question them so they speak to you, but they didn't speak much with each other. Even in the starter they were very quiet. You should encourage them to learn by speaking. Give them permission to talk about the task.'

He considers this.

'Interesting,' he says. 'What if they start talking about something else instead?'

'You have to monitor them to check they're on task,' I explain. 'But train them how to do it, and they will focus better each time.'

He makes a note. He seems to be taking this very well.

'Your lesson, then,' he says, turning to a different page on the clipboard. 'I liked the way you moved around the room.'

I stifle a smile – it sounds like some cheesy pop song from the 90s.

'The class was focused… with maybe one or two exceptions.'

This kills my potential smile.

'Yes, we should talk about Rose.' I sigh. 'She's going through a rough time.'

'If an inspector had been there, they would have wanted to see more decisive action from you.'

'I would have intervened when she was on her phone, only you beat me to it.'

'Sorry,' his tone says 'not sorry at all'. 'I was closer to her.'

'Given that it was my lesson, you should have let me deal with it instead of jumping in.'

'Just don't give special treatment to some kids and not others. Rules are rules and they are for everyone. It's because staff don't follow the systems you have in place consistently that you're in this situation as a school,' he gestures with his hands as if to say– *here, isn't it obvious? This is what is wrong with this school. Why aren't I in charge?*

'Your unfailing belief in the rules and the system astounds me,' I say. 'Surely with your *eight years* of teaching, you must be aware by now of how broken the system really is?'

'With consistency, the system can work,' Michael says. 'At Cassley High–'

'Don't you dare tell me about Cassley High,' I cut him off. 'Their catchment is the wealthiest section of the county. They attract the best staff from the city. They got a brand new building, lorryfuls of computers, and what did we get? David Clark and a few Ipads.'

'People want to work there because it's well managed. If the leadership in this school can get straightened out, then things will improve here too.'

'So I suppose we should be thankful that you so *generously* decided to work here… and how convenient that the Head of Department role has just come up.'

I hate being cynical, but it's the truth.

'Are you applying?'

This man. He is going to drive me to the edge.

'If it means you don't get it uncontested, then yes.'

His eyes widen slightly. And then he smiles, in the way that a tiger bares its teeth.

8

'So what shall I tell Dad?' Katie asks on the phone that night. 'You can't come to Sunday lunch because you have marking, and planning, and now you've also decided to apply for a promotion.'

'Yes, I suppose so,' I say, cradling my phone to my ear while stepping through the obstacle course in my lounge to find the pile of Year 7 letters about plastic pollution I was meant to mark tonight.

'You can't just come for the meal, and then do your work afterwards?'

I sigh.

'You know I want to, but it's never just an hour or so with Dad. It'll take over the whole day.'

'He's all we've got left,' she says, with unsugared brutality.

'Don't do this,' I say.

There's a heavy silence.

'So you really want to be Head of English?'

'I don't know,' I say, finally locating the papers. On the top, a kid called Rupert has addressed his letter to Mr P. L. Astic. 'I don't want *him* bossing me around, that's for sure. If I don't try, I'll never know.'

'You're an awesome teacher,' she says. 'You've got just as much right to get that promotion as he does, if not more. But you've got no life. When was the last time you worked on your story? When was the last time you went on a *date*?'

'I just haven't had any time!' I wail. 'And no one is asking me out.'

'You've got to make time. And you've got to meet people. You're letting school take over your life.'

'Well, it's hard not to when the Head is asking for meaningless paperwork all the time, we've done book scrutinies and learning walks and Michael's observed me, and I'm running this theatre trip on top of everything else.'

'Just get your application done,' Katie says impatiently, 'then make it up to Dad. Take him out for Sunday lunch, or something.'

'Okay,' I promise. 'I'll do that.'

I view the HoD job advert again and download the application form. I read the requirements: qualified teacher status, proven record of classroom management, experience of responsibility, a passion for the subject. I'm qualified and I love English, but my run-ins with the boys' group really undermines my 'classroom management'. With Geoff as HoD and Liz as second in department, I haven't really been given any official responsibility… But because Liz doesn't do anything, I suppose I can list the things she was supposed to do that I helped with, like this Year 8 travel writing unit. I'm really enjoying that actually –a few extracts from Bill Bryson and Gerald Durrell and creative tasks for the students, and I think it will be engaging and stretch them to use irony. Perhaps I should just work on that instead…

I persuade myself to do the easy part of the application first: the data section of my grades and personal details. I was a straight-A student, so no issues there. The form asks for degree qualification, but not which university. I wonder where Michael studied. The familiar curl of dissatisfaction and shame unfolds in my stomach when I think about uni. I could have gone somewhere much better than our nearest city, but… Dad.

I can still remember the conversation I had with Janet Patchell, who was my form tutor, in the classroom where Michael teaches now. The dust in the corners, the musty smell in the book store cupboard, and displays of my work on the walls.

'You could go to any of the top universities,' she said. 'Don't you think it might be good to get a fresh start?'

'I can't leave my dad,' I explained.

She knew what we'd been through. In fact, she had been the one to ask me if I wanted them to apply for special dispensation to the exam board when my mum dropped back into our lives, only to tell us that she had been diagnosed with stage 4 cancer and had months to live. I refused, because I wanted my grades to be my own. I buried myself in studying, because I couldn't play happy families with Mum and Dad as if she hadn't left us to go travelling, paint second-rate pictures and have an affair with a Yoga instructor. Dad forgave her and loved her to the end, and he's still mourning her loss now. One day I might feel less angry, but after she died, I had to commute to lectures from home because I needed to cook meals for Dad and Katie and make sure the house didn't fall apart.

Michael's going to write about his amazing eight years of teaching, pushing educational boundaries and displaying an unfailing commitment to excellence and high standards. The last eight years for me have been about survival. I got through uni, I did my teaching qualification, and I got a job at my old school, because through all of it, I could live at home and look after my dad and my sister.

When Katie started uni, and she did move into halls of residence, I felt that sense of what I had lost. Of what I had given up. The thing is, I don't think Dad even registered it. He was –and still is, to some extent– living in a haze of grief. I moved out a year ago into my greasy bedsit-flat, giving up the luxuries of living in a comfortable 3-bed semi and being insured on my dad's car, because I just needed to find something that was mine.

Each morning when I walk into Whidlock County, a thousand memories of my life are etched upon the walls. Maybe that's why I'm still there.

But I can't put any of this in my application.

Why am I even doing this?

I look at the pile of Year 7 letters and start to read the first one.

Dear Mr P.L. Astic,

I am righting to you today too ask you to Stop using single use plastic for your products. Did you now that over 8 million peices of plastic go into the ocean every year? They end up chokking dolfins and being etten by sea gulls and then they have no room in there stomack for food and they die of starvation.

I smile as I remember the class discussion we had about this. We watched a video clip and they were all shocked at the impact plastic has on sea life. Without fail, children are appalled by anything that causes harm to animals. They say things like 'why don't we just stop making plastic, then?' and in their minds, it's a simple problem with an easy solution. They see everything in black and white. I love that.

The HoD application requires a personal statement. I start to type: *I am a passionate teacher and my job is a privilege. There's no other profession where I can discuss the impact of plastic pollution, the obsessive love of Cathy and Heathcliff and the use of the comma before lunchtime.* As I continue to type, I find I am writing about why I chose teaching, what my strengths are, and what I could bring to the role if I was appointed. It's just a first draft, and it will need polishing, but it's not bad. Not as bad as I thought it would be.

Maybe, just maybe, I have a chance.

9

When I enter the photocopying room first thing the next morning, the larger machine is just finishing a job. I pick up the booklet and examine it: Year 9 persuasive writing. Michael.

I set my handouts copying and flick through it. Some extracts, some technique practice, and planning sheets. It looks thorough, if not very easy on the eye. That man loves Times New Roman way too much.

My handouts finish and I pick them up. I should really take these booklets to Michael's room. Plus it gives me the opportunity to tell him, more officially, that I am applying for the job.

I'm surprised when I get there to see his empty chair. There's a pile of books on his desk that he's obviously mid-way through marking. I find a space to set the booklets down, but then something catches my eye.

It's the HoD application form, printed off, with notes scribbled over it. The handwriting is very familiar to me: it's Geoff's.

It's like a knife twisting in my gut, even though I haven't told Geoff I'm applying… I haven't really told anyone, except to shout something vague to Michael yesterday over my shoulder. But it hurts because clearly, he hasn't considered me for this role. He hasn't sought me out, encouraging me to apply. Michael's asked for his feedback and he's happy to give it, probably glad to know he can hand over his department to someone competent and efficient.

Someone who is not like me.

There are voices in the corridor and I'm frozen like a bank robber caught red-handed as Michael and Geoff walk into the room.

Those eyes of steel assess me in a penetrating glance. Guilty.

'Jennifer,' his tone moves up at the end, like an unspoken question. *What are you doing in my room?*

'I came to give you these booklets,' I say, the fiery blush spreading like a rash over my face and neck. 'Sorry, I don't want to interrupt you.'

I walk hastily towards the door, avoiding eye contact with either of them. Geoff steps back so I can get past.

'See you later,' I call airily, as I head for the sanctuary of my room.

Ugh. How embarrassing.

It takes five minutes before Michael comes bursting into my classroom. I look up from my laptop.

'Can I help you?'

'Jennifer,' he says my name slowly, like the first part of a joke before the punchline. 'There are a few things, actually.'

He moves towards my desk and my hands fall from being poised over the keyboard. I have to crick my neck back as he draws closer until I'm leaning back in my chair. He places his hands deliberately onto my desk and looms forward, locking eyes with me. His eyes are the colour of thunder.

'Were you serious yesterday when you said you were going to apply for the HoD role?'

I blink. This is my opportunity. Be clear, be calm.

'Perfectly serious,' I reply crisply.

I hold my nerve and refuse to look away. I watch a shadow of something –surprise?– pass through his expression before he gives me a cynical smile.

'Lovely,' he says. 'So I'm sure you'll want to have some input into redoing the corridor display boards? I think we can both agree that they are looking a little tired.'

'As much as it pains me to agree with you, I will concede the point.'

'I've been told that you're the best person to come to for resources in this area.'

What he means is that he's asked Geoff, and Geoff has sent him my way.

I push back from my desk and walk over to a plastic box with the lid shut in the corner of my room. Before I can lift it, he's there and lifting it for me. He sets it down onto the desk and we stand over it as though it's a Christmas present and we're kids again. I open the lid and reveal my store of tools.

'Staple gun. Staples. Staple remover,' I pick each item up to show him. Each one has my name written twenty times all over it. Nothing lasts five minutes round here. 'Laminate pouches. The laminator is in the staffroom. The rolls of paper are in the store cupboard.'

I look up and he's rubbing his hands with glee, like Gollum.

'Now listen,' I use my best teacher-voice (assertive but not aggressive). 'These are all my *personal* items which I keep in school for my *personal* use. I don't want anything left out where someone can swipe it. Everything has to be returned to the box and the lid replaced. Do you understand?'

'I understand that you clearly have trust issues,' Michael rolls his eyes. 'You've even managed to write your initials inside the trigger of the staple gun.'

'Maybe it's best if you only use this when I'm around.'

'You know I really think this is a two-person job anyway. How about after school?'

Seriously? I have a job application to write. Or at least, redraft.

But the image of my flat and reheated macaroni cheese isn't something I want to rush home to. And there was that weird moment when he was leaning towards me in the doorway… Perhaps part of me wants to find out what that was all about.

'Maybe,' I say, shutting the box lid with a decisive click.

He raises an eyebrow.

'I'll take that as a yes,' he says. 'Now another thing.'

Here it comes. He's going to accuse me of spying in his room.

'I have hidden a small ornament somewhere in your classroom. When you find it, let me know.'

'Wait, what?' I say, and watch him try to suppress a smile as he turns to leave. 'What kind of ornament?'

'It's a cat.'

I know I should be more organised. It's been my new year's resolution for about seven years now, but I still feel like things just catch me out all the time. Birthdays, favours I agreed to in a moment of folly, household bills… In school, I live a fairly hand-to-mouth existence with my planning and preparation, and it's tough to find any time to focus when emails keep pinging into my inbox, the phone rings with a message, or a student is hovering in the corridor when they should be in a lesson.

The fact is, no sooner than you 'catch up' with your tasks, then something new is happening and you're already behind again.

I don't have time to check my email in my first lessons of the day. When I head into the staffroom, everyone is standing in silence while David is giving an all-staff briefing. Must have missed the email about that. He gives me a pointed look of disapproval while I attempt to fade into the background.

'I want everyone to use the new behaviour policy,' he says. 'If any student breaks a rule, give them a warning, then if they continue, issue one of the consequences. It could be detention, seeing you at the end of the lesson, or in serious cases, sending them to their Head of Year. We need consistency.'

Roger that. Once David's gone, I retreat to the kitchen in relief. There's barely any break time left, but I have a blank lesson for planning after break, so I can take my time to make a cup of tea then tackle those emails. I'm just stirring my mug when Michael stands in the doorway.

'Did you check cover?' he asks.

'No,' I say.

'You're down to cover for Matt's sports group.'

'What?'

'You'll have to take them to a computer room.'

'Which class?'

I look at Michael and I already know the answer.

'It's the boys' group.'

I groan and abandon my tea.

Flustered and turning over in my mind what I'm going to do with the boys' group for a substitute P.E. lesson in a computer room, I arrive at the outdoor entrance to the gym changing rooms to find the boys, with their kit bags, passing a basketball around.

'Sorry boys, we need to go to a computer room as Mr Myers isn't here today.'

There's a lot of grumbling and I hear Tyler say disdainfully,

'I don't know why they've sent *her*.'

I'm ignoring that one.

Once we've arrived at the classroom and the students have all logged on to computers, I suggest that they research different types of cardio exercise while I open my email, hoping to find some cover work for them to do. Thankfully, Matt has sent over some instructions.

'Okay, everyone, Mr Myers wants you to continue working on your write-up of a circuit fitness session.'

I walk around and check that they are all on task. I catch Tyler on a gaming website.

'That's a warning now, Tyler,' I say. 'Stay focused.'

I look through my emails and catch up on the messages about staff briefing, and another one from Natalie to say that some staff are being used for cover as a supply teacher was ill, so that explains why I was on the list unexpectedly. The boys are easier to cope with while they are glued to screens, but then I hear the hiss of a can opening.

'No drinks in here, and you're not allowed these in school anyway,' I say, taking the can of Coke and placing it on top of a cupboard.

'I'm thirsty,' Tyler complains.

'Drinking twelve teaspoons of sugar probably won't help.'

'So pathetic,' he mutters, turning back to the screen.

'You're already on a warning,' I remind him. 'I think you'd better see me at lunchtime.'

'I can't,' he snaps. 'I'm supposed to be with Mr Chase.'

'That's fine, I'll speak to you in his classroom, then.'

'I can't wait.'

'Cut the attitude, Tyler.'

I return to my emails, thinking through what my options are if he continues acting up. His Head of Year is Matt, who is not here, so I can't send him there. Next door is Roger, but there would be no use sending him to work in there. He would probably just play online games the whole time. I guess I would have to ring the office and see if anyone else was available on the senior team.

'Everything okay in here, Miss Baker?'

David walks in, using a rather forced politeness that he never bothers with when it's just me in the corridor. His eyes flick round the room, and he sees Tyler's screen the same time as I do.

'Tyler, close that down,' he barks. 'Is everyone behaving?'

He directs the question at me, like it's some sort of test of my competence.

'Actually, Tyler has been through a warning and received a detention,' I tell him, nodding towards the can of Coke on the side. 'I know Mr Myers isn't here but I think we might need to escalate this if he continues to disregard the rules.'

'Get your bag, Tyler,' David commands with a frown. 'I will take you to work somewhere else.'

David looks annoyed at the inconvenience, but at least it means that Tyler will start to realise there are consequences for his actions.

But when I find him in Michael's room at lunchtime, he doesn't seem very apologetic.

'Do you mind if I speak to Tyler for a minute?' I ask, and then I take a seat from the desk in front of Tyler. 'Tyler, do you understand why I gave you detention?'

He gives a tiny nod of his chin, not looking up.

'What do you think you could do differently next time?'

He shrugs.

'Tyler, could you look at me please?'

His eyes move, but his head stays low on his chest.

'Sit up, please. I want to have a proper conversation with you.'

He straightens his shoulders a little.

'I'd really like you to reconsider your attitude,' I say. 'I find your behaviour disrespectful.'

He rolls his eyes.

'Tyler,' Michael says sharply. 'Apologise to Miss Baker.'

'Sorry,' he says, without looking at me, in a monotone.

'I really don't want to have this conversation again,' I push back the chair.

'Nor do I,' Tyler says under his breath.

10

It takes me until the end of lunch to find the creepy cat ornament. It's a white cat with sapphire blue eyes, about two inches high, directly underneath the clock. It's then that I realise that the clock has new batteries. It must have been Michael. The cat, and the batteries… It feels personal, somehow. Like he's *noticed* me. Perhaps this is Michael's way of being friendly.

I twist the cat to examine it. What to do next? I'll have to hide it in his room and tell him later when we do the display. It makes me chuckle. Where on earth did he get it from?

There's a knock at the door. It's Geoff.

'Hello stranger,' I say.

'Sorry,' he apologises. 'I know I haven't been around much.'

I give him a half smile. I've hardly seen him, except at meetings.

'About the Head of Department job,' he begins, staring at an invisible object just above my left ear to avoid direct eye contact. 'Are you going to apply?'

'Yes.'

He gives a nod.

'That's great.'

He says it in a 'good-for-you' kind of way. Not in a 'great-the-department-is-safe' kind of way.

'You didn't expect me to,' I say. It's a statement, not a question.

'Well,' he pauses, 'David said you'd been struggling with behaviour, and… it's a very difficult job.'

So I asked David for help one time, and now he's going to hold it against me.

'You don't think I can do it?' I automatically place one hand on my hip and stare at him, until he meets my eye.

'No, of course not!' Geoff says, backtracking. 'I just didn't think you would be interested.'

That's even worse.

'Geoff, whoever gets that job is going to be in that position for at least five years. If I don't go for it now, that's my chance gone.'

There's an awkward pause as my hand lingers in the air from gesticulating. Geoff clears his throat.

'If you want me to look over your application–'

He's offering because he feels obliged, not because he thinks I have a chance of getting it. He's mentored me through my first years of teaching, with my many mistakes, and now he can't see me any differently.

'No thank you,' I say it too quickly. I'm offended, and he knows it.

'Good luck, Jen.'

He walks away, and I'm torn between tears or throwing something at the wall.

I meet Michael in the hallway with my box, a roll of black paper, and a red border.

'Okay, let's do this,' I say abruptly.

He looks at me questioningly.

'Are you all right?'

'Yeah, I'm fine,' I snap, in the way that everyone does when they are clearly not.

I grab the roll of paper and shove it into his hands, then pull the roll to stretch out across the display board.

'Hold it in place,' I command. I'm not taking any rubbish from anyone anymore. This school has had the best of me. It's time they woke up to how hard I work and how much they need me.

I press the staple gun to the wall: snap, snap, snap. Michael winces.

'I think you just hurt the wall.'

'I don't care.'

'What's with the black and red, it's very Macbeth.' He closes his eyes as I fire the staple gun. 'Maybe you could let me?'

'No.'

We roll out the border.

'I've hidden the cat in your room.'

I glance sideways at him to see his lips curl into a smile.

'It's probably got some curse on it,' I continue.

'I thought you weren't superstitious.'

'Fair is foul and foul is fair,' I quote Macbeth. 'It may look innocent, but conceal an evil intent.'

'Like school inspections.'

I give a dry laugh.

'Or a job advert where the outcome is already decided,' I focus on stapling the border onto the board. It's got more staples than paper now.

'Jen,' he says, and his quiet tone makes me turn around and stare at him. 'I mean, Jennifer…'

'No one calls me that.'

'I do.'

There's a long moment and I think I've forgotten how to breathe.

'I'm glad you're going for the job too.'

I narrow my eyes. He looks far too sincere.

'After all,' he says, turning away from me to pick up the next roll of paper, 'winning doesn't mean anything without competition.'

I grab the nearest roll of paper and swipe him. He blocks it with his roll with annoyingly good reflexes.

'You're unbearable, do you know that?' I seethe.

'Why should I play the Roman fool, and die on mine own sword?' he says with a smart-ass grin.

Two can play at that quoting-Shakespeare game.

'I have no words: my voice is in my sword!' I return, swiping him again.

'Ahem!'

We both drop the rolls of paper and turn to see Janet Patchell, with her best disapproving stare, at the end of the corridor.

'The cleaners want to know if it's safe for them to enter this war zone.'

I can feel myself burning all over. Ground, swallow me up.

'Yes of course,' Michael has an answer for everything. 'We'll just take these rolls back to the store cupboard.'

He jerks his head at me to follow, so I pick up my roll and sigh at the sound of Janet's heels clicking as she walks away.

'You are a bad influence on me,' I hiss, as Michael opens the door to the store cupboard. What feels like fifty years of dust and mildew wafts out.

'When was the last time anyone cleaned this?' he ignores my statement, taking in the ugly metal shelving crammed with 90s textbooks (the hairstyles on the cover are hilarious) and the filthy floor.

'Probably the flood.'

'You mean, like Noah?'

'No, I mean the actual flood that happened here when the water pipe burst. I think I was in Year 10.'

That was a great day, actually. Sent home before break time.

'You know way too much about this school.'

Michael reaches to place the rolls on the top shelf, his shirt riding up slightly to reveal a lean torso. Look away, Jen.

'Watch out for the spider,' he says, pointing at my shoulder.

I jump and start brushing my top with my hands and then catch him laughing.

'Got you,' he says.

I shake my head and try to recover my dignity.

'You know, maybe you're the one more suited to primary.'

He steps towards me and my heart starts to speed up. He's tall, so tall, and he smells of cologne and he's just inches away now…

'The door's that way,' he says dryly.

'Oh, yes, sorry,' I nearly trip over my own feet as I pivot and hurry out of there.

When I get home, my phone pings with a new message.

Jennifer. This is Michael.

Me: How did you get my number?

Michael: It's on the trip risk assessment.

Me: You need some better reading material.

Michael: I particularly enjoyed the part about the risk of snow and ice. You will have to make sure you choose appropriate footwear.

Me: My footwear is always appropriate.

Three dots appear to show he is writing a reply, but it never comes. Time to ask the WC girls for advice.

Me: Michael got my number and now he's texting me.

Clare: What's he saying? Take screenshots, you might need them as evidence of harassment later.

Me: Not bad messaging… Just… being funny.

Deena: He's trying to get inside your head!! Don't fall for it, girl.

Me: Really?

Clare: As much as I usually disagree with Deena's paranoia, I think I agree with her on this.

Me: Neither of you have met him, remember?

Deena: No need. He's a privileged white guy.

Deena's part Nigerian, and she's had to put up with a lot of rubbish in her office over the past two years — mainly from privileged white guys. She has a point. But maybe there's another side to Michael. I just don't know whether I'll get to see it.

I try to read to calm myself down before sleeping, but I can't concentrate. I keep wishing that Michael would message me again. And I keep thinking about that moment in the cupboard where he was so close he could have kissed me.

11

It's trip day, and I'm wearing the pineapple shirt to guarantee success.

I'm sitting in an oasis of calm at my desk, ignoring the mountain of paper and focusing on one sip of hot, strong tea at a time, when Michael barges in. He sees the pineapple shirt but decides not to comment.

'All set for today?'

I give what I hope is a confident nod.

'Permission slips? Payments? List sent out to staff? Cover work?'

'All done and dusted.'

I take another sip of tea.

'Miss Baker!' two students from the mentor group squeak from the other door.

'Yes?'

'Maizie's sick and she can't come on the trip! She texted me to ask if she can have the money back.'

'Oh, that's a shame,' I say, my calm deflating. 'Well, I can't really give a refund unless there's someone who can take her place. Do you know anyone?'

The girls look at one another.

'We could ask Charlotte.'

'Great, let me know as soon as possible.'

They scurry off, and I press my fingers to my temples. It's not a good day for a stress headache. Not when I've got to drive the bus.

'Do you think she will be able to come at such last-minute notice?' Michael asks sceptically.

'Probably not,' I sigh. 'You got any ideas?'

'Well, I think I remember you telling me this was your trip and you were going to run it. I would have had a sub list in case anyone dropped out.'

I would love to throw my tea all over him, but it would be a waste of a precious commodity. What Happened In The Store Cupboard seems to belong to the metaverse.

'Ok, well, thanks for your help,' I say in my best sarcastic tone.

The day goes on. I get a visit from the girls again, with Charlotte in tow, to say that she's texted her Mum and has been given permission.

'Right, well we need to get the office to call because we don't have a form filled in.'

I send a few emails to sort that out and take a deep breath. Then Tyler appears at the door.

'Mr Chase said I can come on the trip today,' he announces.

'No, you can't, the space has been filled,' I reply.

'Well I just gave him the money.'

'You had twenty pounds in cash on you?' I ask in disbelief. 'Anyway, I don't have a letter from your parents.'

'I can show you a text on my phone from my dad.'

He pulls out his phone and starts scrolling through his messages. I can't help it: I notice the name Ben and I remember the mysterious card I found. Why was Tyler carrying more cash than he would need for school dinners? He sees my expression and I avert my eyes.

'See,' he shows me the message.

'I need to speak to Mr Chase,' I say. 'The bell's going to go any minute, and I'm on duty.'

'So can I go then?'

'I can't magick up another space, Tyler,' I say, more snappily than I intend. 'And if it's between you and the other student, she's not behind on her work for me like you are.'

'What work?' he asks, and the contempt in his tone is enough to make up my mind.

'Just look at your book,' I pull it out from the pile and open it up. 'Half finished tasks, messy presentation… Everything is half hearted, Tyler. You want the rewards then you have to earn them.'

He gives me a venomous stare, and then stalks out of my room. The bell goes.

Making a mental note to find Michael as soon as possible, I hurry down to the canteen. Break time duty is not a highlight of the week. There's already a heaving mass of students and my duty-buddy, Roger from the I.T. department, is notorious at either being late or forgetting completely to turn up.

'Right everyone, line up.'

I start sending in students, checking they are wearing the correct uniform. I send a few away to find their tie or blazer. I can see a few students in my mentor group waiting patiently, and I give them a smile. Then Tyler saunters in, flanked by Ollie and Jayden, and tries to seamlessly cut in front of them.

'No chance, boys,' I say. 'Get to the back of the queue.'

They exchange glances and then turn. Suddenly the queue sprawls forward, nearly knocking me over.

'Hey, what's going on?'

I steady myself and straighten up to see Michael, looking appalled at the mess of a queue, with kids falling all over each other.

Tyler, Ollie and Jayden are standing smugly –no sense of *them* having stumbled.

'Stand back please and straighten the line,' I say, reasserting control. 'Those three are pushing.'

Tyler, Ollie and Jayden erupt in protest.

'We did nothing, we were just standing here!'

I send a few more kids into the canteen to try and get the queue down.

'Did Tyler tell you he has the money for the trip?' Michael asks.

'Yes, he came to see me, but I already arranged for Charlotte to go, and the office has called her mum to secure permission.'

'She doesn't want me to go because she doesn't like me,' Tyler says bitterly.

'He's got a bunch of unfinished work in his book and I don't feel he deserves the place.'

Michael sets his jaw in annoyance.

'You should have spoken to me before you promised him a space on the trip,' I hiss. 'The way he's behaving now is exactly why I don't want to take him.'

'Tyler, this is Miss Baker's trip, and her decision is final,' Michael tells him. 'You did have your chance to get your money in when we first gave out the letters. Next time you'll have to be faster.'

'What's the point?' Tyler swings his bag over his shoulder and storms off.

I look at my watch. Thirty minutes before we leave.

When break is finally over, I frantically take a few painkillers, drink half a bottle of water, then dash to the toilet. I grab my folder with all the forms, my 'teacher bag', which is a thick tote bag stuffed to the brim with papers, my coat, and go to pick up the minibus keys from the office.

The minibus is a bit of a relic and smells of rugby fixtures and gone-off sandwiches. It's a battered, navy colour, and the handbrake is so stiff I need to use both hands to release it. There's a knack to getting the engine started too, where I have to hold down the clutch and press a magnetic fob on a security button for five seconds before the ignition will work.

The kids are making their usual uproar in the back and Michael is watching me go through this process with varying degrees of my-life-is-in-danger horror on his face.

'Do you want me to–' he starts.

'No.'

'Can I–' he tries again.

'No.'

I am not letting him drive this thing.

Finally the engine kicks into life and the kids cheer. I put the gear stick in reverse and the beeping noise begins. I wrestle with the handbrake and then ease the vehicle out of the parking space. It always takes a while to get used to driving it again. I am always in mortal terror of knocking over a pupil while we're on the school site.

'Is it clear back there?' I call.

'Yeah,' Connor shouts.

Then there's a crunching noise. I've just run over Mrs Evans' flowerpots.

'Apart from the flowers,' Connor adds.

'Oh well,' I mutter, putting the gear stick into first gear.

The engine revs and the bus jerks forward. I see Michael's hands clutching at the glove compartment, anything he can find to hold for added security.

'Did you pass the county certificate?' he asks incredulously.

'Yes,' I say, moving up into second gear. 'It's always a bit jumpy till it gets warmed up.'

I slow as we approach the school gate and the bus judders. I put the clutch down and just avoid stalling. I try to ignore Michael and focus on the gates opening. His hands lower from the dashboard but he doesn't relax back into the seat. Maybe he's the sort of guy who never chills out.

Once we're out onto the road, I feel better, and by the time I've gone through the third roundabout, it feels more natural to drive this decrepit machine again. We get onto the motorway and manage to travel at around sixty miles an hour, though the engine sounds like an unhappy lion whose food was waved under its nose then taken away.

'Miss, there's something wrong with the door,' one of the girls calls.

'Ask Mr Chase. I'm driving,' I reply.

'Mr Chase, this just came off the door.'

Someone passes Michael a piece of rubber trimming.

'Very reassuring.'

'Should I open the window to check it's still working?'

'No!' Michael says.

Too late. A gust of wind blows into the bus.

'Nice to have a bit of fresh air,' one of the kids comments.

'It's freezing!' the girls complain.

'Everyone remember the story of the play?' I ask.

'Twin brothers, separated at birth, can't find out they're twins otherwise they'll die,' Connor pipes up.

'That's pretty much it,' I nod. 'A few songs along the way. *Tell me it's not true*!'

I start to belt out the opening number. Michael looks at me as if I've lost my mind.

'Come on, Mr Chase!' I say. '*Say it's just a story*.'

'You're doing fine on your own.'

'You'll all be singing with me on the way back.'

'Great.' He covers his face with his hands.

He reminds me of my dad. Mum loved musicals and was always singing around the house. Dad never wanted to go to see a show. The familiar pang of missing my mother aches beneath my rib cage. I wonder whether it will ever go away.

'What are you thinking about?'

Michael's question jolts me back to reality. I can feel him assessing me again with his gaze, and I deliberately focus on the dashboard.

'Are you the Thought Police now?'

'Are you comparing me to a totalitarian dictatorship?'

I have to look at him now, to check he isn't offended. When our eyes meet, he instantly grins. I can't help it: I smile back, despite myself.

'You don't come across as very democratic.'

'Democracy is overrated.'

Michael made a *joke*. He starts laughing and I join in. Wow, running a trip with someone really does bring down the barriers.

It takes around half an hour to drive to the theatre. Parking the bus is always interesting in the tight city spaces. I get Connor to hop out and indicate how wide the gap is between the rear bumper and the wall as I reverse.

'I'll get out too,' Michael mutters, unclicking his belt and jumping out of the bus as if he's on fire.

My driving really isn't that bad.

We walk en masse to the theatre and I take a group photo for obligatory social media PR, then we are finally in. Michael and I end up next to each other at the end of the row. I collapse into my seat and the lights immediately dim, before a spotlight centres upon Mrs Johnstone, ready to sing.

I love Blood Brothers: it's such a great show and the kids are loving the rude jokes. I even see Michael smile too. There's just one problem: I didn't have time to take my coat off, and now I'm stiflingly hot. I decide I'm going to have to go for it, so I wait until the next song and pull down my zip, then wriggle around, pulling the sleeve taut so I can withdraw my arm. I lose my grip on the sleeve, and my elbow launches into Michael's face.

'I'm so sorry!' I whisper, as he doubles over, clutching his cheek with a muffled cry.

I quickly finish wrangling myself out of the coat then lean over to inspect the damage.

'Is it red?' he asks, taking his hands down so I can see.

'It's hard to see.'

I reach up and brush my fingertips over where I think the impact was. His skin feels hot to touch and for a moment our eyes lock. It's a good job I took my coat off because I can feel my cheeks beginning to burn.

'Sorry,' I whisper again, hastily sitting on my hands to avoid further embarrassment.

He shifts in his seat, and his leg is within grazing distance of mine, but not quite touching. I sit rigidly, feeling an electric charge between us, and I can't concentrate on anything anymore. I'm staring at the stage and the characters, but all I can think about is how close I am to Michael Chase right now.

12

At the interval, the kids queue up for ice cream, and I dash to the Ladies to avoid Michael.

I splash some water on my face. What is wrong with me? It must be the stress. I haven't felt a spark like that with someone since… Well, for a long time. It makes me feel like I'm sixteen again, when I first started going out with Jamie. Being next to him felt amazing, hence why I was his shadow for the two years we were together. He went through intense mood swings, but when he kissed me, it was like the finale of a fireworks display, and all was forgiven. But it's not enough to just have chemical attraction, I remind myself. Don't let your stupid, stress-warped brain imagine that there is something between you and Michael. Deena's words about him trying to get inside my head seem very appropriate right now.

Back in the auditorium, he's holding a carton of strawberry ice cream against his cheek.

'Is it painful?' I ask guiltily. 'Sorry, my arm slipped.'

'It's fine,' he says, then holds the ice cream out to me. 'Would you like it?'

'Don't you need it?' I ask suspiciously.

'No, it's okay.'

I maintain my stare. Is this a truce?

'I figured, given how much you love pineapples, that you would like strawberries too.'

I take the ice cream.

'Well, I suppose it's healthier than chocolate.'

He gives a laugh and then we hear the announcement that Act Two is about to begin. I eat my ice cream and reflect on the fact that Michael Chase just gave it to me. And not an insult in sight. Well, maybe a touch of banter. Talking of touching, I feel compelled to lean more to his side like a magnet, an irresistible draw. My arm is on the arm rest next to his, and I keep shifting uncomfortably, hoping to brush against him and see if this weird chemical tension will dispel or react. I shift my eyes to sneak glances at him, and I feel a jumpy excitement that he's watching me too, but we both just have to sit here and do not touch, do not touch...

The play is well acted and builds to its inevitable conclusion. As we all applaud enthusiastically, I feel a huge sense of relief. This wasn't such a bad idea, after all. As we walk back to the bus, Connor is talking at me about all the parts he enjoyed the most.

'Thing is, Miss, she should never have trusted the posh woman. Rich people do what they like and they don't care about anyone else.'

'*Some* rich people,' I correct. Although it's tempting to agree with him.

'I don't think Mrs Johnstone should have given her own baby away,' Rose says. 'Even if you're poor, families need to stick together.'

'But Eddie had much better opportunities with the Lyons family,' Michael says. 'He went to university, got a good job…'

'He stole his best mate's woman, and then he got shot,' Connor says bluntly, and I snicker with a sense of triumph.

That's what I love about Blood Brothers– kids from our estate *get* it. For once, it isn't all about white middle class people —

although it looks like Michael may have drawn a different moral from the story. Looking at how much the group has enjoyed this show, I make a resolution to do this more often.

Maybe not the part where I elbowed Michael in the face.

It's dark, and the traffic is heavy as I drive the bus out of the city centre. Somehow, the atmosphere feels different now. As much as we all want to get home, it's not the end of the world if we're delayed. I'm looking forward to telling the Head how well everything went when I next see him. Which quite possibly may be at my interview for the HoD role, if I get one.

'How are you feeling about the job?' It's like he's read my mind.

I shrug.

'I'm trying not to think about it too much.'

There's a long pause.

'I wasn't sure you'd be interested.' He turns back to look out the window, to avoid my scrutiny.

'Why?' I wonder what he's going to say next, what damning assessment he's going to give of my capabilities.

He shrugs now, pretending to be casual.

'It's such a data-driven role, all those spreadsheets, meetings with the Head… I just didn't think that was your thing.'

I gulp.

'I can use Excel.'

Why do I even have to justify myself to him anyway?

'I'm not saying you can't handle it, I just think your strength is more the pastoral side.'

'Is that because I'm a woman?' My tone is razor sharp now. The effect of the ice cream has totally worn off.

'No.'

He clearly thinks I'm some kind of hippy teacher who's all about peace and love. I remember the first time I met him with the cat poster. Does the cat poster reinforce this? Perhaps. But I should not have to take down any cat posters just because of what some hotshot thinks about them.

'You're mad at me again now, aren't you?' he says.

I employ the classic tactic of ignoring him.

'Yep, definitely mad at me.'

I flick the radio on to drown him out, and start pressing all the different buttons to get the right station.

'You focus on driving, I'll sort the radio,' he says, waving my hand away.

'It's fine,' I jam some more buttons, swerving the bus and grinding the tyres on the lane markings of the hard shoulder.

'Just. Drive. The. Bus,' he says with gritted teeth, holding on to the dashboard again.

The engine starts making a sputtering sound.

'Check the fuel gauge,' he commands.

Oh no. I don't have to say anything; I can feel him reading my expression.

'How bad is it?' he asks, and starts tapping on his phone to find a petrol station.

'We'll make it,' I say, annoyed at him using a map when I've driven down this road hundreds of times. 'I know where the garages are.'

'Didn't you check it before we left?'

It's exactly the sort of 'you're-so-stupid' comment that I can't stand.

'No, Michael, I was too busy trying to drive and making sure that we had the tickets and the consent forms and everything else! But thanks for your help,' I snap.

'Pull over,' he says.

'It's a *motorway*,' I glare at him. Who wants to be on the hard shoulder with a bunch of kids? 'We can make it to the exit.'

The sputtering sound continues.

'Really?'

His hands are on the dashboard again. We hurtle past a sign which says 'Exit ½ mile.'

I press down on the accelerator. Michael looks like he's on some kind of thrill ride, about to be dropped from a great height into an abyss. He's muttering something to himself which could be a self-help mantra or praying — I'm not sure which.

I move into the exit lane, take my foot off the gas, and coast down the ramp. Like a perfectly executed driving test manoeuvre, I pull the bus into a bus stop just as it grinds to a complete halt. Michael and I both heave sighs of relief.

'What's going on Miss?'

'Why have we stopped?'

'Okay everyone,' I turn to face them. 'We've run out of fuel so I'm going to have to ask you to ring your parents to collect you from here. It isn't too far from the school. If you haven't got a phone, let me know, and I will call them.'

The kids all start making calls and I feel Michael staring at me. I turn back to him.

'Yes? Going to tell me how this would have all been different if you had been in charge?'

'Just wondering how *we're* going to get back.'

It's a fair point.

'We'll have to wait for the kids to get picked up, then walk to a petrol station, fill up a carton and bring it back here.'

'Can't I just go now and get the petrol?' he asks impatiently.

'Ratio,' I reply.

He thinks for a moment.

'What if I take some of the boys with me?'

'You could… Do you think we should ring Roger?'

Roger is the trips coordinator. This basically involves him clicking a button to authorise everything on the online system the County uses. He's pretty hands off.

'Er, Roger is not doing that role anymore,' Michael says awkwardly.

'What?'

'David's taken it off him while he undergoes a capability review.'

Oh great. David's picking the incompetent staff off, one by one.

'Nice of you to tell me. So who do we ring?'

'It would be David.'

We both look at each other. Well, this is his opportunity to drop me in it, that's for sure. There's a pause. He's not picking up his phone yet.

'I don't think we need to ring him unless we can't sort this out ourselves,' Michael finally says. 'Let me go, with some of the boys, we'll get the fuel, and hopefully the parents will start arriving.'

'Look, if you go through the underpass, there's a fuel station only five minutes' walk away,' I show him a map on my phone.

'Great.'

He unbuckles his belt and opens the minibus door.

'Right, I want four of you to come with me to the petrol station. Stan, Marlowe, Lewis…'

'Can I come, Sir?' Connor waves his hand in the air.

'All right. Connor too.'

I watch as the four boys jump out of the bus and head with Michael down the footpath. Connor is moving his hands animatedly and I can tell he's super excited about this latest turn of events. In spite of this massive disaster, I find myself smiling that Michael picked him to go with his group.

'Right, who's going to sing with me?' I turn to the rest of the bus.

After a few renditions of key Blood Brothers songs, parents start arriving. Michael comes back and starts emptying the fuel into the bus. Even though the night is cold, at least it's not raining. No one has a go at me for driving a bus with low fuel; instead most of the parents thank me, and some even offer to take me and Michael home.

'It's all right, honestly, I think we'll get the bus working again in no time.'

Finally, it's just me, Michael and Connor.

'Have you rung your parents?' I ask.

'Yeah, Mum's on her way,' he says.

Michael rolls his eyes, and the two of us stand, shivering in our coats, willing a car to come round the corner.

'Thanks for organising the trip, Miss,' Connor says.

'It was good, wasn't it?' I give a smile.

A car pulls up and Connor jumps into the back. His mum shouts her thanks through the window and then they drive off.

'Great, we can go then,' Michael says, clearly desperate. 'You sure you don't want me to drive?'

'You're not insured without the County certificate,' I tell him for the hundredth time.

We get back on the bus, and thankfully the motor starts. We head back to the school, and it feels like the middle of the night, although it's only 7:00pm. I could go to bed right now. Hot water bottle, cup of tea…

'So do we need to tell David about this tomorrow?' Michael interrupts my fantasy.

'You can if you want.'

I say it casually and look in the rearview mirror to avoid his gaze.

'I think it was all fine in the end,' Michael concedes.

I breathe an inward sigh of relief.

'You did well, organising the trip,' Michael continues.

I'm thrown by this unexpected compliment, and our eyes meet, before I have to return my gaze to the twenty five roundabouts to get to Whidlock. At one point, Michael's phone rings.

'Who is it?' I ask, although part of me already knows.

'David.'

'Maybe one of the parents called him to complain.' My mind goes into overdrive.

'Jen, they don't have his personal phone number,' Michael points out.

The phone is still ringing.

'Are you going to answer?' I ask. The tension is killing me.

The ringing cuts off.

'Looks like I missed it,' Michael says, deadpan.

I can't help grinning. This man.

The phone then pings.

'He sent me a text now,' Michael says. 'Everything ok?'

'What are you going to say?'

My emotions can't take much more of this torture.

'All good,' Michael says, tapping on his phone. 'There. Sent.'

With driving the bus and David breathing down our necks, this trip has taken a few years off my life.

When we finally reach the school, the staff car park is empty apart from one car: a red Subaru. I park the bus and we clamber out. Michael slams the door with considerable emphasis. He strides towards the red car, then looks back at me.

'Where's your car?'

'I walk to school.'

He frowns.

'Well, do you want a lift?'

I want to stand my ground and refuse him, because he's annoying and I don't want to be in his debt any more than I already am since the elbow-in-face incident, the ice cream and then forgetting to put fuel in the bus, but it's late and I'm cold.

'Sure.'

I get into the passenger side and try to sit up with a confident posture, but I am shaking with cold now. He grabs a blanket from the back seat and hands it to me, without a word. I wrap it around myself, aware that I am melting towards him again. It's the way that it smells of him… If he wasn't sitting right next to me, I would smother my face in it to breathe it in deeply. I try to focus on taking in every detail of his car. Unsurprisingly, it's immaculately clean. It looks brand new inside.

'So, where am I going?' Michael's voice interrupts my crazed thoughts.

'To the shops.'

I give him directions and it only takes five minutes to drive there. He surveys the area.

'Where do you live?'

'In a flat,' I reply, undoing my seatbelt and readying to open the door. 'Thank you for the lift.'

'What, so you actually live this close to the school?' He looks at me in disbelief.

'Yes.'

'Don't you see kids everywhere, all the time?' he says, horrified at the thought.

'No.'

That's not strictly true, but never mind.

'How long have you lived here?'

'A year.'

I feel a jolt of pain as I remember moving in. That was a depressing day of my life.

'Do you even have a car?' He scans the car park.

'I don't need one.'

'It probably benefits society that you don't frequent the road space too often,' he quips. 'That time when I offered to help you with the box, you should have just asked for a lift.'

His eyes have softened but I don't want to be pitied. I made this choice for a reason.

'Thank you for the ice cream.'

I open the door and try to step out gracefully, then walk to the entrance of my flat. I feel myself blushing at the loud shouts of people going in and out of the chip shop, and how drab and dingy my home looks. I should have just walked.

I let myself in and once I've closed the door, I hear his car engine roar to life as he drives off.

I put the kettle on for my tea and hot water bottle, then a text from Katie reminds me.

Katie: How's your application going?

Thoughts of an early night vapourize into the steam. I might be exhausted, and my driving abilities questionable, but I cannot stand by and watch Michael sail into Whidlock and snatch a pay rise from under my nose. I sigh and open my laptop.

13

I walk into school feeling exhausted the next day; trips just suck you dry. I keep reminding myself that it was worth it.

I step into the female staff toilets, and Janet Patchell is standing by the sinks, her eyes red-rimmed. I've never seen Janet cry before. She's the sort of woman who's made of solid rock, holding up the school like a balustrade.

'Janet, what's the matter?'

She shakes her head and blows her nose.

'It's fine, it's nothing…'

Judy sails in and quickly assesses the situation while I look on helplessly.

'Come here,' she says, wrapping her arms around Janet and squeezing her. 'What's the bastard done now?'

'I… used the wrong spreadsheet,' Janet says between sobs. 'We just had a meeting and all of the Senior Team were there. He humiliated me in front of everyone.'

'He's a bully,' Judy says, rubbing her shoulders. 'Pay him no attention.'

'But he's the Head!' Janet replies.

'They've put him here to wave his magic wand and then they'll take him away again. You just need to outlast him.'

'Sometimes I wonder why I'm doing this,' Janet murmurs.

I head for the staffroom. I grab Little Miss Sunshine and make my tea, wondering how bad that meeting must have been to make Janet Patchell cry.

'Had that song stuck in my head all night.'

I look up to see Michael, making his beloved coffee, seemingly chipper and humming 'Tell me it's not true'.

'Are you all right?' he asks when I don't reply.

I'm sick of the glass ceiling in this patriarchal school. But what's the point in telling him that? He's part of the problem.

'Just tired, that's all.'

He gives me an appraising look. I move into the seating area to avoid his scrutiny and grab a seat next to Steph.

'How'd it go last night?'

'It went,' I smile. 'We all arrived in one piece. Didn't have enough fuel to get all the way back, but the parents picked the kids up from just outside the motorway exit.'

'Oh no! Did you get back all right?'

'Yeah, the petrol station wasn't that far.'

'Were you alone with *Mr Chase*?' she puts on an affected tone. 'How was that?'

'He was okay,' I start to giggle. 'I accidentally elbowed him in the face in the theatre.'

'Try punching him next time. It might make you feel better.'

We both laugh.

'I heard he went to lunch with the Head to discuss the HoD promotion,' Steph says in a low tone.

'Seriously?'

'Well it was either that or just because he can't stand hanging around the rest of the Senior team. Which, given they are all old enough to be his parents, could be true.'

I want to find out more but then David Clark walks in, his hair sleek with no hint of grey. He definitely can't be forty yet, which is why he stands out so much from the others. His composure annoys me when Janet is probably still crying in the toilets.

'Morning everyone,' he begins with a breakfast TV presenter's smile. 'As you're all aware, I've been attending meetings with Inspire to Achieve and the Local Authority to discuss the future of Whidlock County. My first half term here has been extremely eye-opening. We are all working together for the best possible way forward to improve conditions here for staff and pupils.'

The mood in the staff room is stony-faced and flat. It's been a long half term and everyone's flagging.

'We have decided that we will run an in-house inspection the week after half term. A team from Inspire to Achieve will come in and conduct observations, book scrutiny and interviews with Heads of Department in core subjects. Much like an inspection, you will not know if you are going to be observed in advance. We want to gather a sense of what is happening across the school.'

I exchange a look with Steph. This sounds like a nightmare. Inspections are bad enough, but he is voluntarily organising this. Is he insane?

'Of course, we want a realistic picture of what happens in your classroom on a daily basis. But it is definitely in our interest as a school to impress Inspire to Achieve. This is a great opportunity for us to showcase outstanding lessons and excellent practice.'

I catch Michael's eye, expecting him to be smugly writing in his planner again, but he is looking at me with an inscrutable expression. Almost like concern. I look away.

'Janet, as our curriculum leader, will send out a lesson plan template. All staff are expected to use this for every lesson during the week of the internal inspection. Please ensure that your plans are printed and ready to hand in to any visitors who come to your classes.'

Happy half term. I try not to think about how many hours this will take. It's like a GIF in my head of David Clark snatching away my story manuscript and shaking his finger at me in reproach.

School trip: done. Application: needs to be handed in imminently. Novel: needs serious work and a wad of cash I don't yet possess. Mountain to scale: start ASAP. Social life: Dead On Arrival.

'Come on, Jen,' Steph says. 'I was thinking, how about we do a run before school? Get some fresh air and exercise.'

I can't think of anything worse. But I hate the gym and at least Steph would motivate me not to give up in the first half-mile.

'All right,' I say. 'Let me know when and you can come to my flat.'

I'll probably regret saying that later.

At lunchtime, I catch up with Judy as we eat around the table together in the staffroom. She's going for healthy-looking salads and houmous at the moment. I'm currently eating every type of carb imaginable: bagels, pasta, any form of bread…

'Is Janet okay?' I ask.

Judy nods.

'She's a tough cookie. Just makes me cross, though. He's a sly one, that David Clark. Always knew it. I used to teach him, you know. His Head Boy campaign plastered A3 size posters of his face all over the school. Makes me feel old now!'

'I didn't realise.'

'He knows exactly how to get away with it. He's clever. A bully, but a clever one.'

'He pretended he didn't remember me, when he taught me in sixth form.' It still stings to think about it.

Judy gives a dry laugh.

'So you know not to trust anything he says, then.'

'I was wondering if you could help me,' I say, setting down my bagel. 'I'm applying for the HoD job.'

Judy raises her eyebrows.

'You decided to go for it?'

'I've got to,' I say. 'I can't let Michael get it uncontested.'

'I know I said the other day that you should go for it,' she says, hesitating, 'but I don't want to see you throw your heart and soul into getting this position when you're not going to get a fair trial.'

'Look, I know I won't get it,' I admit. 'But I'm a bit tired of being written off. I want to have at least some say in what goes on around here. If I put my hat in the ring, then they at least have to give me an opportunity to share my ideas, and it may be that they do consider me for Liz's role, if she ends up losing it or not coming back.'

'When's the deadline?'

'Tomorrow.'

'Email me your application tonight and I'll send you feedback,' Judy promises.

Michael sits down at the other end of the table, and I catch his eye for a moment before the P.E. department noisily burst into the room.

'Right everyone,' Steve, the Head of P.E., booms. '5-a-side football starts tomorrow after school. Who's in?'

'The Head's signed up,' Gareth adds. 'You in, Michael?'

'Great, another boys' club,' I mutter to Judy. 'Just what we need.'

The bell rings, and I dash off to face the Year 11 boys' group.

As I approach the classroom, I can hear noise. I open the door and they are all in there, sprawled over desks. One of them is holding a bag of chips. On the whiteboard there is a crude diagram of a woman, stick-figure style but with two circles for breasts. Tyler is sitting in my swivel chair. He looks up when I enter and gives a smile of satisfaction at what must be shock and horror in my expression. The others at least have the grace to look awkward.

'What is going on in here?' I ask.

The room has fallen silent.

'I want every one of you to get outside and line up in silence. Now.'

Muttering and shuffling, the boys start to move. Tyler gives a bored shrug and swivels himself a half-turn before standing. I give him a hard stare.

'You do not sit in my chair. Is that understood?'

He says nothing, staring back at me sullenly, then goes to join the others outside.

I wipe the board clean, trying to calm my shaking rage. Is this about the theatre trip? Is he punishing me? Perhaps I should just remove him from the lesson, ask Michael if he can work in the back of his class… But the HoD application is due tomorrow. What will SLT think if I'm calling for pupils to be removed?

I take a deep breath and go to the door.

'Let me make this clear,' I say firmly. 'You do not enter my classroom if I am not present, unless there is another member of staff with you who gives you permission. Is that understood?'

The boys mumble a response. Some of them tut and roll their eyes.

'You do not bring food into my classroom.'

I look at the boy with the chips.

'You do not write on my board, and you certainly do not draw lewd images on it.'

I try to look at each of them in turn, so that none of them feel singled out, and also to make them squirm.

'Now you're going to walk in and stand behind your desk until I tell you to sit down. No talking.'

I lead the way and stand at the front of the classroom while they come back in. Some of them are completely quiet; others deliberately bang the chairs or their bags against the table. I wait until every last one of them is in position, standing.

'You may now sit down.'

The mood in the classroom is toxic, and there's no way I can launch into a jolly starter activity after that performance. It's time for an impromptu exam practice task. Handing out lined paper, I give instructions as I walk around the room.

'You will complete a timed writing task using an exam style question,' I explain. 'Write about a time when you were unfairly treated.'

As I pass Tyler, I stumble over a sports kit bag that's been left in the aisle. Thankfully I don't completely lose my balance and fall over, but some of the boys laugh and I get the feeling that someone is doing something behind my back. I stand up and see Tyler quickly move his arm and look up with a mock-innocent air.

'Can you please keep bags under the desk?' I say with annoyance.

I move to the computer to take the register and there is some scuffling and muffled noise from the class. When I look up, they all fall silent and start writing hurriedly. Then I notice. All their bags are deliberately placed to block every aisle.

This is not a day when I want to fight this battle.

I pretend that I haven't noticed anything, and stay at my desk, while they complete the writing task. Tyler seems to be writing rather enthusiastically. Finally their thirty minutes are up, and I feel ready to face them again.

'I'd like you to swap your writing with someone else now please,' I call out. 'And you're going to read it and write down one thing they've done well, and one thing they can improve.'

In the general kerfuffle of swapping sheets and the release of talking again after a time of silence, a pen lands on the floor by my desk.

'Whose is this?' I ask, leaning down to pick it up.

'I'd tap that,' a voice mutters, and someone snorts.

I hear it distinctly, and I think it's from Tyler's direction, but I can't be sure.

'Miss, there's a pen on the floor over here too,' Ollie shouts in mock earnestness.

'Then I'm sure you can pick it up,' I say icily.

Thankfully, the bell is going to go soon, so I let them messily appraise one another's work and watch them closely for any other misdemeanours. I watch Tyler the most. I'm sure he's at the centre of this out-and-out rebellion.

'Miss, can you read my work?' Tyler asks, holding his page up.

'Yes,' I say, deciding I need a different tactic.

I carefully make my way over to him without falling over any bags, and take the page. There's sniggering and chit-chat behind me as I scan through his writing, but I ignore it.

It seems that Tyler has written about how his teacher did not allow him to go on a school trip. He's called the teacher Miss Watson but it's obviously about me.

The bell goes and the boys start to head out of the classroom, leaving their papers in a scattered pile on the back desk. Tyler stands up to leave.

'Tyler,' I say. 'I'm sorry that you didn't get to go on the trip.'

His eyes challenge me and he stays silent.

'I will do my best to make sure you get a place next time.'

He turns to leave but his silence is unsettling. I stand and wait for him to go.

At the door, he looks over his shoulder to stare at me once more. Then he gives a smile of triumph before walking out.

14

I'm sitting at my desk, staring at my application, but all I can feel is a hollow sense of failure.

Who am I trying to kid? I'm not HoD material. I just had a mutiny from one of the most important classes in the school, the key marginal boys' group. If we don't turn those D grades into C's, then it'll be another nail in the coffin for Whidlock County.

'Jennifer?'

Michael clears his throat. I look up to see him come in through the side door.

'Yes?'

'I wanted to say… two things, really. Firstly, well done on organising the trip. You worked really hard, and it was a big success. I shouldn't have moaned so much about the petrol situation,' he takes a breath, pulling on his collar to loosen it. 'Secondly, good luck for the job. I'm sorry about what I said before.'

'You mean when we did the display or in the minibus?' I narrow my eyes.

'Both.'

I blink. I'm not sure I can handle Michael being nice to me. Not after the day I've had. Looking at me, he steps closer.

'Are you okay? You seem stressed out.'

I'm either going to scream or burst into tears. I choose anger; it's less humiliating.

'Stressed out?' I repeat. 'Yeah, I'm stressed out. I just worked my guts out to get that trip off the ground, I haven't finished my application, and now the Head just announced he's arranged an inspection. But you probably knew about that, given that you're such good buddies.'

His jaw sets and he doesn't say anything.

'I knew it.'

'I've worked with David for a few years. I can't help what he tells me.'

'I bet he's taken you out to lunch and told you exactly what to say in your application.'

'He didn't tell me anything,' he says, too quickly, in complete contradiction to what he just said.

'Did he take you to lunch?' I press.

'Just as friends. Friends can have lunch together, can't they?'

He's starting to look uncomfortable. Good.

'What about when he's on the interview panel, will he be your friend then, or just your boss?' I fold my arms.

'David is always very professional…'

I roll my eyes. There's no point listening to this.

'Oh, come on!' I snap my laptop shut impatiently. 'I don't know why I'm even bothering, this is such a set-up. It makes me sick.'

'It's not a set up! If one of us gets that job, it will be because the panel decides it. It's not just David, it's the governors too, and Geoff.'

'How do you know who's on the panel?'

He gives a defeated shrug.

'I didn't come here to argue with you.'

'Then why did you come here?' I stare at his face, discerning a slight flush of embarrassment as he looks down to avoid eye contact with me.

'I wanted to apologise…' he runs a hand through his dark hair. It's not waxed like David's, which I like. But that's not the point. 'I also wanted to ask if you'd join our 5-a-side team tomorrow.'

I just took a swig from my water bottle and I gulp it down the wrong way, coughing.

'Who, me?'

'It, it could be fun,' he says, and I've never heard him falter before. I look at him incredulously. Is he… nervous?

Maybe if I do it, I can tackle David Clark and pretend it was an accident.

'Sure,' I reply, taking another sip of water, and this time recalibrating my thoughts to consider what I'm going to wear. Sports top, leggings… Need to dig out a sports bra…

'Great,' Michael says with an unexpected smile.

He almost looks like a normal human being.

I turn back to my desk and gather up my planner and pens.

'See you tomorrow then,' he says.

I open my mouth to give some sort of barbed reply, but I haven't got the energy.

'Bye,' is all I say, exhaling.

I stuff my laptop into my already-rammed-full bag. May as well finish this application at home. It's going to be a long night.

When my alarm goes off at 5:30am, I groan and briefly contemplate texting Steph to wimp out of our run. But then I remember that I also signed up for 5-a-side, and she would – rightly– feel slighted if I chose the beefy P.E. crew over her. So I'm faced with the inevitability of two bouts of exercise in one day, when usually the only running I manage is for the bus, when it's pulling away from my stop.

It's dark and cold outside, and after layering two sweaters, I huddle up on my faded sofa with a bowl of porridge. I've got a stress headache and it's not even 6.00am. All I can think about is my application. I just wish I had more time to polish it.

I hear Steph's car pull up outside and sigh. Taking a swig from my water bottle, I lock up and zip the key safely into my pocket. The corridor smells of yesterday's chips.

'Morning, partner,' Steph says, as I meet her on the street. 'Ready to go?'

We jog along the pavement, grateful for the hazy glow of the streetlights. Apparently sunrise is at 6:20am. I'll be lucky if I'm still alive by then.

'Keep your pace steady,' Steph instructs. 'You should still be able to talk to me.'

'I'm trying to focus on not falling off the kerb.'

'Relax! Just put one foot in front of the other.'

'You mean as opposed to going backwards?' I puff. 'You'll be pleased to know I'm doing 5-a-side tonight as well.'

'Wow, you're really pushing the boat out,' Steph rolls her eyes, barely breaking a sweat. 'What's made you want to join in with Steve and the macho crew?'

'David's going to be there,' I explain, gasping for breath. 'And Michael.'

'The job is Head of English, not P.E.! You think you're going to impress the Head with your football skills? I seem to remember last time you played, you were goalie and you let in twenty-one goals.'

'When it's down to the goalie, it's a sign that the *team* has not been doing their jobs properly.'

'Right.'

'I thought you'd be supportive,' I say. 'You're always telling me to do more exercise and not let work take over my life.'

'When was the last time you did something for yourself? Something you enjoy?'

Cue montage of the past few weeks: me at school. Me sitting in my flat, marking. Eat, sleep, repeat. How depressing is my life?

'Exactly,' Steph says, as if she's read my thoughts. 'The thing is, Jen, it doesn't stop. There will always be a David who tells you to type thirty-six lesson plans and have them on your desk ready for an impromptu visit; there will always be a Liz who doesn't show up and you have to fill the gaps. If you don't set boundaries, they will take and take until you've got nothing left.'

'I want to be good at my job,' I frown, and brush my hair away from my sticky forehead. 'I'm not doing this for David. I'm doing this for Connor, for the kids who can't even spell their own names right.'

'And you do a great job,' she says. 'But if you don't put on your oxygen mask first, you're going to suffocate.'

'I could certainly use one right now,' I say, wheezing and coughing.

The daylight has slowly seeped through the heavy layer of cloud –a rather imperceptible sunrise– and I can see my breath in the cold air as we stop for a breather at the top of the hill. Whidlock sprawls below: council houses and double-parked streets, speed bumps that crunch the underside of cars, and gardens full of broken fridges and brambles. In the distance are the high-rise apartment blocks going into the city, which is surrounded by leafy suburbs and easy access to the motorway. Up here, Whidlock gets the leftovers that nobody wants.

'Beautiful, isn't it?' Steph jokes.

'A certain urban mystique.'

'Right, we've got to quicken the pace to get back to yours now. Go go go!'

I keep forgetting Steph's alternative job choice would be personal trainer.

Back at my flat, we take turns to shower and get ready for work. I choose a black pencil skirt and a pinstripe blouse, and stand in front of the mirror applying layer after layer of gel to slick my hair back. Steph pops up over my shoulder, making a face.

'Very serious,' she mocks. 'What's with the suit? You're not trying to fit in with Michael 'Moss Bros', are you?'

'If I'm applying for this job, I need to look the part.'

Steph assesses me in the mirror.

'You look boring,' she says bluntly.

'That's what they want,' I shrug.

'It's not what Whidlock needs,' she replies. 'Especially not with Roger's explanations about how to use an interactive white board!'

That was a particularly disastrous in-house training session, where they were really scraping the barrel.

Steph drives us to school, the sixties' concrete block building so familiar that I don't often consider what it looks like to outsiders. It's barely changed since I was a student –except for ageing– and the black metal railings and grey expanse of car park and yard blend with the breezeblock exterior, a line of square-cut windows exactly spaced. It strikes me now how much it resembles a prison.

As we walk towards the main entrance, I catch a glimpse of Michael's classroom. He's at his desk, marking books. I check my watch: 7:45am. I'm fifteen minutes earlier than usual, so I probably won't cross paths with him as I make my tea and battle with the photocopier. I shake off what feels almost like disappointment to remind myself that I need to check over my application one last time before I send it in.

I open my laptop and there's a message from Judy with feedback on my application so far.

Dear Jen,

This is great so far. Well done! You're nearly there. I think you should add more about your focus on creative writing, and how that helps raise students' attainment. I have a friend who's a published author and she does school visits to run creative writing workshops. Why don't I give you her contact details and you could organise something? It will really help you to stand out.

Judy

Hmm, maybe she can give me some tips on how to actually get back to my writing. I sip my tea and try not to feel resentful and grumpy. I haven't opened my story document up in weeks, and it makes me think about what Steph said earlier. Maybe it is my fault that I'm not doing more things I enjoy.

Focus, Jen.

Would a focus on creative writing really help my application? Surely David would just read it and roll his eyes. He wants grades, not cliched reworkings of the latest action film in a poorly worded scrawl with no full stops (which is what Connor does. Every time.).

But creative writing is engaging. How else can you get a class to imagine themselves on another planet, describing the smell of Martian air? Kids love stories. And if I'm going to choose a hill to die on, I want that to be it.

I consider how it might work. How about a whole-school creative writing week? A bit like a writing festival? My brain starts whirring through the possibilities and I type quickly.

'Hey, Jennifer?'

I jump in my seat and knock my mug over, spilling tea all over my planner.

'Oh no!' I spring out of my chair and collide with Michael, who's moving forwards at the same time to grab the mug, and I watch in slow motion as it slips through his hands and crashes to the floor, breaking into pieces.

'I'm sorry,' he says, as I stare at the mess. 'I didn't mean to scare you.'

I place a hand on my hip and look at him incredulously, then follow his gaze to my laptop screen, my application open for all the world to see. I slam the lid shut and grab some tissues, dabbing at my planner. Was he just here to spy on what I was writing? How much did he see?

'I'll get you a new mug,' he says, stooping to the floor to pick up the china.

'Well as long as it's not like yours,' I retort, and it sounds ruder out loud than it did in my head.

'What's wrong with my mug?'

'It's totally plain. IKEA's finest.'

'Not all of us like cartoon characters.'

'I suppose you were born quoting Shakespeare.'

'Methinks the lady doth protest too much,' he says, without missing a beat. And, just like that, I feel tears burning in my eyes.

'Hey,' he says, in a softer tone, his hand reaching out and his fingers just grazing my wrist. 'This isn't just about the mug, is it?'

I pull away from him, finding a tissue to blow my nose and subtly dab my eyes, my back to Michael. He doesn't move.

'I actually came to tell you something,' he says. 'They've extended the deadline for the HoD applications.'

'What?' I spin around to face him again.

'You can check on the advert if you like,' he says, gesturing towards the laptop. I was so lucky the tea didn't soak it; it would be like losing my right arm.

'When's the new deadline?'

'Friday.'

Relief, sweet relief, floods through me, and I smile, but then I sob and I realise that I am crying too.

I am crying in front of Michael. He is standing there watching me cry. This is probably his worst-case scenario. Like it's an out-of-body experience, I can hear my ugly crying noises and just want myself to shut up, but I can't hold the floodgate back any longer.

Suddenly, as I sniff back my streaming nose, I can smell cologne and he's there, he's standing right in front of me. I can just about see the lapels of his jacket, through the blurriness of tears. One hand softly presses my back, and I cave, I cave forwards and my shoulders shake and I don't care if I get mascara on his white collar, he broke my damn mug and he can… he can…

He wraps both arms around me and I can't – think – straight; when was the last time someone held me like this? I'm still sniffing and crying and if I look as bad as I sound then it's really bad, but he's strong and there and he's folded around me like he *cares*, but this is Michael, this is *Michael*…

I place both hands on his chest and shove him so that he stumbles back.

'What the hell do you think you are doing?' I say it so loudly, I'm almost yelling.

'I was just… trying to help.'

'By sneaking around, reading my application so you're always one step ahead? I'm so sick of you! You think you're better than everyone else.'

'I think you're a bit upset right now—'

'Yes, Sherlock, you want a medal for that observation?'

He's looking so shocked, and for once he has nothing to say. It's so absurd I start to laugh.

'How about I make you another cup of tea?' he offers.

Our eyes lock. He knows my weakness. I can't refuse.

'Okay.'

15

As I stand next to Michael at the back of the hall in our mental-health-awareness assembly, the irony isn't lost on me that the teaching profession is full of advice for how students can look after their wellbeing, and yet none of us seem to follow this ourselves.

Drink more water. Get enough sleep. Make time for things you enjoy. Somehow I don't think that dosing up on caffeine is really the solution I need, but there's not much a hot cup of tea can't solve. Even if Little Miss Sunshine has bitten the dust.

'Next slide please, Roger,' Janet prompts him. Michael and I watch Roger, unfortunately located on the stage in full view of the whole school, bumble around with the PowerPoint.

'I don't think this assembly was good for Roger's mental health,' Michael leans close to speak in a low tone into my ear. The electric charge is back, fizzing from my neck to my stomach. I hate the fact that I like it.

'It's going to be a video next,' I predict, correctly. 'Let's see how long it takes him to press play.'

Roger, visibly sweating, shakes the computer mouse vigorously before finding the cursor and navigating it to the play button.

'Seven,' Michael and I whisper in unison.

I shuffle minutely to the right so that my shoulder touches his arm. And I stay there.

Apparently, telling Michael you're sick of him does nothing to put him off being around you, because he seems to walk into my classroom every five minutes to check I'm not sobbing again. And he brings me another cup of tea at break time. Where does he find all these mugs?

I email Geoff and Michael, suggesting that we each create lesson plans for the inspection week with the schemes of work we were already updating– that means I would only need to sort Year 8 and Geoff would sort Year 7, Michael Year 9. Then it would just be the older groups, but I think we've got enough resources in the department to cover that.

I develop my proposal for a Writing Festival week and when Michael appears *again* at lunchtime, I click save and shut the laptop with some satisfaction. He hangs back, obviously keen to avoid being either accused of reading over my shoulder, or physically assaulted.

'How, er, how are you feeling?' he asks. Again, hesitancy. Not usually Michael's style. 'Are you going in the staff room for lunch?'

I make a face and shake my head.

'I'll just get the third degree from Steph once she sees me. She'll just know I'm upset.'

He shrugs as if to say 'Well, it is obvious'.

'Do you fancy going for a walk around the block, just to get some fresh air?'

The run this morning was enough fresh air to keep me going for a month, but it's kind of thoughtful that he's willing to be with me even when I'm a nervous wreck.

'Sure.'

For the second time in one day, I find myself walking the streets of Whidlock. There's more people around now that it's the middle of the day, and cars with noisy exhaust pipes screech past us as we head for the park.

'So is this where you grew up?' Michael asks.

'Sort of,' I reply. 'I lived on the outskirts of town, near the golf club. It's quieter out there, next to all the fields.'

'Is it weird, teaching in the school you went to?' It's more of an open question than the quick-fire interrogation I'm used to from him.

'Well, not many of the staff are still there now.'

Apart from David, but let's not go there.

'I know Whidlock gets a lot of bad press,' I continue, 'but it's really not a terrible school. The kids may not be affluent, but they're honest and –when you get them on side– they are willing to learn.'

I expect him to disagree, to launch into a tirade of negativity, but he nods and looks thoughtful.

'Connor spelled his name right the other day,' he says, and then gives an actual smile.

Michael's face is so different, with the edges of cynicism washed away, that I smile back.

'There you are, then,' I say. 'Progress where you least expect it.'

We walk a lap of the park and then alongside a graffitied wall. I remember coming here with Jamie at lunchtimes, when we'd pick up a bag of chips and sit outside together even if it was freezing cold. How sad is it, that my lingering memories of a meaningful relationship are a teenage romance conducted mainly at school and in Whidlock park? I'm a grown adult, for goodness' sake. Now I'm walking here with Michael, and I'm feeling the same shivery excitement. Am I just deluding myself?

'I've got a question for you,' Michael looks sideways at me, and I hope he can't read my mind.

'What?' I ask nervously.

'What's your favourite book?'

I relax. An English teacher's safe ground.

'*Wuthering Heights.*'

He considers this.

'Do you find it romantic?'

'No. Would you dig up a corpse? Who does that?' I shake my head. 'You don't read Emily Bronte for romance. You read her work for the unflinching portrayal of a destructive obsession.'

'Nice. Can I quote you on that?'

'Okay, smarty pants, what's yours?'

'*Bleak House.*'

He says this without a trace of irony.

'Dickens? I did not expect you to say that.'

'It was the first book we studied at uni, and I had a really great tutor who unpacked all the layers in it.'

'Interesting we both chose Victorian novels. Perhaps we're both old-fashioned.'

'Or Bronte and Dickens were modern in their outlook.'

'Now you've found something else to argue with me about,' I laugh.

'As long as you're laughing, I'm happy,' he says, and he holds my gaze for a moment before I look away. I'm worried I'm going to start blushing. Act like an adult, Jen.

'Do you want me to find someone to fill in for you at football, or do you want to go ahead with it?' he asks, breaking the silence.

It's a choice between being with Michael or being without him. And I know which one I'd rather.

'I'd like to do it,' I say.

The school gym hasn't changed since Whidlock opened in the 1960s. It's panelled with orange varnished wood, a squeaky floor and a line of windows across one wall that make it freezing in winter and roasting in summer. For the second time today, I don my trainers – this time with leggings and a T-shirt. It's a smart (mostly *unworn*) sporty style in red. Didn't want to look like I was trying too hard, but the only other option was my neon orange one. If Michael couldn't handle the pineapple shirt, he might spontaneously combust with that one. I check my hair, and thankfully the style has held up well thanks to the gel (no idea what that's stuff made of, but it feels like concrete).

It rather dismays me to find that I am the only girl. Honestly, out of a staff of 60, does no one else want to challenge the male dominance of popular sport? Of course, I overlook the fact that I am doing this to get more attention from a guy. Hardly a win for feminism.

Why exactly do I want Michael's attention anyway?

Pushing the thought from my mind, I assess my team and the opposition. Michael seems to have sniffed out the most athletic staff who aren't in the P.E. department: Jason from Music, who looks like he lifts weights in his spare time, and Will from Science, who I actually thought was in the P.E. department for a while. And then me: a curve ball to say the least.

The P.E. guys are wearing exactly what they wear every day of the year (including December), which is shorts and T-shirts with fleece jackets. Only they've swapped the fleeces for red bibs. There's Steve, Gareth and Matt, and then Joseph Vermont, the new Maths teacher, who looks suitably weedy.

The door opens, and Michael walks in with David. They're both in polo shirts and shorts, and my stomach gives a little flip when Michael catches my eye straight away and smiles. He looks more relaxed than in his usual suit, and as I register his open collar and follow his shoulder line with my eyes, all I can think is that he held me against his shoulder today, and why am I so desperate for him to do it again? I run my hand nervously over my collar bone, and try to look clued-up as Michael draws us in for a team huddle, but in reality I'm measuring the distance between us in inches; let's see if I can get just a little closer…

'Okay,' he begins, and his tone indicates he's in classic-Michael-control-mode. 'Jason, you're in goal. Everyone else needs to pick a player to mark. Spread out as much as possible.'

'I'll take Vermont,' I say, sounding a lot more confident than I feel. Best to choose the one who doesn't look like he could mow me down.

'Great,' Michael nods. 'I'll take David.'

We all get into position to begin, and I'm starting to feel nervous now. It's been a long time since I played football. It's only 5-a-side, how hard can it be?

The game begins. The P.E. guys are straight into action: dribble, pass, run, pass, and they're shooting for the goal in what seems like minutes. They don't score though, and as we regain possession of the ball, Michael's shouting instructions whilst running all over the place. I'm 'marking' Joseph in the sense that both of us are standing rather half-heartedly on one side.

'Into the space,' Michael commands me, and I hurriedly leap to the left, just as Will passes the ball to me.

I can see Michael running and waving to me so I boot it over in his direction. So far, so good. David attempts to tackle him but he skilfully out-manoeuvres him and charges towards the goal. He shoots, and misses. Then I realise that I'm staring at him instead of marking Vermont, who is suddenly over the other side of the gym.

'Jen, over here,' Jason gestures for me to run into a space.

I dart over obediently, just as Steve intercepts, passes the ball to Gareth, and Joseph is running and calling his name –darn it!– so I try to block him. Gareth passes it, and I fight with Joseph to get to it first, and though I manage to get the ball, I only scuff-kick it so it goes skittering rather pitifully away for a few yards, before being met by Steve, who charges towards the goal. He shoots –on target this time– but Jason saves it. Steve looks back towards Joseph in annoyance and as David claps his back in commiseration for the missed goal, I hear him mutter about there being two girls playing tonight.

Steve's friendly enough in the staffroom, and I don't mind his banter, but it's comments like this that really annoy me. What also annoys me is that I'm not very good at football. I'd love to buck the trend and blow away all of their expectations by being stunningly talented, but the truth is, the pace of this game is way too fast for me. I feel about three steps behind every move. I'm also puce in the face and making a wheezing noise like I'm hyperventilating.

I get the impression generally that 5-a-side is a bit of fun. It's not serious football; it's for a bunch of work mates, half an hour after finishing time, to run about and have a laugh. But as the score is still nil-nil, the laughter dies out and I can see Steve's team getting more and more stressed, and Michael getting increasingly competitive too.

The 'half time' pep talk goes like this:

'Right guys, we really need to push them hard now and get some goals. Move it forward, use the space, and don't miss any opportunities.'

It sounds more like a hedge fund manager addressing stock pickers. I turn to the window to check my hair, looking at my reflection in the grimy glass, and as I raise my arms, I catch David looking over at my reflection too. Only I don't think he's looking at my face. He clocks that I've noticed and looks away.

Sigh.

I'm tired now and the long day is catching up with me. My reaction time is deteriorating and it wasn't great to begin with. Perhaps that's why, when I'm standing near the goal, Michael calls my name, and I turn at just the right time for the ball to smash into my nose.

I let out a cry of shock at the sharp, searing pain and then cup my hands over it, feeling the warm stickiness of blood.

Michael rushes over to me. 'I'm so sorry, I kicked it too hard…'

'Lean forwards,' someone else says. 'I'll get an ice pack.'

'I think she needs to go to A&E.'

Brilliant.

'Should we call an ambulance?'

'No, it'll be quicker if I take her.'

Michael hands me a towel and I bury my face in it. I don't want to cry in front of him AGAIN.

'Jen, let's go to my car. David, go and get her bags.'

That's probably the best thing I've heard all day. At least in my humiliation, I've turned David into a bellboy. Justice.

Michael's arms (for the second time today) support me as he guides me towards the door. I can't see very well, due to trying to keep my head down so that blood doesn't run down the back of my throat. Matt gives me an ice pack and there's a general commotion as a bunch of guys try to help escort one damsel in distress to her knight in shining armour's steed. Except the knight was the assailant. The analogy is flawed on many levels.

Maybe this injury transported my brain back into feminist critique mode of medieval tropes.

I can hear Michael confirming that David has secured the right coat and bags, and he opens the car door for me to get in. To his credit, he doesn't seem bothered by the potential mess or the idea of my nosebleed staining his pristine car interior. I could be facetious and say that it was all his fault, but everyone makes mistakes.

I really hope this stinging pain goes away. My entire head is hurting.

The car judders as the boot slams shut. Michael opens the driver door and sinks into the seat, creating a surprisingly intoxicating waft of sweat and deodorant. He clicks his belt and starts the car, casting a worried glance at me. Outside the window, David stands with the other guys, looking miffed that his footie was cut short. I snort into my towel (let's face it, Michael won't want it back after this), instantly regretting it due to the stabbing pain. Michael thinks it's a sob and worriedly says,

'It won't take long to get there.'

'Do you not see how ridiculous this situation is?' I say, muffled slightly by the towel, but I lift my head so that he catches my eye and sees my amusement.

'The only thing that's ridiculous is how competitive I am,' he says grimly, putting the car into gear and pulling off towards the school gates.

'Hey,' I say, touching his arm for a millisecond, then pulling my hand back hurriedly because the car lurches to one side.

'Sorry,' he mutters.

'At least I wore a red shirt.'

Our eyes meet and this time he smiles. The car lurches again.

'Now focus on driving,' I command. 'After all the stick you gave me about mine! I don't want to end up in A&E for something more serious.'

'Sorry,' Michael repeats.

I have a feeling he's going to say that a lot this evening.

16

'I don't think I'm ever going to do exercise again,' I announce to Michael after we've been in A&E for two hours, waiting for someone to check my nose.

It's stopped bleeding, and I've lost the will to live now, so I just want to go home. Michael being Michael insists that we stay until a doctor can verify that it's not broken, and then maybe he'll stop apologising. It's driving me crazy.

But I'd be lying if I said this was the worst day of my life. In some ways, I blame myself for wanting to see more of Michael – I definitely got my wish. But the guy –who let's face it, is going to be ripped apart by every one of our colleagues who hears about this in the staff room tomorrow, if not already via some Whatsapp group– can't do enough for me. He bundled me into his car, ice pack clamped on my nose, and drove me to the hospital, and in the past two hours has provided me with tea, chocolate, a sandwich, and the pleasure of his company. I'm not even joking. Waiting to see a doctor in A&E is not one of life's best experiences, but we've been playing the random-facts-about-my-life game and I'm not bored yet.

'I was in an orienteering club at uni,' Michael confesses.

'Where did you go?'

'We did some competitions in the Lake District.'

'I've been to Windermere. What do you think of Swallows and Amazons?' This question is crucial and my opinion of him will drop if he doesn't like it.

'I loved it when I was a kid. I would have sailed off and lived on an island on my own if I could have.'

Tick.

'Where would you go, if you could go anywhere?'

'A field in the middle of nowhere. Maybe a forest.'

'You'd have to take your suit off for that.'

'I'm not wearing one now,' he points out. 'Instead I'm wearing a white polo shirt with nose bleed stains on it.'

'I'm not apologising for the injury *you* caused me,' I joke, then regret it as it sets him off again.

'Jennifer, please believe me, I'm so sorry–'

'Stop! I can't take any more,' I place one hand over my eyes. 'Wake me up when the doctor comes.'

'Are you tired? Here, let me put something under your head.'

He rolls up his sweater and tries to stuff it on the back of the chair, but they are the short, brown plastic kind.

'You might have to turn slightly,' he says, his hands gently twisting my shoulders.

It's like a shot of the drug I'm addicted to since he put his arms around me this morning. I sink back and lean on him, putting my feet up on the next chair. I breathe out slowly –that's the one benefit of mindfulness assemblies– and imagine myself on a beach, with water gently lapping the shore.

'Jen.'

I open my eyes, feeling the confusion of sleep and did Michael just call me Jen not Jennifer?

'The doctor can see you now.'

Yes, it's definitely Michael. I swing my legs down and stretch out my arms. Better not hit him in the face again.

'Have I been asleep?'

'Yes, for approximately forty-five minutes.'

'Come this way please.' A nurse ushers me to a cubicle to see the doctor.

'It's not broken,' the doctor says. 'What happened?'

'I got hit in the face with a football.'

'Oh,' she says. 'Ouch. Well, it will be sore but it should feel better in about ten days' time. Just keep taking painkillers.'

'Thank you.'

I feel like I've wasted their –and my– time. Oh well.

'Just one moment.' The nurse pulls me over in the corridor. 'I just wanted to give you this.'

She hands me a leaflet: *Are you suffering from domestic violence?*

'I know your partner brought you here, but if you have any concerns, there's a helpline you can call.'

'He's not my partner,' I state hurriedly.

She looks like she doesn't believe me.

I'm too emotionally 'done' now to argue, so I take the leaflet and walk back to Michael, gingerly touching the bridge of my nose. I remind myself that she's just doing her job, and she probably sees a lot of "accidents". Michael springs up to his feet when he sees me.

'It's not broken,' I say, before he can ask. 'Can we go now?'

As we walk back through the car park, I avoid eye contact with other people, including the crew of smokers in hospital gowns outside the main door. Do they think that we're together? Do they think that he beat me up? I'm emotionally overloaded just trying to consider these possibilities. Michael, meanwhile, is opening the car door for me and constantly staring at me. Maybe he's worried about how bad the bruising will be, because of what people will think of him. My cynicism fades, though, as his concern seems genuine. On the journey home, I lose count of the amount of times Michael asks if I'm okay.

'You asking me that repeatedly is making me not okay.'

'So you're not okay?' he looks panicked.

'Michael, I'm fine. My nose is sore, but I'll survive.'

'Will you be able to get your application done?'

'Yeah, it's pretty much there now.'

'Good, because I don't think David would give another extension.'

'What do you mean?' I sit up straight.

He doesn't say anything.

'You asked David to extend the deadline. Didn't you?'

'I knew you had a lot on.'

I'm actually speechless for a moment.

'Jen?' he says. So he's definitely using my proper name now. 'Are you mad at me?'

'Did you tell David that I couldn't make the deadline?'

'Of course not. I said that with the trip, things had been rushed, and I would appreciate an extra day.'

'You asked for an extension for yourself so that he wouldn't know it was really for me?'

He doesn't say anything, just grips the steering wheel a little tighter.

'I don't know what to say.' I slump back in the chair again.

I sift through my feminist principles to try to work out how I should react to this. Firstly, I am supposed to be given a level playing field, not special treatment, otherwise this diminishes my achievements. However, in organising the trip, I had a lot of extra work on, which meant that I needed the extension. David doesn't know the extension was for me. Therefore he will not think any less of me. Michael was being gallant –possibly even chivalrous– by taking the hit for me, but do I want him to do that? Do I want him to feel he has to take on that role? Can't I fight my own battles?

'I don't want you to think that I need you to save me,' I say finally. 'But I do really appreciate what you did. Thank you.'

His grip loosens. He's practically sweating with relief.

'Okay. So we're okay?'

We're? I look at him questioningly.

'I have something else to ask you,' he says. He's definitely looking nervous now. 'I'd really like to make all this up to you. Would you like to go out for dinner with me tomorrow? Then I can take you to the end-of-term drinks afterwards.'

I'd almost forgotten about the drinks. The staff head to an upmarket bar in the city centre, because most of them live in that area and commute to the school. It's an annoying distance for me, though, and I usually have to take the bus.

Wait – is Michael asking me on a *date*?

'I can drop you home later, if you like,' he carries on. 'I'm not planning on drinking.'

He's trying his best to examine my expression while still paying attention to the road.

'You don't have to ask me to dinner because you accidentally kicked a football in my face.'

'I know,' he says with a sheepish smile. 'I'm asking you because... I wanted to ask you anyway.'

'Since when?' I'm enjoying staring at him for a change, watching his discomfort.

'Since I got your number from the risk assessment. I nearly sent you a message so many times these past few days, but I just…'

'Chickened out?'

'Something like that.'

I bite back a smile. He keeps glancing sideways to check my face.

'So, are you going to give me an answer?'

He can't wait for a single minute, this guy.

'Yes, I will.'

He flashes a proper smile at me and I can't help but smile back.

When I get into my flat, I text my sister: I think I just agreed to go on a date with Michael.

What??? she replies within a minute.

Me: He's taking me for dinner before staff drinks tomorrow. Then driving me home.

Katie: What are you going to wear?

Maybe, I reflect later as I hang three different outfit choices up in my window, this was a deliberate ploy to get me distracted away from my application.

It worked.

'So it's either the black dress, the black jumpsuit, or the jeans-and-a-sparkly-top combo,' I tell Katie.

'No jeans,' she says immediately. 'Which dress do you mean?'

'It's the one I wore to Steph's party last year.'

'Is it short?'

'Kind of.'

'Sounds good. The jumpsuit is a bit hit-and-miss if you ask me. Well, maybe you should wear it if you're not that into him. I mean, I thought you hated him.'

'Hate is a strong word,' I say, trying in vain to find vocabulary to describe how I feel towards Michael.

'Do you find him attractive?'

'Yes,' I say. 'But I need him to be more attracted to me than I am to him. Then I can manipulate him to do what I want, for a change.'

'That's dark for you!' Katie laughs.

'I don't want him to think he has any power over me,' I say, picking up the black dress and holding it in front of my body. 'I want him to be the one who's speechless and awkward because he's so blown away with how amazing I am.' And wrap his strong arms around me and pull me close against his perfect pinstripe suit… I clear my throat to get back on track. 'I want him to realise that he can't just take that promotion like it's a cherry on a cake. With his name on.'

'So you're fighting the patriarchy… by wearing a little black dress.'

'Something like that.'

My words echo his from earlier. I smile to myself.

'How's your application? Doesn't it have to be in by tomorrow?'

'Yes,' I remember our conversation in the car. 'He's the one who asked for the extension. For me.'

'Seriously?'

'I know. He told David that he was the one who needed more time.'

'Wow. That's actually… really decent of him.'

'I know.'

'What does he look like, again?'

'He's… muscular,' I reply, picturing Michael in front of me with his crisp shirt and tie combo. 'Pretty lean. He's tall, he must be six-five or something.'

'You sound like you've memorised his vital statistics.'

'Isn't that term reserved for women's figures?'

'Hashtag everyday sexism,' she laughs. 'I think I need to readjust my mental picture of this guy. From what you said to me before, I got the impression he was half-man, half-robot.'

'He is a machine,' I confirm. 'He said he's not drinking tomorrow because he's doing some training programme. Probably going to run a marathon while I eat my weight in chocolate over half term and write lesson plans for the inspection the Head just volunteered us for.'

'David Douche Clark.'

'My thoughts exactly.' Katie always makes me smile. 'Right, I need to get my application done.'

'Yes, that is correct. Get your application done, and then pack your kick-ass outfit and make-up. Don't forget to take a good pair of shoes!'

'Obviously.'

A text comes through from Michael.

Michael: Amidst all the excitement, I forgot to tell you. The cat is in your room again.

Me: That explains why you came in about twenty times today, then.

Michael: Yes. I'm also spying on you. Very subtly.

Me: Did you use autocorrect for how to spell subtly?

Michael: Possibly.

I give my hair special treatment before I go to bed, washing out all the gel with my most expensive shampoo, and lathering it with leave-in conditioner and moisturiser. I tell myself this has nothing to do with my date tomorrow with Michael.

17

In the morning, there's bruising over my nose and it feels tender, but nowhere near as bad as yesterday. It isn't too obvious and I don't even think someone would notice from a distance. Phew. I'm glad for myself but also for Michael. After his effort yesterday in helping, I would feel really bad if he was vilified by the whole staff as a result of my injury.

My hair looks *amazing*. Katie's right, I should take the time to use the moisturisers more often. I section off the front, sweep it to the side, and make sure I've got my combs and sprays for later. I pack up my cosmetics and outfit too, feeling a constant fizz of excitement. It's Friday, and I'm going on a date with Michael tonight.

There's a small box waiting for me on my desk when I get into work. I open it to find a white porcelain mug, patterned with black flowers, and the quote 'Whatever our souls are made of, his and mine are the same.' *Wuthering Heights*. It must be from Michael. Be still my beating heart. A guy who can quote Shakespeare AND Bronte. I send a picture to Katie and the girls.

Clare: he's definitely into you.

Deena: still don't trust him.

Katie: can't work out if he's a stalker or really romantic.

I click send on my application, pick up my new mug, and enter the staffroom with a spring in my step. It's nearly half term, I'm going to look awesome tonight and Michael, for once, will be lost for words.

I can't wait.

He's in the kitchen with his coffee machine, but judging from the way he looks up when I enter, he's been waiting for me.

'Jen,' he starts forward, 'how is your nose?'

He moves closer to examine it, and I inhale his aftershave.

'I'm so sorry,' he begins his apologies again, but I laugh, half-drunk on the fumes.

'It's fine,' I reassure him, then hold up my gift. 'Thank you for my mug. It's beautiful.'

He gives a nervous smile.

'You still okay for tonight?' he asks.

'Definitely,' I say, opening the fridge with a flourish. Maybe the cool air will calm down my cheeks.

Everyone, staff and students, is counting the hours till the final bell. We all move dutifully through the day, not doing much in lessons, and at break there are doughnuts in the staffroom.

'Thanks Janet,' Steph calls out, then mutters to me, 'There's no way Clark is behind this.'

'Happy inspection… Have a doughnut,' I say, biting into pink frosting.

'So are the rumours true?' she asks, staring at the bruising on my face.

For a heart-stopping moment, I think she's talking about Michael taking me out tonight.

'What rumours?' I stall.

'Michael hit you in the face with a football.'

'Oh. That.' I swallow more doughnut. 'It was an accident.'

'Looks nasty. As if you didn't already have enough reason to hate that guy,' Steph frowns, then breezes on before I can contradict her. 'Have you got a ride sorted for tonight?'

'Uh huh.'

This is going to be so awkward when I tell her… maybe I won't have to… She's scrutinising my face… Look deadpan, Jen!

'There's something you're not telling me…' Steph continues to stare, waiting for me to crack. 'Wait a minute, who's giving you a lift?'

I consider lying, denying… but in the end I look down and mutter the answer.

'Michael.'

'Michael *Chase*?' Steph nearly spits out her doughnut.

'Shhhh, I don't want the entire staffroom to know.'

'How long has this been going on?' Steph demands, thankfully lowering her voice.

'Nothing is going on. He's just giving me a lift, that's all.'

'What are you wearing?' her eyes narrow. This is the ultimate assessment of my intentions. I avoid answering by taking another bite of my doughnut.

'It's a little black dress, isn't it?' How does she do that? 'Is it the one you wore to my party?' Again, how?

Steph folds her arms.

'There clearly is something going on then. I knew it!'

'What do you mean, you knew it?' I hiss. 'There is nothing going on!'

Well, maybe something. I hope there is something going on.

'I've seen him looking at you.'

On cue, Michael walks in, and his eyes find me straight away. He looks at Steph next to me and evidently isn't brave enough to approach us together. He takes a doughnut and starts a conversation with Joseph Vermont, on the other side of the room, but I know he is still following me with his gaze.

'He's hot. If you ignore his personality.'

'He's probably lip-reading everything you're saying right now.'

'What is he, a tortured James Bond type?'

'More like the Terminator.'

'And you're still both fighting over the promotion?'

'Yep. I just figured it was time for a change in tactics.'

It's not a complete lie. Steph raises her eyebrows and sips her coffee.

'I hope you know what you're doing.'

I finish the day with my lovely Year 8 class, reading *Stormbreaker* and exchanging recommendations for half term books.

'Can we start a writing club after half term please?' Beatrice asks, flanked by two other girls who add their pleas.

'Sure,' I say. 'How about Monday lunchtimes? We can have cake.'

They nod eagerly and when the bell goes, I'm smiling as I amble around my classroom, picking up stray pens and tidying the bookshelves. So what if there's an inspection? If I can't run a writing club, then there's no point being an English teacher.

'Hey.'

This seems to be Michael's way of saying hello to a friend rather than an enemy. He leans in the doorway, his head grazing the top of the frame.

'Hey,' I try to match his casual tone. 'We made it to half term.'

He gives a smile, his face instantly softening.

'It's been quite an experience.'

I can finally see past the mask to something real. It catches me off-guard.

'So, are you ready to head?'

I grab my handbag, my bag with my outfit, and we set off to his car.

I try to wear a blank expression, like this is just what I do every day: walk through the corridor with Michael Chase. I feel ridiculously self-conscious, though I don't think anyone notices there's anything out of the ordinary with us. Except when we get to the main door, David Clark is standing next to it with Joseph Vermont. He looks from me, then to Michael.

'Coming to drinks?' he asks casually.

'Yeah,' Michael replies, perhaps more curt than normal.

'See you there,' David says, but he's staring at me the whole time.

I ignore him and move forward. Michael jumps to open the door for me. My cheeks are on fire now but I try to walk out with dignity, as if I am unaware that David is seeing it all. But he is. I can practically hear the cogs turning in his tiny, calculating brain.

I quicken my pace and Michael matches my stride. At least I know which one his car is. I get in and take a moment to breathe and check my hair in the mirror.

'Are you okay? You seem flustered.'

'I just don't like that man.'

'Who, David?'

'Mmm.'

'Why?'

'He's a creep.'

'Why do you say that?'

'He's back-stabbing, manipulative and passive aggressive.'

'You don't even know him.'

'He taught me, remember? As much as he pretends to forget it.'

'Are you just annoyed that he doesn't remember you?'

'Michael, he knows exactly who I am. He used my work to prop up his teaching for years after I left. He was the worst teacher I ever had and it makes me mad that he's now the one running this school. I don't know how he's managed to fool everyone else but he's not fooling me.'

Michael absorbs this for a few seconds.

'Maybe he's changed… It's a long time since you were a student here.'

'Not *that* long ago.'

He gives me a wry smile.

'Okay, can we just… call a truce for tonight? Please? I don't want to argue with you.'

'What are we going to talk about then?'

'Anything except work.'

He starts up the engine and the radio kicks in. I lean back in my seat and smile.

By the time we get to the parking area, not too far from the bar, I have discovered the following: Michael has a younger sister, his parents live about an hour away near the coast, and he lives in a house in a suburb about halfway between the city and our school.

'I keep thinking I ought to get a lodger, but I never get round to doing anything about it.'

'It must be nice to have the space to yourself.'

'I suppose. Where did you live before your… flat?'

'With my dad. My sister was starting uni and I didn't want to abandon him… but last year the flat came up and I thought how much easier it would be, to be close to school, and I wanted to have my own space.'

'Is your mum not around?'

'She died while I was in Sixth Form.' I look down at my nails.

'I'm sorry.'

He's turned the engine off and we're just sitting there in the quiet car. It's weird, I don't mind just sitting next to him. I don't even mind the fact that I've just told him personal information. Part of me *wants* to open up to him, in spite of my strategies and plans. I don't know how, but he's made me feel safe somehow.

'That must have been a lot for you to go through,' he says.

'Yeah,' I sigh. 'It was complicated. My grandparents died suddenly in a car accident. They were from Jamaica. My mum decided she wanted to go there and 'find her roots'. She got on a plane and we didn't see her for six months. Then she came back and told us that she had stage four cancer. She died a few months later.'

'That's terrible.'

He's looking at me and his eyes connect with mine, and it's like I can take a breath of air again because I've told him, and now he knows, I don't have to hide anymore.

'My sister's seven years younger than me,' I continue. 'She was just starting secondary school. I decided to stay at home, and commute to uni. I only moved out a year ago, once she'd gone to uni.'

'That must have been really difficult.'

He's a surprisingly good listener.

'Don't feel sorry for me,' I tell him. 'Do you want to know something really bad? I often wished my mother hadn't come back from Jamaica at all.'

We sit in silence for a long moment.

'I can understand why,' Michael breaks the silence. 'It's easier to keep people at a distance. If you let them in, they can hurt you.'

His hands are resting on his knees, his fingers pressing slightly against them. His body is rigid and it's only in his eyes that I can see the storm beneath. My breath catches in my throat and I can't help imagining his hands wrapping around me, his mouth on mine...

I need to get this evening back on track and stop killing the mood.

'Shall we go?' I ask.

He's got to crack first. It's not going to be me.

We walk side by side down the street to find somewhere to eat. It's early evening and most places are only just opening, or very quiet. I'm carrying my bag with my outfit and when my arm brushes his, I don't avoid it.

There's a bistro with fairy lights in the window and we both seem drawn to it. I scan the menu: not too formal, but includes goat's cheese. Always a winner for me.

'You want to go in?' Michael asks.

He actually looks nervous, as though he wants to make sure I'm happy. This is nothing like when we're in school.

I'm enjoying this.

'Yes,' I smile and he opens the door for me.

It's warm inside with low-hanging over-sized lights, polished wooden furniture and colourful prints on the walls. It's got some soul. It surprises me that Michael seems to like it too; I associate him with all things corporate. Jazz music plays quietly in the background and the waiter efficiently takes our orders and fetches us drinks. I head to the Ladies to complete my transformation.

My heart is literally thudding against my chest with excitement. I replace my work skirt and blouse with my black dress. The laced flowers form a round neck and then the material falls in a skater cut. I braid the front section of my hair to the side, and put on some eye liner and lip gloss. It's not too much, but it's definitely more of a polished look than my usual appearance. I pout to the mirror. My brown eyes sparkle alongside the dark eye liner, and draw attention away from the bruising around my nose. I smooth the dress. I'm not skinny, but I'm slender enough to pull it off. I pack my work clothes away then realise: I nearly forgot the shoes. I slip out of my pumps into the heels. Very glam. I take an obligatory selfie and post it to the girls' group.

Clare: You look amazing! Irresistible xx

Deena: I'm starting to question your motives here.

Me: Why? I am taking control.

Deena: Whatever. Like the braid x

I inspect myself for a final time, then shrug. Deena's always going to be suspicious.

When I walk back into the restaurant, I feel like a movie star. Michael's eyes widen and he looks as though he's going to choke on his drink. He starts to cough and I slide back into my seat, as if I'm used to having this effect on guys. He coughs a little louder and I look at him more closely. He is actually turning puce.

'Michael, are you okay?'

He nods, but he can't speak because he's still coughing. He takes a glug of water and then seems to be able to breathe again.

'I should tell you I don't know any first aid.'

'Always reassuring,' he croaks, then clears his throat. 'Jennifer…'

I raise my eyebrows.

'I mean, Jen… You look amazing.'

I didn't expect him to say it out loud. Even though it's exactly the reaction I wanted, I can't stop myself giving a goofy grin and blushing. Keep it together, Jen!

'I'm trying to think of a million excuses why we don't need to go to the drinks, so I can keep you all to myself.'

'It's nice to be here, away from it all, and forget about work,' I say.

I don't know what the plan is anymore; I'm melting from the smouldering heat of his eyes. Mayday, mayday!

Perhaps I'm just a natural at this; I move my chair to be closer to him. It's a round table anyway. His proximity has a magnetic draw, like when we were sat next to each other in the theatre and I was so aware of his presence. I just want to touch him and feel that spark again.

The food arrives way too quickly and we both try to make it last as long as possible. It's getting dark outside and more people start to come in, a buzz of chatter beginning to drown out the music.

'We should probably head now,' Michael says, but I know he doesn't want to break the spell either.

Once we get to the drinks, we will be Michael and Jen again, rivals and enemies.

He pays the bill, so this is definitely a date. Why do I feel so happy about this?

'Can I leave my bag in your car?' I ask, as we put our coats on and move towards the door.

'Of course.'

This time, he puts his arm around me to steer me through the crowd. There are people standing around the entrance and spilling out of the door. Once we are out into the night, he doesn't remove his arm. We saunter towards his car, not in a hurry.

Once my clothes are safely inside, my hands are free and I have to restrain myself from reaching out for him. Let him make the first move. Wait, wait… We stand next to the car, and the distance between us is closing. I can barely breathe and I'm watching his face draw nearer and nearer to mine.

'Michael!'

David Clark's voice rings out over the car park. Michael freezes.

'Don't tell him anything,' I whisper before he pulls away.

David walks towards us with a rapid pace, giving us his fake smile and ignoring my look of distaste.

'I thought you'd be here before me; you left hours ago.' He says this to Michael, who doesn't respond.

'I had to get ready,' I say. 'Let's go inside, it's freezing out here.'

The three of us walk to the bar together. At least now it won't look suspicious to everyone else, but I would prefer everyone else knew me and Michael had arrived together rather than David Clark.

The staff take over a large section of the bar, in varying degrees of drunkenness. We just missed Happy Hour apparently. David ushers Michael into their guy group, so I find Steph and try a sip of her cocktail.

'So, how's it going?' she asks, with a meaningful glance at Michael.

I sigh.

'It was great until David arrived and stole him from me.'

'Don't look: he's looking at you now.'

'Who: Michael or David?'

'Both of them.'

I groan and keep my eyes averted.

'What are they saying?'

'David looks annoyed… Michael looks annoyed too… Is this generally how guys relate to one another?'

'Well I don't want to sit here being watched by them.'

I head for the Ladies, clutching my handbag crossly. The door marked 'Toilets' leads into a long corridor and I find the womens' door around the corner. It's empty inside so I can gather my thoughts for a moment and examine my make-up. Once I feel a little calmer, I steel myself to go back out there. I'm going to go to Michael, and talk to him, and David can go and find somebody else to hang out with.

I push open the door back into the corridor and then a voice calls out my name.

'Jen!'

I spin around, and David Clark is waiting for me. He peels himself away from the wall where he's been leaning and walks up to me.

'Can I have a word, please?'

'Only one?' I ask lightly.

'I know what you're doing, Jen. It's not going to work.'

'I don't know what you're talking about.'

'Michael is my friend and I don't want you to think you can–'

'Wait a minute,' I interrupt. 'Are you speaking to me as Headteacher, or something else?'

'I'm going to give you a friendly hint. It's not too late for you to withdraw your application for the HoD position. Michael will get the job; I will find something else for you.'

'Like what?' I'm interested to hear how he's going to figure this one out.

'I've a pretty good hunch that the role for Additional Learning Needs is going to come up soon. If you hold off on the HoD job, you will be top of my list.'

The maddening thing is, part of me would love to do ALN. It's a whole-school role. But it's the principle of it. How can he just lie in wait for me outside a toilet, tell me to withdraw my application and set it all up like some kind of school-based mafia system?

'Why can't I apply for the HoD?'

'I brought Michael with me to Whidlock County and I promised him that there would be opportunity for progression.'

'So you took away Geoff's HoD responsibilities deliberately to create a post for Michael. Unbelievable.'

'I'm just trying to use everyone's experience in the right place. I'm here to help the school improve.'

'You've got an answer for everything. Why have you got a problem with me coming here tonight with Michael?'

'You're applying for the same job and now you're trying to seduce him.'

'What makes you think that?'

He raises an eyebrow and looks me up and down pointedly.

'That's none of your business really, is it?' I say coolly.

'He's my friend.'

'Well you can't pull rank on me and tell me to withdraw my application because you're Michael's *friend*.'

'I'm trying to do you a favour. I know you would love that ALN role. If you carry on with the HoD application, things are going to get messy. You're going to put yourself through a lot of hassle that you could just avoid by withdrawing.'

'It's my right to apply for it if I want to,' I grit my teeth.

'Sure, if you want to. I mean, there'll be the observed lesson, the panel, the data analysis test...'

'You know, if Michael is really the right person for this job, then surely he will get it anyway?'

'I'm not questioning whether Michael will get it.' It's David's turn to clench his jaw with suppressed anger. 'I'm just concerned that any… involvement between the two of you will not end well and will just create further complications.'

'Well that's the friendliest warning I've ever heard,' I give a sarcastic smile.

'I'm only speaking to you because Michael asked me to.'

My fake smile drops immediately as he delivers this blow. I stare at him silently for a moment while this sinks in.

'What do you mean?'

'I mean that he's concerned about your mental health, and he asked me to speak to you and encourage you to save yourself the extra stress and pressure by withdrawing your application.'

'My mental health?' I repeat dumbly. 'What?'

'There's no doubt that teaching is a difficult, demanding profession. I know you've got a challenge with teaching the Year 11 boys' group, and after half term there's the internal inspection. He's just thinking of your best interests.'

'How can I trust anything you say?'

Surely this can't be right?

He pulls out his phone and swipes a few times, then holds up a message for me to read.

I don't think she's very stable. HoD is too much for her to handle.

Michael's name is clearly at the top of the text feed. It feels like a slap in the face. Mostly because it's exactly what I've thought myself. I push the phone back towards him.

'You still have no right to tell me what I can and can't apply for,' I state coldly.

He holds up his hands in mock surrender.

'I'm not telling you what to do, Jen. If you want to go through with it, be my guest.'

He gives me a longer, appreciative stare.

'Nice dress.'

He strolls back into the bar. I wait until he's gone before I cry.

18

Think, Jen, you have to think.

I was sitting in the car with Michael pouring my heart out, then wishing he would kiss me senseless, and all the time, this is what he really thought of me. Unstable. Unsuitable for promotion. It hurts, but it hurts because I believe it too. The past few days have been a rollercoaster and that was just with getting the application form in. I grab a tissue from my bag and wipe my smudgy eyeliner. I have to get out of here.

I move in the opposite direction of the door back into the bar. Round the corner there's a fire escape. Without hesitation, I push the bar down and feel the cold air blast my face. At least I'm wearing my coat. I start walking quickly. I need to find a bus stop that's far enough away that if Michael comes looking for me, he won't find me.

Messages come through from Michael.

Michael: Where are you? Are you okay?

I ignore them.

I push past crowds of people who are waiting for the nightclubs to open. I ignore the catcalls and stay focused. I don't know this area very well, but if I get to the main city centre, I can get a bus home.

I feel a pang like a physical sickness gnawing in my stomach. I could throw that romantic dinner right back up again. *'Let's not talk about work,'* he said. What a joke. He was probably just pretending to find me attractive. I thought I had the upper hand for once, but he was luring me into a false sense of security. I can't face messaging the girls, because Deena will just say I TOLD YOU SO.

I can't believe I actually thought he cared.

My phone rings: Michael. I press the red button to decline the call.

I angrily brush the tears off my cheek and spot a bus on the other side of the road. I check it's going in the right direction and hop on, relieved I've made it this far. It's not that late and I can find my own way home; I don't need Michael Chase.

I have to wait for longer at the city centre stop for my connection, and I huddle into my coat and keep my eyes down. There is a group of rowdy boys waiting around too, and I wish their bus would come. Being a girl is just so unfair at times. I bet Michael and David have never known what it's like to feel vulnerable standing at a bus stop in the dark. David would never consider telling a male applicant to withdraw from a promotion and fob him off with a different role. He would never compliment a male colleague's physical attire in the same demeaning way he did to me. Would Michael have observed Geoff and texted David about concerns for his mental health? Is it because I'm a woman that I must be hysterical?

It doesn't help that I really want to bawl my eyes out crying, and that really would reinforce their impression of me as crazy, along with the whole bus queue.

My phone rings.

I look at it: Steph. I swipe to answer.

'Hey,' I say weakly.

'Jen, where are you?'

'I'm getting the bus home,' I say, choking up.

'What? Why?'

'I… Found out something. About Michael. I had to leave.'

I can hear her speaking to someone in the background. The sound is muffled but I can still hear her.

'What the hell have you done? She's really upset.'

'Let me talk to her.'

It's him. I know she can't see me but I'm shaking my head.

'No, Steph!'

'Michael wants to speak to you,' she comes back onto the line.

'I can't,' I sob.

I hear her sigh and visualise her shaking her head at him.

'Jen I'm worried about you, can't I help?'

The bus arrives with dazzling headlights.

'My bus is here. Call me tomorrow.'

I hang up and climb on board.

It's a pretty miserable journey home. I spend most of it sniffling into my tissue, dabbing at my eyes, but I'm a mess and there's not much I can do to change that. I send a few texts to Steph to reassure her that I'm alright. Nothing else from Michael.

As the streets become more familiar, the bus pulls into a stop by an old railway tunnel. Out of the window, I see a few cars with teenage boys standing next to them. Suddenly I recognise Tyler, and in the same moment, he sees me.

My stomach churns as I simultaneously process the fact that I look upset and he's seeing me like this, and also that I heard this tunnel is where the drug dealers go. It's no consolation that Tyler does not look happy that I've seen him either. He says something to his friend, points directly at me, and then they get into one of the cars, looking frequently back towards me. The car engine starts and the lights come on. I'm willing the bus to move on, and finally it slowly starts to pull away and move back onto the road. I look behind and see the car begin to follow.

I start to panic. What is he going to do? Attack me when I get off the bus? Don't be ridiculous, Jen. But why is he following me? What am I going to do when it's my stop? At least my stop is the shops area. I can go inside the fish shop as a refuge. But I can't stay there forever.

I keep trying to crane my neck around to see if the car's still following. It's too hard to see.

I look at my watch. Is it too late for me to call Dad? What am I going to say: Dad, there's a kid I teach who I think might be dealing drugs and he's following me home?

Only as a last resort.

I know one thing: I can't go into my flat if Tyler is watching to see where I live. I'll never feel safe again.

We arrive at the shops and I shakily stand up and ring the bell. The bus heaves and lurches into the stop space, and I stumble with my heels on down the aisle. I tremble as I walk down the steps and find the pavement. The bus pulls away, and I'm facing the car park by the shops. The car with Tyler in swerves into a space, the lights blaring so I can't see the driver.

'Jen!'

I turn to see Michael, stepping out of his car at the other end of the car park. He must have been waiting for me.

I've never been so glad to see him.

I break into a run, nearly falling because of my heels, and I hurl myself at him.

'Please, let's drive away from here,' I gabble incoherently as his arms wrap around me.

'What's happened?' he asks, squeezing me tightly against his chest.

I pull back and start trying to open his car door.

'We have to leave now,' I sob.

'Okay, okay.' He opens the door for me and helps me inside, then climbs in on the driver's side.

'Tyler's followed me here,' I say once his door is shut. 'He's waiting in that car over there.'

Michael looks out of the window.

'Why is he following you?'

'Just drive please, Michael!'

He starts the car and reverses back, then zooms out of the car park. The car with the headlights on doesn't follow. I lean back against the seat and realise that my cheeks are wet with tears. I brush them off and let out a sob.

Michael looks at me in alarm and I can see him scan the area for somewhere to stop.

'Don't stop!'

'Where shall I go?'

'Anywhere away from here.'

'Are you going to tell me what's happened?'

I don't hold back; I tell him everything, from finding the mysterious card, to noticing that Tyler carried cash, and then I tell him about the grudge he has since the trip and the lesson he boycotted with the lunchtime antics, the drawing on the board, the bags in the aisle, throwing pens for me to pick up and the sexual comments.

'Now I've seen him with the druggies, he's going to hunt me down.'

A fresh wave of despair hits me and I sob harder.

'Why didn't you tell me about any of this?' Michael asks, clenching the steering wheel so hard his knuckles are white.

'Because I don't want you to think I'm a failure!' I cry an ugly snotty cry, my face smeared with tears and make-up.

'Jen, this is totally unacceptable; we have to do something about him. I think we should call the Police.'

'And say what?' I ask. 'None of it's bad enough for him to really get into trouble. He hasn't *done* anything to me.'

'If you are worried that he is trying to find out where you live so that he can intimidate you, then that's harassment.'

'But I'm sure he can come up with excuses. 'I was just going to the chippy'. Who's to say he was there because he was following me? I have no proof.'

'There must be CCTV around there.'

'Again, he hasn't done anything wrong… yet. But I can't have him find out where I live, Michael.'

'He won't,' Michael says, his jaw set in a firm line.

I look at the road ahead.

'Where are you taking me?'

'To my house.'

I turn to stare at him.

'I'm not trying anything, please believe me,' he says hastily. 'You can ring Steph and tell her where you are if you like. I'm slightly scared of her.'

'She already hates your guts after tonight.'

'You're going to tell me all about that too when we get there.'

I get my phone out and send Steph a quick text.

Michael came to get me. I'm going to his place.

It takes her a minute to reply. ???

Me: I know. Long story.

If I didn't feel so emotionally exhausted, I would be freaking out by now about going to Michael's house. But I'm drained, and I just curl up in the passenger seat and lean my head against the headrest. He keeps darting glances at me and shifting with agitation.

Finally we stop in the driveway of a semi-detached house.

'Here we are.'

Michael gets out and walks round to my side, opening the door and holding out his hand towards me. I take it and he pulls me up, then supports me with his arm and leads me to the door. He turns his key and then we're inside a warm, carpeted hallway.

I slip off my heels and he holds his hand out for my coat. As I take it off, I feel strangely bare and exposed before him, quite a contrast to my strutting around earlier.

'Come here,' he takes my hand and we enter the lounge. He flicks a switch and a lamp gives a warm glow to the room. He ushers me to the sofa and then puts a woollen blanket around my shoulders. 'I'm going to make you some tea.'

I hear him clatter about in the kitchen, and I look round at each corner of the room. The walls are pale and the sofa is a rich charcoal colour. I find myself sinking deeper into it, pulling the soft blanket tighter around me. There's a rug on the floor and a fireplace, and a bookcase I really want to nose through. Predictably, everything is neat and tidy, and fairly minimal.

He comes back in and hands me a steaming mug, then sits on the sofa by my tucked-up feet. He runs a hand through his hair. I've noticed he does this when he's stressed.

'I'm sorry for commanding you to drive me like that,' I say, sipping my tea.

'I'm glad I was there. What were you going to do?'

'Go to the chip shop. If they didn't leave, I was going to call my dad… as a last resort.'

'I don't like the thought of you in that flat on your own.'

'I don't want a Year 11 boy to drive me out though.'

'Why did you leave the bar?'

It's the big question he's been waiting to ask. I drink more tea and marvel at how much better I feel already.

'David waited for me outside the Ladies'. He told me to withdraw my application for the HoD job. He said that's what you wanted, because you messaged him to say I was unstable and couldn't handle it.'

'I didn't,' he says immediately, with a strength of indignance that makes me believe him.

'I saw the message.'

He frowns and shakes his head.

'What exactly did it say?'

'I don't think she's very stable. HoD is too much for her to handle.'

Even as I say it out loud, my cheeks grow hot with embarrassment. Perhaps he will remember sending it. His fingers are pressed into his forehead and all I can think is how much I hope that he doesn't have such a low opinion of me now.

'It sounds like something I said about Liz, before she went on the sick.' He lifts up his head and looks at me.

Now it's my turn to consider. I didn't look at the date on the message.

'Given my behaviour tonight, I'm beginning to doubt how stable I really am.'

He looks at me more earnestly.

'There's nothing wrong in the way you've reacted. I know I'm constantly offending you and I broke your favourite mug. I'm not surprised that you thought I said that about you, but please believe me when I say that I didn't.' He runs his hand through his hair again. 'I can't believe David outright lied to you and used a text I'd sent about someone else…'

He wants me to believe him. Is it just so he can keep his cover and continue to manipulate me? That's Deena talking. As much as part of me would like to keep him at arm's length, another part of me is hypnotised by his stormy grey eyes and his desperation to make things right between us.

'It just… made me wonder if you'd been watching me and talking about me to him all along.'

I watch him carefully. He shakes his head.

'No, I honestly haven't. I wouldn't do that to you.'

The clock, the cat, the mug… All the little moments we've shared make me realise that I do trust him. I'm sitting in his home, wrapped in a blanket, and I feel safe. I want to stay here forever.

Michael, though, jumps up in restlessness and paces to the bookcase.

'I can't believe David asked you to withdraw.'

His sense of outrage is cute, but it's frustrating that this is his first inkling that there's something rotten in the state of Denmark.

'I can,' I take another sip of tea. 'He'll do anything to get what he wants. He offered me the ALNCo role.'

'Really?' Michael looks impressed. 'You would be great at that. Not that I'm saying you should accept his offer.'

He's back to pacing again.

'It's just the way he does everything that bugs me. It's… entitled,' I say this and simultaneously hope Michael won't take offence, but that he will also apply this to himself. 'He also had the cheek to tell me not to seduce you. And then his parting shot was 'nice dress'.'

'*Are* you trying to seduce me?' Michael stops pacing and awkwardly presses the back of his neck. He almost looks *afraid.*

'Well I'm not doing a very good job at it, am I?' I jiggle my blanket and put my mug down on the coffee table. 'I haven't seen my face, but I've got bruising *and* runny mascara.'

Michael's arm relaxes at his side and he stands still for a moment, looking at me. The next thing I know, he's back on the sofa beside me, as if irresistibly drawn back. He's even closer this time. He reaches over and rubs his thumb over my tear-stained cheek.

'You look beautiful to me.'

I can't help it; I start crying again. I am a complete emotional wreck.

He folds his arms around me and draws me into his warmth. It's like the mug day, but this time I don't fight it. He smells too good.

'Am I mentally unstable?' I ask when the sobs have subsided.

'You're just tired and upset,' Michael reassures me.

'What time is it?'

'Nine o'clock.'

Wow. It feels like it could be midnight.

'That's lame. You should be partying in the bar now instead of having me drown your sofa with my meltdown.'

'Jen, the only reason I was planning to go to the bar was because of you. Once you left there was no incentive for me to stay.'

He gives me a wry smile. I think he actually *likes* me.

'Really?'

'Yeah. It's not my kind of thing. Plus Steph looked like she was about to start torturing me for information when I had no idea what I had done wrong.'

'Did David speak to you?'

As soon as I ask this, his expression changes. I can see his jaw tighten.

'He made a few comments.'

'About me?' I press.

If I lean forward any more, we're going to bump our foreheads together.

He doesn't answer, and he's avoiding eye contact.

'Tell me.'

I reach out and touch his shoulder to get his attention. It works; he finally looks up.

'He sort of suggested that this,' he passes his hand from me to him, 'shouldn't go beyond tonight. That if I wanted to 'have some fun' with you, then I should let it cool off over half term so that the inspection and the interviews run smoothly and professionally.'

'What did you say?' I'm thoroughly expecting him to voice total agreement, and my heart sinks.

'I said that *this* is none of his business and he would only have a right to discuss it with me if my behaviour was unprofessional.'

'And what is *this*?' I copy his gesture.

'I don't really know,' he confesses. 'I mean, I'm not sure if you hate me. I'm getting pretty mixed signals.'

'I don't hate *you*. I don't want to be a bit of fun for you, and I don't want to be used like a pawn in some race-to-the-top for you or for David.'

'I don't want to use you.' He looks straight into my eyes. 'I haven't dated much… I'm not used to playing games.'

'I haven't had much impression that you liked me,' I say. 'Apart from when you bought me the ice cream. And when you saw me in my dress tonight.'

'I nearly stopped breathing.'

We both laugh. Was that just a few hours ago? It feels like a lifetime.

'I think I realised I liked you when I first saw you wearing that pineapple shirt for the first time.'

We set off giggling again.

'Seriously?'

'Absolutely,' he smiles. 'Jen, you're pretty, funny, intelligent, bold and creative. I could never be like you. I'm just a total bore compared to you. If you agreed to go out with me, I worry I would bore you to death.'

'Are you asking me out?'

'I guess I'm trying to. If I did, would you say yes?'

'That's not asking me properly!'

'Okay, okay. Jen, will you go out with me?'

'Do you mean, on one date so you can see how you feel about me? Or do you mean, to enter into a state of relationship?'

'What?'

'Do you mean, let's go out this week on a date. One date. Just to see how it goes.'

'Didn't we just do that already?'

'Well, yes, I think so, but I don't know what you're thinking about it.'

'I had a great time with you. Before David ruined the evening.'

'It's not been the best night of my life,' I admit. 'But at least I'm here now, with you, and we're not still stuck in that cocktail bar.'

'You still haven't answered my question.'

'You still haven't outlined your terms and conditions.'

He leans his face closer to mine.

'Do I need to get you to sign a contract?'

We stay there for a moment, an inch of breath between us. I wonder why he isn't kissing me already. Then I remember my injury—maybe it's better that I take control of this. I tilt my head to avoid bumping my nose, and meet his lips with mine. There's a split second of surprised hesitation before he joins in. All I can think is how soft and warm his mouth is, when I always thought of Michael as cold and immovable as iron. Now he's like molten lava and every inch of me is on fire.

'I knew you would crack first,' he mutters, before kissing me again.

'Wait,' I pull back and press my palm against his chest, desperately trying to focus on what Deena or Clare would say about this situation. 'So what kind of asking out is this again? I need to know.'

'Run me through the options again.'

I groan.

'So it's either I am asking you out on *one* date,' he says, his eyes glinting, 'or I'm asking you to be my girlfriend.'

'That sounds about it,' I say, my voice half disappearing.

'Jennifer,' he kisses me again, 'I can tell you right now that one date isn't going to be enough.'

I love the feel of his mouth on mine and I wrap my arms around him even tighter.

'Are you going to give me an answer?'

I give him another kiss.

'That means yes,' I say.

19

This is definitely not where I expected this evening to end up, but I'll take it over cocktails anytime. Maybe this is the other side of Michael that I thought I'd never see: the smouldering version. Maybe it wasn't all in my head in the store cupboard…

'What do you want to do about Tyler?' Michael asks.

Okay, maybe it was just in my head.

I look at him quizzically. Most guys would have started removing my clothing by now. I examine Michael's face. He definitely looks flushed. It's not all in my head. But he's pulled back a little and he's not pushing this any further.

'I don't know,' I finally answer. 'He may well have gone off somewhere else now.'

'I suppose he can't wait around for you,' Michael frowns. 'Even so, I think I'll feel happier if we install some better security at your flat. I don't want you to go back there tonight.'

Aha! Classic romantic trope. Maybe there's only one bed here and we'll just have to share it? I move in closer, about to kiss him, but he pulls back again and places his hands on my shoulders, keeping us slightly apart.

'J-Jen,' he stammers. 'I didn't bring you here to take advantage of you.'

I smile. He's genuinely sweet underneath the Terminator persona.

'I know,' I tell him. 'I was the one who told you to drive me away, remember?'

'And this is all happening quite fast…' he continues, looking slightly panicked. 'I don't think we should… I mean, we need to take things slowly.'

'I'm not in a rush,' I give my best suggestive eyebrow arch.

'Nor am I,' he says, in a final sort of way. He clears his throat. 'I am happy to drive you to your dad's if you'd like to go there, or I have a spare room here.'

I blink as my various imagined romantic montages vanish. He doesn't want to sleep with me.

Is this a good or a bad thing?

'Is there a particular reason…' I begin and trail off, looking at him questioningly. 'I mean, do you not find me attractive?'

He gives a wry smile.

'I thought you were intelligent,' he teases. 'Of course I find you attractive. Is it really that unusual for a guy to want to take things slow?'

'Uh, yeah. In my experience.'

Cue montage of Jamie, George and Ryan. Ugh.

'Why don't I show you the spare room and then you can make a decision?'

I follow him upstairs, enjoying the soft, luxurious carpet way too much. My eyes are darting faster than someone in hyper-vigilance mode as I make a mental inventory of every paint shade, picture and plant pot. Everything is convincing me that he is the Real Deal. In every part of his life, Michael has got it together. I wonder what he would think of my flat.

'Just in here.'

He flicks a light switch to reveal an immaculate bedroom, painted sky blue with crisp white bed linen. The bed looks expensive with its solid wood frame; such a contrast to the cheap futons in my friends' spare rooms, which are always piled up with laundry and junk. Last time I stayed with Deena, there was nearly an entire gym in her guest room. I tripped over the cycling machine when I needed the toilet in the middle of the night.

Michael obviously mistakes my silence for reluctance, as he hurriedly says,

'But no pressure. I really don't mind driving you… anywhere, really.'

I look at him and grin.

'Do you have any spare pyjamas?'

It's definitely surreal, changing into Michael's PJs and being in his spare room. I open the drawer of the bedside table, almost expecting to find a Gideon's Bible, just like a hotel. There's a towel, soap and a toothbrush. Does he have many guests? It all looks very… unused. There's an unopened box of tissues and it makes me think that this room isn't often occupied.

'Do you need anything else?' he calls from the landing.

I empty my handbag. I definitely did not foresee this scenario when I packed lip gloss and a free perfume sample.

'Do you have a phone charger? My battery's almost dead.'

I wish I had a silk scarf for my hair, but never mind. Katie always lectures me about taking better care of it. This reminds me that I haven't told Katie about the revelatory turn this evening has taken. I pull out my phone and send her a text to update her on my new relationship status.

Katie: Ahh! When can I meet him?

Me: Give me a chance!

I'm not ready for those worlds to collide yet.

Katie: Does he have a brother?

Me: No. Get back to your revision.

'Jen?' Michael knocks the door.

'Come in,' I call, discarding my phone.

He steps inside and offers me a charger, clearly both happy and terrified that I'm here, in his pyjamas in his spare room. He obviously didn't expect this to happen either.

'I hope everything is okay,' he manages to say, blushing and hovering near the door.

'This is perfect,' I say. 'Thank you so much.'

'I hope you sleep really well,' he says, rearranging the bathrobe hanging on the door hook. 'I was going to go out for a run in the morning. I'll try not to disturb you.'

'Sure,' I say, amused at the idea. I could hardly imagine Michael barging in when he was clearly struggling to even get past the threshold. 'Are you going to give me a goodnight kiss?'

He steps over and brushes my cheek with his lips.

'Don't look at me like that,' he warns me in mock-seriousness. 'Any more than that and I won't be able to sleep.'

'You know where to find me,' I say flirtatiously.

Michael blushes a fiery red and I laugh.

'I'm joking!' I reassure him. 'Well, a bit.'

'Goodnight, Jen,' he says, and closes the door.

I shake my head. Who'd have thought that Michael would be the one to hold back? All my great plans of seduction have well and truly come to naught. And yet, I don't feel unhappy. Michael didn't betray me to David after all. He asked me to be his girlfriend. Instead of being alone in my greasy, cluttered flat, I'm in Michael's five-star spare room.

I sink into the bed and close my eyes. This is what amazing feels like.

Morning light pierces through the curtain when I wake up, so I know I've had a solid night. I grab my phone to check the time: 8:30am. I'm momentarily confused by the absence of clutter on the bedside table, and the scent of fresh linen, and then I remember: I'm in Michael's spare room!

My raw stream of consciousness is a mass of confusion: Michael likes me I hate David Clark I'm wearing Michael's PJs his house is perfect I want to stay here forever I kissed Michael last night what is he going to think when he sees me I need to get to the bathroom and sort myself out I hope my hair is ok.

I throw off the sheet and I'm just about to stand up when I see it. Blood.

This can't be happening!

There's a red stain seeping through Michael's jog pants, and there's a blot on his pristine white sheets. Dammit.

I'm going to have to make a run for it.

As I tiptoe-dash out of the door and shut myself in the bathroom, I reflect on my emotional state last night and feel a sense of relief. I'm not crazy; I just had PMS. That's why I was crying all the time.

I use a load of loo roll to create an improvised wad. Michael's bathroom is well stocked, but I think he hit his limit at female sanitary products. What am I going to do? I'm going to have to find a corner shop or something.

I steel myself and open the bathroom door. Nothing.

'Michael?' I call.

No reply. He must have left for his run already.

Well, at least he doesn't have to see this. I go back to the room to survey the damage. I'm going to have to chuck it all in the wash. I start stripping the bed and then consider what I'm going to wear to the shop. Do I wear the black dress and look smutty, or Michael's dressing gown and look slummy? It's got to be the dress, with a coat over the top. Plus I need to wash Michael's joggers as well.

I throw on my dress, bundle up the pile of laundry, and head downstairs. I shove it all into the machine and grab the detergent. I press a button and it whirs into action, though the duration of the cycle flashes up as three hours. Oh well.

I look around for something to write on to leave Michael a note. A Specsavers advert will do.

Gone to shop.

After consideration I add an 'X'. Then I grab the back door key and slip out.

Walking around this estate in daylight, it looks very well-kept and expensive. My flat is truly a hovel in comparison. I have no idea where I am, so I load up a map on my phone and amble in the direction of where I think there may be a shop.

I make a few different circuits before I finally find something. Everything's extortionately priced, and as I deliberate between brands which make increasingly implausible promises, I hear a voice which turns my blood cold.

'Do you have any aspirin?'

It's David Clark. I'd know that slimy voice anywhere, but I still look over to see him standing at the till. What is he doing here?

'There's more options in the aisle over there,' the assistant says.

I quickly look at the shelves. Feminine hygiene is right next to painkillers. Makes sense.

Like a bad pantomime, I whip myself round to the dried goods section and pretend to be very interested in overpriced muesli as I hear my nemesis find himself some medical relief. Maybe a short, sharp blow to the head would do it. There's a slightly damaged box with a reduced price sticker on it, and the reduced price is double what a normal cereal would cost. It makes me strangely nostalgic for the chaotic newsagents next to the chip shop, where Nikos has a huge trolley full of KitKats that are three months out of date, and an endless supply of leaflets.

I listen to David's footsteps and hear him pay at the checkout. Once the door opens and closes, I exhale. Does David live around here? Did he and Michael buy houses off-plan together? If they were neighbours, it would make more sense of Michael's desire to stay on David's good side. You wouldn't want to tell David off for raving in the middle of the night with 90s music blaring. However, you wouldn't want to be forced to attend David's parties either.

Feeling spooked at this near-miss, I grab the cheapest packet and head to the till. I hurry back to Michael's and let myself in through the back door. I'm about to shout something like 'Guess who I just saw' when I hear David Clark's voice. Again.

'It's not just a game of golf,' he says. It sounds like he's in the hallway. I breathe in, even though it makes no difference to my overall body mass, and press myself against the wall. 'I think he wants to tell me the plans for Whidlock and I really want you to be there.'

'I don't think I'm free,' Michael says.

'Do you mind if I just use your bathroom?' David asks.

'Um…' I can hear the panic in Michael's voice –he must think I'm still in the spare room– but David doesn't wait for an answer.

I hear the stairs creak as he walks up, and I've never been more grateful for my period than this moment. I walk through the kitchen to the doorway, where Michael, red-faced and sweaty from his run (still hot, though!), double-takes when he sees me. I wave my arms around and he signs for me to go into the understairs cupboard. It's like charades but there's no TV option. I crush myself in amongst ski jackets and shoes and pray that David won't open the door.

I can hear the floorboards creaking overhead. How long does it take to use the bathroom? Why is David walking around up there?

Then it hits me: he's looking for me.

He's supposedly 'called in' – at nine a.m. on a Saturday, the first day of half term– because he's expecting to find me, possibly naked in Michael's bed. I shiver at the thought. Focus, Jen.

He's not going to find a trace of my existence, but while bringing a measure of relief, that doesn't make standing in Michael's shoe cupboard any better. What am I, a criminal? I'm plastered into a coat rack holding a pack of sanitary towels when I really need to go to the bathroom to actually use them, and here is David snooping around Michael's house like he's in a crime drama.

Finally I hear the noise of David coming down the stairs — or rather, I feel the vibrations, given that the wooden underside is inches from my face.

'I've —er— got to get showered so…' I hear Michael awkwardly trying to end this spontaneous catch-up.

'Sure,' David says. 'Enjoy half term.'

The front door closes and I hear a car engine outside. Michael opens the cupboard door and I stumble out.

'Sorry about that. I panicked,' he says.

I straighten my coat.

'Clearly. Please tell me that you can see now that he was coming here to spy on you, to catch us out.'

'Really?' Michael looks incredulous. 'Why would he bother coming out here unless he was genuinely on the way? He told me he's going to his mum's, and she lives in this area.'

'Well, he won't have seen anything,' I say. 'Although we might need a more long-term strategy than jumping in cupboards.'

'Sorry,' he says again. 'Do you want some tea?'

'Yes,' I reply automatically. 'And I'm going to the bathroom, because I –unlike David– actually need it.'

'What's all this stuff in the washing machine?' Michael asks when I come downstairs.

'I just… thought you'd want to wash the sheets.'

'You didn't have to do that.'

Actually, I did.

He hands me a mug of tea and I can see sweat glistening on his forehead. It's quite attractive in a primal sort of way.

'Glad I saw you from the hallway,' he continues. 'If I'd come home and seen the bed stripped, I would have just assumed you ran away.'

'I left you a note,' I hold up the Specsavers advert.

'That's completely unnoticeable. Where have you been, anyway?'

'To the shop.'

'Why?' Classic Michael. Doesn't know when to stop.

'You know… Women's problems.'

I hate that phrase but what else do you say?

If Michael was less red, he would probably go pale, but as it is, he remains a slightly different shade of puce.

'I put the wash on and maybe I should get the other set of clothes out of your car.'

'Sure. Key's on the hook.'

Once I'm dressed in my crumpled work clothes, I help myself to breakfast and wait for Michael to emerge from his toilette. The cereal selection is somewhat lacking so I degrade him from five stars to four, making a note to recommend broadening his range. Should have bought that expensive-but-reduced muesli after all.

When he enters, in jeans and a T-shirt, it's so different seeing him in casual clothes. He looks so much more… human. I don't know what aftershave he wears, but it makes the adverts showing women falling over themselves (which I wrote off as male fantasy) look suddenly plausible.

'You're quiet. What are you thinking about?' he asks, grabbing some bran flakes.

'Nothing.'

After breakfast we climb into his car and head back to my flat, stopping off to get something for 'added security' at the retail park on the outskirts of town. The DIY store is a huge warehouse with a polished floor and seemingly endless aisles of paint, tools and building materials.

'This looks good,' I select a fairly cheap CCTV camera and turn towards the checkout.

'Wait a sec,' Michael picks up a different box. 'Let me just compare them…'

I guess everything in life gets subjected to the Michael Chase scrutiny. Just then, a guy rounds the corner into the aisle with a slightly familiar face. This is the problem with teaching in the area where I grew up. He could be a parent… Or maybe someone I went to school with? There's a lot of people to bump into around here.

As I struggle to eliminate possibilities, a girl follows him, pushing a trolley. Rose. She's got earbuds in and she's glued to her phone screen, so hopefully she doesn't hear me as I yelp and dash into the next aisle.

Michael probably hasn't noticed I've gone.

I stand in an aisle with a range of adhesive signs: toilets, fire exits, beware of the dog… The only noise I can hear is the tinny music from the store speakers. I'm wondering if Rose will notice Michael, and if she does, whether she will speak to him.

'Jen?'

Michael stands at the end of the aisle, so I grab his hand and pull him into mine, then put my finger to my lips.

'Ssh! Rose,' I point to the other aisle.

Like spies, we tiptoe through the signs and then we're into the bathroom section. We're using the fake wall to hide behind, with a toilet right in front of us.

'Right, I calculated that this one, although slightly more expensive, is more cost-effective,' Michael holds out the box.

'That's fine,' I say dismissively. 'Let's get to the till and then out of here before we meet the whole class.'

Furtively, we check both directions before joining the shortest queue at the front of the shop. There's just one guy in front of us buying light bulbs…

It's Joseph Vermont.

'Hi,' I say awkwardly, as he takes in my creased left-over-from-yesterday outfit. I mean, who would choose to wear a skirt and blouse on a Saturday?

'Hi,' he says. It's the most he's ever said to me, and it's only because Michael is standing right there. 'You guys are out early.'

Oh no. He thinks we had a… *thing* last night.

'Michael's helping me install this at my flat,' I gabble. 'I have some security issues, really urgent.'

Michael gives me a 'stop talking' look.

'Uh… great,' Joseph looks unsure how to respond. Thankfully, the cashier gives him a receipt and it's his cue to leave.

'Have a good half term,' Michael says, half-heartedly, then runs his hand through his hair and sighs as Joseph walks out of the exit.

'He thinks we're sleeping together,' I say.

'What does it matter what he thinks?' Michael says, when clearly he's rattled as much as I am.

'You're not the one dressed in yesterday's work clothes,' I indicate my crumpled shirt.

'You don't even know him,' Michael says.

'I know that he's probably texting David right now, rendering my hiding in your cupboard completely pointless.'

'Do you want to buy that?' The cashier is looking at me with raised eyebrows.

'Oh, yes, sorry,' I hand her the box to scan.

We return to Michael's car, and I'm still scanning every direction for signs of pupils or colleagues. It's a small world around here, and not in the cute sense: more in the creepy repetitive Disney song way.

Once I've climbed inside and buckled my seatbelt, Michael starts the engine and looks questioningly at me.

'So what are we going to do when we get back to school?'

'I don't know,' I say, 'but I don't want everyone to think I threw myself at you and moved in with you on our first date.'

'Not sure exactly how I can clarify that.'

'Don't treat me any differently in school. Treat me the same as everyone else.'

'I don't hang out in anyone else's classroom. Only yours.'

'When you say 'hang out', you really mean 'walk straight through it'.'

'It was one of the ways I got to see you more.'

Smooth. I roll my eyes.

He drives to my flat, and while I can finally take a shower and give my poor hair some attention, he fits the camera. I'm beginning to think he can do anything.

'So if Tyler decides to pay you a visit, you'll have evidence to prove it.'

'Do you think he will?' I ask with a stab of panic.

'I don't know. It depends what he's involved in, really.'

I sit down on my mustard-coloured sofa, which has my favourite quilted blanket draped over it. It's the thought of being sat here, on my own at night, and the noise of someone outside the door… It terrifies me. I know it's only Tyler, but who will he bring with him? What will they do? What if I need to go somewhere, and they follow me and attack me once I'm in an empty street? My movements are pretty predictable.

'You're worried about it.'

Michael comes to sit next to me, lifting the blanket to examine it first.

'If they show up, what should I do?'

'Call the Police and explain it's harassment.'

'But if they've just shown up outside my door, that isn't a crime, is it?'

'The Protection from Harassment Act defines it as causing alarm or distress, so yes, I believe it would be.'

'How do you know that?' I look at him in surprise.

He flushes.

'I did a joint degree: English Literature and Law.'

I stare at him for a second. There is a LOT I don't know about him.

'That actually makes sense given a number of your characteristics,' I muse. 'Sorry, did I say that out loud?'

'I'd ask you what that's supposed to mean but I don't think you'd give me a favourable answer,' he smiles.

'Do you want some tea?'

Classic avoidance tactic. I head into the small kitchen area. Steph texts, asking me how I am.

Me: Better. Don't worry about me. Catch up soon x

When I return to the lounge, Michael's engrossed in his phone.

'You don't take sugar, do you?'

'No. Thank you.'

He takes the cup and places it on the table, then turns to face me.

'I've got an idea.'

20

'You're WHAT?' Katie shrieks down the phone and I hold it at arm's length from my ear. 'You've been going out with this guy for approximately eight hours and you're going AWAY with him?'

'He suggested that we go and stay somewhere quiet, somewhere where no one knows who we are…'

'Somewhere he can kill you and hide your body and no one will ever find out.'

'He's not like that!' I protest.

'All you've told me about him is what a jerk he is.'

'I think I've probably given him an unfair press.'

'Where exactly are you going?'

'Not far, I think it's some place in the country.'

'Very specific.'

'He's arranging it. He's even paying.'

'Well I should think so; he's the only one of you who's coming back alive.'

'I'll have my phone, and I'll send you the details of the place. Please can you trust my judgement for once?'

'When have you *ever* been right about a guy?' she pauses for effect. 'Jamie– too clingy. George– not serious. Ryan– total waste of space.'

'I don't see you with an excellent track record yourself,' I hiss down the phone.

'Look, if it was me calling you, how would you feel?'

'Admittedly I would be concerned. But Michael and I are older than you; we're not students anymore. We want to get away and relax in a cottage with a real fire in the middle of nowhere.'

'Sounds great… until he kills you.'

'Will you stop that?'

'You probably won't even get a mobile signal. You won't be able to call for help even if you needed to,' she continues. 'And anyway, where does he get all his money? You say he's got a house all to himself in a posh part of town, and now he's booking you a last-minute holiday. Isn't he on the same salary as you?'

'He's been teaching for longer,' I explain. 'He probably gets a bonus for being a 'leading practitioner'. Anyway, he works so hard he probably doesn't ever spend much money.'

This is more tenuous, but I'm going to run with it.

'Hmm.'

'Look, it's better than staying in my flat, worrying about whether one of my students is going to turn up.'

'Don't you have a ton of work to do? I know it's half term but you've got to plan for that inspection next week.'

'We'll take our laptops. We can work together.'

'Sure. Like that's going to happen. Again, what would you say to me if I told you I was going to take my laptop to a guy's place to 'study together'?'

'Well I know you, and you are very easily distracted.'

'So you two are just going to be discussing educational psychology while planning lessons, are you?'

'Look, it's my time of the month so nothing's going to be happening in that department, and he knows it.'

'Just don't throw yourself at him. It feels like you've gone from nought to sixty in twenty-four hours. I mean, all the guy did was buy you an ice cream!'

'With Michael, everything's nought to sixty,' I sigh. 'He's just that kind of guy. He's always on the move, always planning something, always one step ahead.'

'Don't let him get ahead of you. If it turns out he's taking you away to manipulate you into giving up on the HoD job, I will be the one burying a body in the woods.'

Typical Katie: always so extreme.

'How was your sister?' Michael asks from the doorway of my bedroom.

My holdall is open on the bed and I've strewn some clothes messily all over it. He walks in and starts folding everything.

'She thinks you're going to kill me,' I say.

'I think I could have done that by now if I wanted to.'

'How reassuring,' I reply, watching him at work. 'Instead you're rolling the air out of my sweaters. Where did you learn to fold like that?'

'Summer job at a department store one year.'

'You are full of surprises.'

He gives a dry laugh.

'I keep telling you, I'm as boring as you first assumed when you met me in September. But I want to be different for you.'

'You don't need to pretend with me.'

He carries on rolling and folding and I reach out my hand to stop him.

'Michael?'

He sighs and looks at me.

'Don't you ever just want to be someone else?' he asks.

'Not really,' I answer flatly.

'When I'm with you, you make me feel like a different person.'

'Is that a good thing?'

'Yes,' he says decisively.

'I don't get you,' I say, turning to pull socks out of my drawer. 'You've got everything: an amazing house, car, job…'

'Yes, but the only thing pencilled in my calendar for this week is potentially playing golf with David to network with other school leaders.'

'And you're not going to go, because you're with me?'

'I'm not going to go, because finally I have something way better with you.'

'That's sweet. You must have other friends, though.'

I hope he's not clingy like Jamie. He might turn out to be a Heathcliff, raw and passionate on the windy moor, calling my name along the howl of the wind, digging up my dead body (that's Katie intruding on my train of thought again)…

'Jen, most of my friends are lawyers. They don't get half terms.'

'Oh.' I shove away Katie's infectious paranoia. 'Mine too, actually.'

Maybe we have more in common than I realise.

I've packed everything now except my underwear. I stand and wait for him to go.

'Anything else?'

'Yes but I'm doing it.'

'Remember to roll…'

'Go out there and I'll be with you in a second.'

'That is literally never a truthful statement but okay.'

Once I've packed, I check my phone and Clare has posted.

Clare: How did it go last night?

Seeing my selfie, it feels like a million years ago already.

Me: Dinner was great. Then we had some issues with the Head at the drinks. He's not keen on us dating, so we've gone away to escape for a few days.

Clare: Wow. That sounds intense.

Deena: Let me guess: everything is under control, right?

Me: Absolutely.

Me: The Head wanted me to withdraw my application.

Clare: No! What did you say?

Me: I refused. But he made me feel rubbish.

Deena: What does Michael think?

Me: That David has no right to tell us what to do, unless our behaviour is unprofessional.

Clare: Yes, but if you two are still going for the same job, isn't that going to be awkward?

Me: I think I was originally applying because I didn't want Michael to get it. Now I'm refusing to withdraw to make a point.

Deena: Still not sure you should be fraternising with the enemy. Didn't you say he was all buddy-up with David?

Me: Maybe I misjudged the situation.

Clare: Be careful.

Their warnings sober me up a little, but the truth is, I'm feeling reckless with the prospect of release from the heavy pressure of this term, and actually getting away, when I didn't really go anywhere all summer. I've also finally found a guy with a house and a car who's willing to take me away. I'm not going to turn that down for the sake of 'we've only just started dating'.

In the car we play the interrogation game.

'Favourite chocolate bar?' I ask.

'I don't really buy them.'

I bury my face in my hands.

'If you had to.'

'Um… just dark chocolate. 90% cocoa.'

'When you go to the cinema, what is your preference: sweet or salted popcorn?'

'Salted. Though I don't really go that often.'

'I will have to drag you to a rom-com. It's obligatory.'

'Do I get to ask you some questions now?' Michael says with a glint in his eye.

'If you like.'

'Do you really like cats?'

'Yes.'

'Would you ever own one?'

'It's on my list of life goals. Once I've bought my own place.'

He winces slightly.

'Would you say you were an animal person?' he continues.

'Yes. My sister is training to be a vet. Why are you asking me so many questions about animals?'

'I can't stand them,' Michael says bluntly.

'What, all animals?'

'Pretty much.'

'What about dogs?'

He wrinkles his nose disdainfully.

'They smell. When I go out running, and people's dogs jump up on me… It's awkward.'

'Please don't say that to my sister.'

'Noted.'

I think about what is going to happen when Katie meets Michael.

'Why are you screwing your face up like that?' he asks.

'No reason. Ask me another question.'

He thinks for a moment.

'Did you always want to be a teacher?'

I laugh dryly.

'Did you?'

'I asked first.'

I sigh.

'I always wanted to be a writer. But after my Mum died, I had to think more clearly about earning a salary.'

'Do you still write?'

'Yes…' I falter. 'But school gets in the way.'

'It does that.'

We both sit, considering how much school consumes our lives, a hungry monster that's never satisfied.

'Will you let me read some of your work?'

I look at him. Now he's really asking to see shades of me he's never seen before.

'You have to be nice.'

He sighs.

'I'm not a 'nice' person, Jen. You should know that by now.'

'You've been really nice to me,' I say sincerely.

'Even when I kicked a football in your face?'

'That was an accident, right?' I grin. 'You changed the batteries on my clock.'

'That wasn't kindness, just compulsive behaviour.'

My phone buzzes, and I look down. It's Dad calling. Katie's probably tipped him off that I'm eloping. I slip my phone back into my handbag and return to staring at the increasingly rural landscape around us. We're off the motorway and surrounded by autumnal colour, the trees spaced over rolling fields.

'Not far now,' Michael says.

I gaze covetously at the large, detached properties with climbing roses. There are occasionally 'for sale' signs, but I can't even afford a garage around here. If only I could get out of that flat. I scowl at the people in Audis and 4x4 trucks, picking up organic meat from the deli and coffee from some special grinder that sings. They don't need to hide their teabags in a filing cabinet.

'Everyone here's going to be wearing posh wellies and gilets,' I moan.

'Didn't you pack any?' he gives me a sideways smile.

'Yeah, because of all that country walking I do from my flat to school every day.'

'It's about time you got some fresh air.'

Stepping out of the car, the breeze is cool and the afternoon sun is low in a grey sky, but it feels cleansing to breathe air that is nowhere near the radius of school. The house is on an ordinary residential street, and I am fluttering with nerves as I meet Michael at the boot of the car.

'I've got your bag,' he lifts it out easily with his own.

I wrap my coat around me more tightly and follow him up the path. The garden is well kept and the front door is primrose yellow. I take this as a good sign.

Michael lowers the bags and is just about to ring the doorbell when the door suddenly swings open.

'Hello!'

It's a lady well into retirement, and she's wearing a gilet. Her accent sounds like the Queen.

'You must be Michael. Come in, come in.'

Her name is Sylvia. She introduces herself, smiling eagerly, with bright blue eyeshadow and pink lipstick freshly applied. As we enter the hallway, there's a large dresser filled with ornaments. Most of them are ducks. Not cute Beatrix Potter style, but expensive and delicate bone china, solid gold beaks, painted in garish colours with beady eyes. I repress a shudder.

'Do you like my collection?' she gestures as we walk past.

I nod and follow as she strides on into the kitchen. It's authentically vintage, the expensive kind rather than the bric-a-brac kind. Blue and cream measuring jugs and brass scales.

'Now feel free to use the kitchen whenever you need it,' Sylvia continues. 'I'll take you out to your room through my yoga studio.'

She leads us into a small, bare room with large patio doors. On the walls, there are several certificates for yoga instruction, aromatherapy, and breathing (presumably for something more than just the automatic intake of Oxygen we all do ten times a minute.) The laminate floor is squeaky and polished, with a few rollmats in the corner and a CD player.

'You are welcome to join in my sessions anytime,' Sylvia says. I try to imagine Michael doing yoga and stifle a laugh.

We cross the room and walk along a short corridor to a back door, where Sylvia steps into some wellies. I give Michael a Look and suppress another giggle. As she rustles the keys to unlock the door, we hear barking and some scuffling.

'Is there a dog?' Michael asks immediately.

'Two,' Sylvia says airily, wrestling with the keys. 'Donald and Daisy.'

'Like the ducks…' I make the connection.

'I, er, don't –' Michael begins, but it's too late: she's opened the door.

A huge greyhound bounds in, followed by a yapping whippet. I don't know how they know, but they both go straight for Michael.

'Donald! Daisy!' Sylvia scolds them in an 'ah bless' kind of way.

Michael gives a muffled cry, holding the bags up by his head as Donald crashes around him, while Daisy looks about to tear into his ankles.

I push him out through the door, hoping that if we go outside, the dogs will scatter. They swarm around us and run under our feet, moving with us like a dust cloud that blurs our vision. Added to this is a sudden cacophony of noise from a group of ducks, gathered near a pond at the bottom of the garden. When I say garden, it's more like the size of a bowling green.

'Just along here,' Sylvia leads us through the lawn, hopping on some small hexagonal patio slabs. 'I won an award for this garden. It's a zen garden. Very relaxing.'

I register the stone sculptures with tiers of cascading water and Buddha statues while Michael tries to keep the bags out of the dogs' reach, and avoid his trousers being torn off.

'Do you like dogs?' Sylvia asks innocently.

'Yes,' Michael says through gritted teeth. 'Though perhaps if you could restrain them...'

She grabs onto Donald's collar and starts fussing him.

'You are so exuberant, aren't you?' she says, with such affection that I wouldn't be surprised if she kissed him. 'Go on in, the door's open.'

I finally notice the cabin. It's smart with wood panelling and pretty little windows. Michael practically dives inside to get away from the dogs. I follow and it's so perfect my jaw drops.

It's small, but it isn't cramped somehow. There's a wood burning stove, a sofa, and a neat desk area fitted into an alcove. There's a small bathroom and a kitchenette.

'This is amazing!' I turn to smile at Michael, who looks relieved but also keeps darting glances at the patio doors. The dogs are chasing each other and the ducks are mildly interested, squawking to each other as they observe.

Sylvia joins us, and thankfully leaves the dogs on the lawn.

'If it feels chilly, light the stove and you'll soon be snug in no time,' she says. 'You just fold down the sofa to turn it into a bed. The bedding's all tucked away over here, Jane.'

'It's Jen,' I correct, exchanging a smile with Michael.

'Oh, sorry! Head like a sieve. Anyway, you're always welcome in the house.'

She adds this on hopefully.

'Thank you,' I say.

She hangs on to prattle for a few more painful minutes, and when she's finally gone, Michael sinks onto the sofa with a groan.

'It didn't say there were dogs. Or ducks.'

I put the kettle on.

'This place is lovely. You did a great job finding it.'

'Why do people have dogs?'

'She probably likes the company.'

'She's nuts, isn't she?'

'Just a little quirky,' I fish around for teabags. 'She's very thoughtful. We won't have to see much of her.'

'I think we should barricade ourselves in.'

Michael starts to build a fort of cushions around himself.

'Just listen,' I say, and he stops. There is a beautiful silence. 'See? We came here to get away from it all, and it's the perfect escape.'

I hand him a cup and settle next to him, sipping my tea.

'If that dog jumps up on me again, I will not be held responsible for my actions.'

21

We go for a blustery walk, past the shop and a take-away, and trudge over fields and paths covered in fallen leaves. The trees are rich with colour, and the gentle hills roll into the distance, the landscape dotted with farms and occasional houses. The air is cold, but I'm wearing my matching bobble hat and scarf. It's one of my favourite times of year. I still can't believe I'm here with Michael.

Katie: Has he killed you yet?

Me: Go away.

It's getting dark and we make our way slowly back. Now that there's no chance of us seeing anyone we know, we can hold hands, laugh, and chatter away, and no one will question it. The knot of anxiety in the pit of my stomach that tightens when I think about work is gradually unravelling.

We reach the shop and just as we're about to go inside, Michael stops and frowns.

'What's the matter?' I ask.

He points towards a van, parked a short way up the street. The driver is reading a newspaper.

'That van was parked up there before, when we went along this street earlier.'

The van looks pretty generic and the driver looks to be in his late forties, not much hair, and a bored expression.

'So?'

'Don't you think it's a bit odd?'

'Not really.'

I manage to steer Michael inside the shop, so we can choose food for dinner, and I throw a few packets of biscuits into the mix. Michael offers to pay, so I walk over to the ATM to get some more cash out. I'll let him get this, but I can't let him pay for everything. It's at the front of the store by the window and there's a guy standing in front of it. He turns around, sensing me waiting there, and it's the van driver. He looks annoyed.

'You want to use this?' he asks abruptly, pointing at the machine.

'Yes,' I say, keeping my tone light. 'No rush, take as long as you need.'

'Easier if you go first,' he says gruffly, stepping aside.

'Thanks,' I say, slightly confused, as I take his position by the machine.

I put my card in, and decide that it might be a good idea to check my account balance. As I press the buttons and go through the different processes, I can hear the van driver huffing impatiently behind me. Once I've finally got the cash, I step away from the machine to zip up my purse, and already the driver is in my place, muttering obscenities. And then I hear 'f***ing slag.' I look up, my eyes wide with shock.

'Excuse me?' I challenge. 'Is there a problem?'

'Ready to go?' Michael appears, carrying the shopping.

The van driver is now ignoring me. I shake my head.

'What's wrong?' Michael asks.

'Tell you later,' I sigh.

My phone starts to ring. It's Katie.

'Hello?'

'You okay?'

'Well I haven't died yet if that's what you mean.'

I roll my eyes at Michael, but he's outside on the street looking up at the van again.

'Ha ha,' Katie replies. 'Dad was trying to ring you.'

'I couldn't answer.'

'Mm,' Katie's not convinced. 'Look, I don't want to interrupt your lovers' getaway, but I've been talking to him and we both think this incident is a Sign.'

'A sign of what?'

I'm out of the shop now, and standing on the pavement while people give me funny looks as they walk inside.

'That flat is a disaster. Why don't you come home?'

Even the word tears at my heart savagely.

'I don't want to talk about this right now.'

'You never want to talk about this, but you can't run away with your boyfriend forever. You need to sort this situation out.'

Nothing more annoying than a little sister bossing you around.

'I am sorting it out,' I protest. 'I've got a camera installed now…'

'Why won't you speak to Dad?'

'I will,' I counter.

'When?'

'I'll go and see him when I get back.'

It's a bit of a rash promise but I don't know what else to say.

'Great,' Katie says with finality. 'I might be able to pop down too.'

This makes the thought of going home slightly more palatable.

'Okay, tell Dad for me and I'll see you soon.'

After ending the call, I walk forward to join Michael.

'Stop staring at the van,' I hiss. 'That guy already hates me.'

'What do you mean?' he asks.

'Let's get going and I'll tell you on the way.'

Needless to say, my recount of the van driver's unnecessary rage at the ATM does nothing to dampen Michael's interest in him.

'I should go back there and speak to him,' he says, beginning to turn around.

'Michael, it's not like telling off Year 8,' I drag his sleeve to pull him back in the right direction. 'Leave it.'

'How was your sister?'

'Fine,' I say. I avoid discussing the idea of moving back home because I think Michael will agree with her.

In Sylvia's kitchen, where thankfully the dogs are absent, we prepare spaghetti bolognese. As with everything, Michael is meticulous when cooking. He models how I should chop the onion and peppers, then takes charge of the pans with the manner of a sous-chef in a Michelin restaurant.

'I have cooked spag bol before,' I remind him.

'Thirty more seconds and the pasta will be *al dente*,' Michael says, looking at the timer on his phone.

I stir the sauce, and when Michael's timer bleeps, he picks up the saucepan of spaghetti to drain it. With the noise of the extractor fan, we don't hear Sylvia come in. Michael is just stepping away from the sink when the dogs run in, barking loudly. Michael stumbles over the smaller one, and drops the pan with a clatter. Michael and I watch in horror as the dogs eat our pasta. Sylvia hurries in and shoos the dogs towards the door.

'So sorry,' she apologises, shutting them out and then grabbing a dustpan and brush.

Michael is speechless, for once, so I tell him to put some more spaghetti on while we clear up the mess.

When we've finally sat down to eat, I suddenly remember my dad making bolognese for my birthday one year. I shove the thought to one side.

'What's your family like?' I ask Michael.

He smiles.

'Quite… quiet. My parents love books. They're both solicitors.'

I swallow a gulp of water. Meeting them might be somewhat intimidating.

'So why did you become a teacher then?'

He raises his eyebrows and sips his drink.

'I think it was the most unexpected decision I ever made. I went to the careers fair, fully intending to head to the legal stalls, but I got accosted by the teaching fast-track programme guys first. If I was honest with myself, I enjoyed the Literature part of my degree more than the Law side. So I signed up, and I never looked back.'

'What did your parents say?'

'They were surprised,' he grins. 'But they didn't say much, really. They don't tend to tell me what they think.'

'If you became a lawyer, we wouldn't be sitting here together now,' I gesture with my fork.

'Unless you believe in inevitability,' Michael says. 'Perhaps our paths were always meant to cross.'

He lifts the glass to his lips.

'Or —what was it you asked when you observed my lesson? Does history repeat itself? I've often wondered why you asked that.'

I roll my eyes.

'You never forget anything, do you?'

I lay my cutlery down.

'Sometimes,' I begin hesitantly, 'I worry that I'm too much like my mother. That I'm going to turn into her, or make the same mistakes she did.'

'What kind of mistakes?'

'Always thinking that there's something better out there. Something I don't have.'

'That's called the human condition.'

'So sorry about Donald.' Sylvia blusters in and shuts the door. 'He's been a really naughty boy today.'

I catch Michael's eye and choke down laughter, gulping down my water to crush it.

'Would you like some food, Sylvia?' Michael asks, gesturing to the pan.

'Oh! Well, if you don't mind,' she smiles. 'That's very kind of you.'

Michael serves her a generous helping, and pours her some wine. I've noticed he's thoughtful like that.

As we sit round the table together, a candle flickering in the centre, it feels like a long time since I've eaten in this kind of setting. Just an ordinary meal, in an ordinary kitchen, but with the comforting company of friends. I consider Dad's missed call again. I will go and see him.

Once we've finished the meal, we tidy up the kitchen (Michael fixing a problem with Sylvia's dishwasher, to her delight) and then head back out to our cabin.

It's well and truly pitch black now, and a tapestry of stars has unfolded in the clear night air. We never see this many in Whidlock – too much pollution. Michael and I stop and gaze up at the blinking lights, so far away. In this moment, the silence is so rich, it's like the universe is singing.

'Want me to grab a blanket?' Michael asks. He guides me to a garden chair, then brings out a blanket and drapes it around me.

'This is magic,' I breathe. 'Is this your tactic with all your girlfriends?'

Michael laughs.

'Is it working?' He takes my hand. 'To be honest with you, Jen, I've never had a girlfriend before.'

I try to scrutinise his face, but the only light is from the windows of the main house.

'Are you serious?'

'Yes.'

'Why?'

'Different reasons,' he says.

'Tell me.'

'I've always been really busy with studying or work. Relationships seemed like too much effort, with not a lot of payoff.'

'You're making a lot of effort now,' I clasp his hand. 'I hope you think it's worth it.'

'I still can't believe you actually like me,' he says. 'Any minute now, I expect you to come to your senses. Find a more normal sort of guy like… Joseph Vermont.'

We burst into laughter.

'Not if he was the last man on earth,' I say. 'I don't know how I'm ever going to look him in the eye again after he saw us today.'

'It's not him who's the problem, it's David.'

'Hey, we said we weren't going to talk about work tonight,' I remind him.

'True,' he says, but in the quiet, I can tell he's still thinking about it.

It's strange how familiar he is becoming to me already, in such a short time. I don't want to go back to how things were before. Just thinking about what's going to happen when we're back in school turns my stomach. I remind myself that we're here to escape. I don't need to think about anything.

Back inside the cabin, I find a CD player with a random collection of albums.

'Retro,' Michael comments.

'I've got an idea to help us relax,' I say, dimming the lights. 'Go and lie on the rug.'

He rolls his eyes but obeys, his tall body stretching out over the floor. I press play and then lie down next to him. Keyboard synth sounds ring out, among the lapping of waves and the crash of the sea.

'What is this?' he asks.

'Whale music.'

We lie on our backs as the soothing sounds fill the room. I close my eyes and breathe.

Teaching must be one of the few jobs where everyone's holidays are the same, creating an odd bubble of term-time franticness, then breaks when everything stops for everyone all at the same time. It's not the only stressful job; I know I'm not the only person who struggles with deadlines and urgent situations. As I lie there on the floor, I picture myself, precariously balancing my box of marking and wobbling down the steps. The picture sums up my entire career. Each term, I feel like I'm carrying an impossible weight. I crawl through, struggling just to tread water, aiming to make it to half term. And when it finally arrives, it takes days to unwind from the tension that I've been carrying.

One good night's sleep is not enough for me to beat the state of exhaustion my body's in.

I don't want to be like this. I don't want to be a workaholic. I don't want this binge-work and binge-rest kind of lifestyle; I just want normality. Steph and Katie are always telling me that I need better work/life balance, but it always feels so impossible to achieve. Lying here next to Michael, I make a promise to myself. I have to change this.

I open my eyes and Michael is propped up on one arm, smiling at me.

'What?' I ask.

'Just looking at you.'

'You really are a romantic goofball.'

We giggle.

'Are you feeling better?' he asks.

I pause before answering.

'Do you ever feel like you're on a treadmill, but you don't know how to get off?'

'Are you talking about work?' he asks. 'Are we allowed to talk about work now?'

'For the purpose of this conversation, yes,' I clarify.

'You've had a lot thrown at you this term,' he says.

'And you. It can't have been easy, starting at a new school.'

'There are perks that I didn't foresee,' he says with a grin. I swat his shoulder.

'I just feel this… heavy exhaustion, where I've got a permanent headache and no motivation. I could go to sleep right now for 12 hours straight and it still wouldn't be enough.'

'You'll feel better tomorrow.'

'I hope so. But I don't want to be in this kind of state all the time, do you?'

He sighs.

'My dad always told me not to waste time. I should always be productive. I find it hard to sit still, to just… be.'

I watch his changing expression. His eyes darken. I want to know everything he's thinking, every experience he's been through. I want to understand him better.

'You know when you said about *Wuthering Heights* being about obsession?' he asks.

'Yeah,' I don't know where this is going.

'Well, I should warn you: I have an addictive personality.'

'What does that mean?' Maybe Katie was right and he is a serial killer after all.

'I love the rush of finishing a task. I always want to do more and more, because I thrive on achievement. It's hard for me to lay down any boundaries.'

'Right. What's this got to do with *Wuthering Heights*?'

'When Heathcliff finds Cathy, she's the only person he can cling to. He's obsessed with her because he has nowhere else to direct his emotion, and he has no boundaries on his love, even when she marries someone else, and even when she's dead.'

Well THIS is an intense conversation.

'What I'm trying to say,' he continues, 'is that I've never had a girlfriend because I've never met anyone worth the effort. But now I've found you, I'm terrified of losing you. I don't know how to do anything with less than 100% involvement. But it scares me because I live and breathe work and I don't know how all the pieces fit together.'

We lie there, holding hands, and the whale song fades. It's just the sound of the ocean remaining.

'We don't need all the answers, Michael,' I say. 'We just need to remember what's really important.'

When he kisses me, it's like a buzz of exhilaration that makes the satisfaction of work seem like a bad support act to a headlining rock star. There's no comparison.

Once the CD has finished, Michael folds down the sofa, then pulls out a spare mattress from underneath.

'I can go on the floor,' I volunteer, grabbing the bed linen.

'No, no,' Michael says, taking it from me. 'You should have the bed… in your condition.'

'I'm not pregnant, Michael.'

'No but…'

He arranges the duvet. Settling down for the night, I feel this unfamiliar sensation of safety and comfort before I fall asleep.

Then I am jolted awake with an almighty crash at two a.m.

22

'What was that?' I speak into the darkness, straining my eyes to see Michael.

I realise he's standing by the edge of the curtain that covers the patio doors.

'Michael?'

'Something's going on out there,' he says grimly. He starts pulling on a sweater. 'I'm going out to see.'

'What?' I croak, rubbing my eyes.

'I'll be back in a minute.'

He unlocks the door and I hear the crunch of it opening, then a click as it shuts. Silence.

I try to breathe. What could have made the noise? What is Michael doing?

I really don't want to go out there.

But my curiosity has been piqued, and I can't sleep, so I turn the duvet aside and grab my coat, slipping on my trainers.

The side gate is slightly ajar, so I walk forwards. A hand grabs my sleeve and pulls me back into the shadows.

'Stay back.'

It's Michael.

'You're lucky I didn't scream.'

'Look.'

A JCB is outside the shop, and the window is totally smashed. Some men are moving the ATM cash machine onto a trailer. I can see the guy who swore at me earlier.

'I knew there was something odd about that van,' Michael whispers.

'Have you called the Police?' I ask.

'Yes.'

'Right. Shall we go back to bed, then?'

'You can if you want. I want to stay and watch.'

'What if they find you?'

'The Police might need me to give evidence. I tried filming but it's too dark out here. I'd have to get closer.'

'Michael, just come inside. The Police can handle this.'

He's got that glazed look of determination. Why is he so obsessive about this stuff? Perhaps Steph was right with the James Bond analogy.

The sound of sirens echoes down the quiet street. The men start shouting to one another and the JCB starts moving.

'How can they get away in a JCB?' I whisper. 'It's a bit obvious, isn't it?'

The Police cars swerve round the corner and block the road off. Officers start appearing and the men scatter in all directions. One is heading straight for us.

'Keep back. I'll get him,' Michael hisses.

Oh, no. Definitely James Bond.

A guy in a balaclava and black jacket speeds towards us and rushes into the garden gate. Michael is off immediately to pursue him.

'Hey!' I call to an officer nearby. 'He went through the gate.'

The officer follows, and I run along behind. I am not cut out for this TV cops thing.

On the lawn, Michael is restraining the guy with his hands behind his back and holding him down by pressing his knee into his back. The officer handcuffs the man and Michael helps to escort him out to the Police car. With some satisfaction, I recognise the man who swore at me earlier, once they remove his balaclava. I'm tempted to snap a pic to share on the WC chat, the antithesis of holiday shots, but I don't think they'd see the funny side. And Katie? She's probably already tracking me by my phone's GPS and got the local police on speed dial. I sigh and head inside again. Time for a cup of tea.

It is nearly morning by the time the officers have taken our statements, and the whole street is swarming with Police cars and tape to cordon off the damaged area of the shop. Michael is buzzing with excitement, using phrases like 'clear intention' and 'co-ordinated crime outfit' and basically shadowing the officers wherever he can. It's driving me crazy.

'I'm going to go to the main kitchen and see if Sylvia's up.'

I enter the house. For once the dogs don't bowl me over, and they half heartedly sniff me before returning to their baskets. Sylvia appears in a dressing gown. Without make-up she looks more frail.

'What's going on out there?'

'JCB smashed the shop window to get the cash machine.'

'Oh!'

Sylvia sits down in shock. I quickly make her some tea. Donald pads over to Sylvia and rests his head mournfully on her lap. Daisy brushes against my legs and I find myself reaching down to stroke this dog that I don't really like. It's soothing somehow.

'Never had anything like that round here before,' she says.

'Someone tried to steal my mum's canoe once.'

'Do you live near a river?' Sylvia seems interested. I figure it's a good distraction from the crime-just-outside-the-door.

'Near a canal actually. My back garden ran down to it. We kept a canoe tied up. One day we were walking on the canal path and we saw someone trying to untie it.'

I smile as I remember.

'My mum said, 'Is that your canoe?' The guy said 'Yes.' She said, 'That's not your canoe. I know that because it's *my* canoe!'

Sylvia laughs with me.

'Your mum sounds quite a character.'

I take a gulp of my tea.

'She died a few years ago.'

I don't know why I am saying this. I don't often mention Mum and this woman is almost a complete stranger, and definitely bonkers.

'What happened?'

'Cancer.'

'I'm sorry.'

Sylvia's eyes look misty, and the genuineness of her sympathy makes me choke in an unexpected sob.

'Here,' she hands me a tissue. 'It's okay to cry, you know.'

'It's been eight years now.'

'That doesn't mean it hurts any less.'

It turns out Sylvia is a trained volunteer bereavement counsellor.

She may talk like royalty and wear expensive wellies, but she's a fantastic listener. Sitting at her kitchen table, I find myself telling her all about Mum, Katie, Dad, and the struggle of living at home while studying for my degree, then helping Katie with her applications, sending her off to live on campus, and finally moving out into my own flat.

'How's your dad been coping on his own?' she asks.

I look down at the table.

'He just… withdraws into his shed all the time. He wants to pretend that nothing's happened. I know I should visit him more often, but he just talks about Mum as if she was a saint. I know she's gone now, but I still feel so angry at what she did.'

'You're not wrong to be angry,' Sylvia says carefully, 'but if you allow that anger to become a barrier in your relationship with your dad, who's the only parent you have left, then that seems sad to me.'

Outside the kitchen window, there are birds all over the feeding station. I watch the sparrows and robins flitter about, and a fat wood pigeon lands in the bird bath and scatters them.

'After Winston died, I hated being alone in the house. That's why I started renting out the cabin,' Sylvia says, sipping her tea.

I sigh. I should definitely ring Dad and arrange to see him as soon as we get back.

'How long have you and Michael been together?' she asks.

I shift in my seat.

'Not long at all,' I reply.

'He's a bit like Action Man out there.'

Sylvia nods towards the window, where Michael is still with the Police Officers. Maybe he did choose the wrong career.

'I don't think Michael knows how to sit still,' I say it without thinking, really. My guard is down.

Sylvia places her cup down on the table.

'People are so busy these days,' she comments. 'You remind me of my daughter, she's always rushing around.'

She points to a photograph on the wall, where a blond, athletic girl is on a sailing boat.

'Just make sure you're not so busy that you can't enjoy life with the people who matter the most to you,' Sylvia says. 'Would you like to join me for some yoga in the studio?'

'Sure,' I drain the rest of my tea and set the mug down.

Why not? I might discover I actually like it. Given the events of the past forty-eight hours, nothing can surprise me now.

23

Sylvia has obviously tried very hard to make her yoga studio an Insta-worthy space. It has the perfect combination of natural wood, mood lighting, and neutral colours. It would be the ultimate serene escape, if Sylvia herself wasn't verbalising her own stream of consciousness.

'I'll just change the CD… Track seven, I think… Perfect… Would you like a mat? I've seen this new one online and thought I might order some more…'

But it's quite nice, for once, to not be the teacher. I can sit on my mat, copy Sylvia, and let her count our deep breathing. I don't have to speak, or think. I feel my shoulders dropping into a more relaxed state from basically being hunched up to my earlobes. My mind finally clears from all the buzzing, nagging thoughts that seem to multiply every minute I'm in school. By the time the CD ends, we're sitting in blissful silence. Through the patio doors, I can see birds fluttering their wings, glimmers of water droplets catching the sun. The ground is dewy and there's a faint mist in the air, like everything's in soft focus.

Michael opens the side gate and steps into the garden. I feel that ripple of attraction just looking at his tall frame and the way his dark hair falls across his forehead.

Then the two dogs rush at him, barking. Sylvia and I watch through the patio doors for a moment in grim fascination as Michael attempts to fend them off, almost falling over in the process.

'I'll get them in,' Sylvia mutters, opening the patio door and calling to them.

Donald and Daisy skitter across the studio floor, and Michael notices me as I get to my feet.

'Didn't realise you were in here,' he says, with a playful smile.

'We were just finishing,' I reply.

The spell's well and truly broken now.

'Maybe we can do this again?' Sylvia suggests.

'I'd really like that,' I nod. 'Thank you, Sylvia.'

'Do you fancy a cooked breakfast?' she asks Michael.

'Absolutely,' he grins.

A short while later, I leave him with Sylvia heaping third helpings onto his plate, and call my dad.

'I've been trying to get hold of you,' he says, as soon as he answers.

'I know. Sorry.' I transfer my weight from one foot to the other.

'Where are you again?' he asks.

'The Cotswolds,' I answer. 'Just for a few days.'

'I've been to check your flat,' he says. 'Looks all okay from the outside. That's a fancy camera too.'

'Thanks,' I say.

'The trouble is, it's not a great area,' he says, and he sounds like he's rehearsed this (perhaps with Katie). 'I don't like the idea of you in there on your own.'

I bite back a sarcastic laugh. This is the dad who checked out of several years of my life, while I cared for him and my sister. That was almost as lonely as my life in the flat.

'I just want you to know that the door is always open,' he speaks with a sort of finality: that must be the final punchline of the spiel.

'Thanks Dad, I do appreciate it,' I say. 'How about I come and see you when I get back?'

He seems happy with this, and by the time I end the call, I feel more positive about the whole thing. About everything, actually. Having a clear head gives me fresh resolve. When Michael and I return to the cabin, I grab a notebook and start scribbling down my thoughts and ideas.

Make the effort to see Dad.

Stop working and breathe.

Get back to writing.

But when I look at my laptop, I can't bring myself to open it. My eyes start drooping and I lower my head to the pillow — the sofa bed is still made up and dishevelled from when we left in the middle of the night — while Michael sits at my side, starting up his laptop.

'Aren't you tired?' I yawn.

'Just want to get a few things done,' Michael replies.

It's well into the afternoon by the time I wake up. It takes me a minute to remember where I am. As I look beside me, I can see Michael, his laptop at a funny angle and the screen has gone black. He's asleep, but positioned awkwardly. I gently reach over, close the laptop and lift it onto the floor. Then I pull his shoulders, guiding his body so that his head is better supported by the cushions. I watch him, enjoying the moment of closeness. We've barely had time to stop over the past few days, let alone the chaos of the whole term.

It's all so surreal. I never imagined this is where I'd be a few days ago. And yet, in another way, being with Michael feels so natural. He's just gradually become a part of my life, and I'm more used to his abrupt humour and driven nature. He never gives up on anything. But maybe, looking at the laptop, he needs to learn to let go.

It is a real oasis here. I can hear the birds singing in the garden, and I'm just enjoying the smooth sheets, the soft pillow, and the feeling that I don't have to be anywhere or do anything. But it isn't long before unwelcome questions pepper my peaceful consciousness. What do I do when I go back to my flat? What do we do when we're back in school? What am I going to do the next time I see David Clark? How am I going to plan all these lessons for this review coming up?

This is the problem with sitting still. Your thoughts are still racing like Formula One.

After giving my hair a comb, I leave Michael and wander over to Sylvia's house. In the kitchen, I automatically put the kettle on. I could've made tea in the cabin but it may have disturbed Michael. To be honest, I'm quite keen to see Sylvia again. She's good company and there's just something about a female companion. I feel like she understands.

'How are you doing, Jen?' she asks, coming down the stairs and into the hallway. 'Did you get some rest?'

'Yes, thanks,' I reply. 'I'm really enjoying how peaceful it is here.'

'I'm so glad,' Sylvia beams. 'Do you have any plans for this afternoon?'

'Not really. Michael is finally asleep, so I don't want to wake him.'

'Why don't you come into town with me?' she asks. 'I was just going to go in.'

'Alright then, if you don't mind.'

I grab my bag and follow Sylvia out to her car. Thankfully she's not bringing the dogs.

The town isn't big, but there's a great charity shop, and I spend a happy hour rummaging through books, DVDs and clothes. I find a pair of brushed velvet trousers in a beautiful plum colour and a really warm stole that I put on immediately. I also bag a retro cookbook with hilarious pictures, a copy of *Wuthering Heights* for Michael and a 1000 piece jigsaw puzzle of some brightly coloured beach huts.

I snap a picture of the menu at a pizzeria, then meet Sylvia back at the car to show her my spoils.

'That stole is gorgeous,' she says. 'I've got a pair of gloves that would match it exactly, if you want them.'

Sylvia hurries when we get back to show me her American style, walk-in closet, which contains around fifty pairs of shoes (no more wellies in sight up here), and retrieves the gloves. They are a soft sheepskin.

'Are you sure?' I check, smoothing my fingers over them.

'Of course,' she says. 'I've got too much stuff anyway.'

I was so quick to judge her, and now I'm astounded at her generosity. It makes me think about Mum. She would have given away the last thing she owned, she was that free-spirited. I always judged her, too.

Later, Michael and I share a pizza and manage to catch up on missed sleep by getting an early night. So much for the party lifestyle. I join Sylvia in the studio the next morning for yoga again.

She's quieter this time, maybe because she's more relaxed, but we spend a peaceful hour together stretching and listening to music.

'I told myself I would never do yoga after my mum ran off with her yoga instructor,' I tell Sylvia.

'We all say rash things when we're hurt,' Sylvia says. 'But it would be a bit sad, if you couldn't enjoy something because of a choice that your mum made.'

'I just couldn't understand why she did it,' I say.

Sylvia thinks for a moment.

'You don't have to understand, or approve, of her choices in order to love her.'

My eyes sting with tears. I hate crying about Mum.

'Avoiding going home, never talking about her… You aren't going to erase your feelings that way,' Sylvia says.

It's like she can read my soul.

'I don't know what else to do,' I admit, brushing a tear from my cheek.

'Remove the thorn, and the wound will heal.'

Now she's turned into Yoda.

'How do I do that?'

'Only you can do it,' Sylvia says sagely. 'But you've got to stop hiding and running away.'

I thought I was here for a romantic getaway. Instead it turns out I've had a spiritual retreat.

This is not entirely a bad thing, but Michael's been obsessively creating lesson plans, and he's still in the fast lane where I've tried to take a slip road off the motorway. Even the jigsaw puzzle poses a competitive challenge.

'I love beach huts,' I say, fishing around in the box for brightly coloured pieces.

'Hmm,' says Michael, turning over some pieces on the table. 'Have you found any edges or corners?'

I leave him to it and grab my laptop. Talking about my mum has reminded me of my story, and I feel like I've finally got the headspace I need to go back to it again. I know that I have to find it in myself to go back there, to go over the words I wrote in the summer when I could do nothing else except think and imagine all over again. I knew it was good for me. But this term I just haven't wanted to reopen those wounds again, not when I've been putting out fires day after day with Tyler's rebellious class and trying to look like a serious contender for a Head of Department.

I open up my laptop and instead of going to the usual work files, I load up my work-in-progress (WIP on the social media groups).

'I shared my docs with you today,' Michael says, arranging puzzle pieces.

'Thanks,' I say. 'I'm not working now, though.'

'Is that your story?' He sits up straighter, and looks towards me. 'You said I could read it.'

'I don't recall saying that exactly,' I stall.

'What's it about?'

I smile.

'It's like 'Alice in Wonderland' but Alice is an assassin, and she falls in love with her target, who's a prince.'

'Is there a White Rabbit?'

'Kind of,' I wrinkle my nose. 'She's actually trying to find her mother, who's disappeared.'

'I'd like to read it.'

I hover in indecision for a few seconds, then hand him the laptop. My story begins with Alice finding her mother's silk scarf, and falling through a tree trunk into another world. My stomach churns as I watch him read the first few pages. If he's into Cormac McCarthy, he probably thinks it's terrible.

'It's good.' His eyes flick to mine. 'It's pacy and you have meticulous attention to detail.'

I smile in relief.

'I can see it all in my head, like a really vivid dream. This is the furthest I've got with any story. But I know I need to give it much more time to redraft it and make it better.'

'You should do it,' he says, affirmingly.

He's so certain about everything. It's very attractive.

I take the laptop out of his hands, place it onto the table, then lean over his chair to kiss him. He pulls me down into his lap and I wrap my arms around his neck. This heat is like when we were standing within breathing space in the cupboard, or almost touching in the theatre. It's the spark of when he saw me in my dress, kindling into a flame now we're away, and we're alone, and he pulls me in closer…

Then his phone rings. It's on the table and buzzes, moving towards the edge. I break off and catch it, looking at the name on the screen. It's David Clark.

24

'Hello David.'

Michael's eyes are on me as he answers the call.

'No, I wasn't planning on it.'

It must be that golf thing he told me about. I thought he'd already told David that he wasn't going?

'Oh. Oh right. Well, I was just…'

I watch as Michael's brain struggles to be creative. He's not very inventive when it comes to making excuses. I motion washing my hair. He shakes his head.

'No, I'm not stressed about that, don't worry.'

He's going to crumble. I can see it.

'Hold on a sec.'

He presses the phone against his shoulder.

'He wants me to join him for golf tomorrow. Joseph's pulled out and it's just him with the councillor from the LEA.'

We were leaving tomorrow anyway.

'Where is it?'

'The golf club near the school.'

That's right by where my dad lives. Maybe this is providential.

'Say yes then. You can drop me off at my dad's.'

He lifts the phone back to his ear.

'About what time?'

We pack up in the morning (including dismantling the puzzle, which I abandoned at one a.m. but Michael persevered in completing). Sylvia gives me a big hug and a card with her number.

'If you ever want to chat,' she says.

'Thank you.'

As we load up the car, we see Donald in a most uncompromising position with Daisy.

'Ugh, I think I'm going to be sick,' Michael says.

No softening towards the furry friends, then.

In fact, Michael seems to change over the course of the car journey. The closer we get to Whidlock, the more his jaw sets.

'What are you thinking about?' I ask.

He looks at me and tries to remove his frown.

'Nothing.'

That means he doesn't want to tell me.

'Are you nervous?' I try a different tactic.

'Why would I be nervous? I've known David for years,' he says, gripping the steering wheel.

'Well, why are you stressed, then?'

'He's my boss! And this councillor is pretty important.'

'This is just a game of golf. It isn't a conference,' I roll my eyes.

'Yes, but it matters. It must matter or he wouldn't have called me.'

I take issue with this on several levels. Firstly, David doesn't seem to mind calling Michael at any hour of the day. Case in point: the trip. Secondly, David calling doesn't necessarily equate to *something that matters.*

'What, do you think he's planning to sweet-talk the councillor into getting us funding for a new building?'

'Don't be flippant, Jen. He's a young guy, and he feels out of place with all those senior figures from the Local Authority who are close to retirement. He needs some back-up. Whidlock County's in trouble. As much as you dislike David, he is trying to help.'

'There's only one person David cares about helping, and that's himself.'

I look out of the window at the familiar roads and scenery.

'And anyway,' I begin again, 'I don't see why you're so afraid to speak your mind. He may be your boss but he's just another guy. He doesn't own you.'

'What, so you wouldn't care if it was you going out to lunch with him then? You'd just breeze in and grab a sandwich?'

'I would never socialise with someone like him out of choice,' I say pointedly. 'But yes, if it came to it, I would eat my sandwich and I wouldn't care if he ordered caviar.'

We turn into the cul-de-sac and I grab my handbag.

'I'll hop out, you stay there.'

I give him a brief kiss and then fetch my holdall from the boot.

'Have fun,' I say with a touch of irony, waving him off.

With a sigh, I turn to face my old front door. The familiar emotions churn up: love, anger and regret. I try the handle. Unsurprisingly, it's open.

'Dad?' I call, as I step inside.

The air feels thick and dank, but it's the same as ever: sage green paint, parquet floor, hooks overloaded with coats. I dump my bags and carry on through to the kitchen. It's so quiet when Katie's away.

I try the back door and step out into the sunny afternoon. The beech tree is covered in copper leaves and the grass is scattered with them. The light in the shed is on, so I head towards it.

'Dad?'

He's wearing his old jeans, with his dog-eared forest green fleece, and his white hair is long, needing a cut.

'Oh, hello love,' he says distractedly, while he lays some wires into position. I can smell the acrid solder iron and the musty wood. 'Do me a favour, can you cut this off for me?'

Automatically I take the string and grab a pair of scissors. It's as if I've never been away.

'What are you up to?' I ask.

'Just wanted to fix this light. The sensor's broken. Thought it could be good for your flat.'

My eyes brim with sudden tears. He does care.

'Thanks, Dad.' I lay my hand on his arm.

Growing up, people wouldn't even think he was my dad, because he was white. We look nothing alike, but in this moment, he looks up, and his eyes are watery too.

'I'm glad you came.'

I watch Dad potter around for a bit, then I head back inside to make some tea. Once I've left his mug on the workbench, I sit on my own in the lounge and lean back into the silence.

I grab my laptop and open it up.

I read over my opening chapter, and I start seeing things I want to change, words I want to improve. It's all so vivid again, even after such a long break. My fingers start to fly over the keys and it feels like hardly any time has passed when my dad comes back inside.

'Do you want some food? I've got salmon.'

I check my phone. Nothing from Michael.

'Sure.'

I continue typing while Dad bustles about in the kitchen. He's always been a great cook, and he cuts his own herbs from the garden. That's what the house smells like: rosemary, basil and mint.

'School okay?' Dad asks as we sit at the table together. He seems more attentive than usual.

'It's been busy,' I say, pouring some water. Dad always forgets the drinks.

'Katie says you're going for a promotion.'

'I probably won't get it,' I say, gulping from my glass.

'Good to try, though. Bit more money for you. Any thoughts on the flat?'

I make a face.

'Look, if you don't want to move back in here, why don't you start looking for somewhere nicer?'

'I might do.' Although it's proved handy to have a boyfriend with a clean and tidy house.

As if he's reading my mind, he says casually,

'Are you seeing someone?'

I look at him in surprise. Dad never asks personal questions.

'Katie told me,' he says when he sees my face.

'Well, it's only been a few days.'

'What's he like?'

'He's…' I try to think of some adequate adjectives. Intense. Relentless. Determined. All too scary. 'Motivated.'

'Motivated?'

'I mean, he is really good at his job.'

Much better than me.

'I'm not asking for his credentials,' Dad says, waving his fork in the air. 'I meant his personality.'

'That is his personality,' I say.

'So you can be workaholics together, then.'

'I'm not a workaholic,' I say automatically, although I've been thinking exactly the same thing.

'You don't seem to do much else.'

I remember my resolution and sigh.

'Well, I just spent some time now working on my story.'

'Good. You should do more of that, you know.'

He looks off into the distance and I can tell he's thinking about Mum.

'You always think you have time, all the time in the world, for the things you want to do. But suddenly, you run out. Nobody gives you a warning,' he says.

Silence hangs in the air.

'Sorry I haven't been here for so long,' I finally vocalise an apology.

'I know you're busy.' He doesn't want to dwell on it, and I'm grateful for that. 'Katie's doing well.'

'Yes, I think she'll have no problems finding a job.'

'I wonder where she's going to end up?' he muses.

'It's quiet without her,' I say.

Maybe that was why I left; I couldn't cope being here without her.

'It's always quiet around here,' Dad says. There's an unexpected edge in his tone.

'I thought you liked the quiet.'

He raises his eyes and blinks.

'Yes,' he says. 'But sometimes the silence gets too loud.'

Just like Sylvia told me. I finish my food but I can't get rid of the stab of guilt in my gut.

On the subject of silence, my phone is still dull with no new messages or calls. Maybe the guys are eating at the golf club. Dad and I sit in the lounge together and watch the news. I consider updating Deena and Clare but I know they were sounding alarm bells anyway, so it feels pointless. I text Katie instead; no secrets from my sister. Then a new message comes through from Michael.

Michael: Something's come up. Can you stay at your dad's? Sorry Jen.

I feel my eyes sting with disappointment. Something's come up?

'Dad, do you mind if I stay tonight? I'm just going to go and ring Katie.'

As I thump my way up the stairs, I swallow back a sob. Something's come up, and I bet it's something to do with David.

'So what, he's just ditched you? With no explanation?'

'None,' I sob. 'It must be David...'

'Look, you know the measure of that guy. But if Michael is the great person you've been telling me, then there probably is a good reason why he's left you tonight. He's not breaking up with you.'

'I hope not. But it's weird.'

'Well if it turns out that Michael is actually the jerk that you originally thought he was, then it's better to find that out sooner rather than later.'

'That's not very comforting.'

'Sorry,' Katie sighs. 'Look, spend a few days with Dad. Get all your work stuff done and write more of your story. Then I'll get the train down on Friday and we'll stay at your flat together to get you used to being there again.'

'And hope that I don't get hunted down by a drug dealer.'

'Stay strong, Jen. You don't *need* him.'

But it feels like I do.

25

I follow Katie's instructions and stay with Dad. It's actually kind of nice. I've been living in the flat long enough to have forgotten what it's like to be in a house with a garden, and instead of annoying me, Dad's actually really sweet. Not much conversation, and we avoid talking about Mum, but then, I've got a lot to get on with anyway.

Here's my plan to save the world: write kick-ass lesson plans and an amazing book.

My reward for each lesson plan is to work on one chapter. By the time it's Friday, I've done the plans and I've worked through a decent chunk of my story. Not bad.

I get a text from Michael, saying he's been roped in to the Duke of Edinburgh expedition because someone flaked out, but then hear nothing for several days. He surely can't have gone totally off grid? I keep picking up my phone to start typing a new message to him, but what exactly do I say? *Hi, are we still together?* The radio silence is killing me, but Katie tells me not to crack. This is the test to see if he's *really* interested in me.

'It's no good if you're the one chasing him,' she says on the phone. The irony, given his name. 'Take a break and give him time to think. You'll definitely be seeing him on Monday anyway.'

If he doesn't contact me by then, I may *see* him but I will not be *speaking* to him.

Is it all just in my head? When we were together, it felt so… right. He was warm and kind and… less like a robot, more like a human being. I felt that he really cared about me. When we kissed, he seemed to feel the spark too. But why hasn't he called? Silence from a boy is never a good thing.

'What if David told him that he isn't allowed to see me?' I suggest to Katie.

'He can't do that,' she replies. 'If Michael allows David to have control over his life like that, then that's a problem. His problem, not yours.'

'He just seems totally in David's power all the time.'

'Well, maybe he should go out with him instead then.'

'Ha ha, not funny.'

'If he's letting his boss dictate his love life, then he's just not worth it, Jen.'

'What am I supposed to do about working with him?' I push my hair back from my forehead.

'You didn't seem to have any problem working with him and hating him at the same time before all this stuff happened,' Katie points out.

'True. But it's not just going to be a normal week next week. It's inspection, followed by interviews.'

The thought of it turns my blood cold in my veins.

'Look, as hard as it is, you've got to separate the work stuff from the Michael thing,' Katie instructs. 'Teach your lessons. Do the interview. Whether you're still dating him or not, it shouldn't affect what you do.'

'Maybe not what I do, but I can't switch off how I *feel*,' I moan.

'You're going to have to,' Katie says plainly. 'Or you'll be a total nutcase.'

Always count on your younger sister to give you the truth that hurts.

When Dad and I arrive at the station, it's such a relief to see her with her bags. Even if her advice is brutal, she's still my sister and she's come for me.

We celebrate with a takeaway, all three of us at Dad's, and then he drives us back to my flat. I feel nervous butterflies going back there again, but at least I'm not on my own.

'Time to watch a rubbish movie,' Katie says, settling into the sofa.

I unpack my bag and start sorting out clothes. I'm definitely glad to be back home with my own wardrobe again. I start making a laundry pile when my phone buzzes.

Michael: Sorry I haven't been in touch. Are you OK?

I stare at the screen as excitement, anticipation, then anger pulse through me. No, I'm not okay. You went off to play golf and never came back. This is the first text you've sent me in days but before you dropped me home, everything was great between us. Were you lying? Were you just pretending? How am I supposed to answer this text now?

I sigh and jab a reply.

Me: Still alive.

Michael: I thought you might need some space before next week.

Seriously? This was all for *my* benefit?

Me: Why?

No instant response. Why does a minute feel like an hour while I'm waiting for his reply? In a sort of superstition, I lay the phone down and turn away from it to sort more clothes, thinking that if I watch it, a message won't arrive. My phone buzzes again.

Michael: Some things David said… Gave me a lot to think about.

I type quickly.

Me: So you needed the space, not me.

Don't try to fob me off, Michael Chase.

Michael: Yes. Sorry.

'Stop saying that!' I realise I've said it out loud as Katie calls over.

'What?'

'Not you,' I call. 'Michael texted.'

She leaps over the sofa to read the messages.

'It's all very cryptic,' she says, handing my phone back. 'What do you think he means?'

'I have no idea.'

'What are you going to do?'

'I don't want to ditch you when you've come all this way to stay over,' I say. 'I'm not calling him. He can speak to me in school if he wants to.'

'Good for you. Now where's the chocolate?'

It's great having Katie around. I don't feel freaked out in my flat anymore and we have some fun time with Dad, too. We even get him out of the house for a walk before we have to drop her off at the station.

'Thanks so much for coming,' I squeeze her tightly.

'It was good to see you,' she says. 'Next week you'll be fantastic. But Jen?'

'Yeah?'

'Whatever happens with this job, you need to know that you're a great teacher. Don't let what that Head guy says get to you.'

'Thanks.'

I feel slightly sick at the thought that it's Monday tomorrow.

When my alarm goes off, I dress myself in the new outfit Katie picked out. No pineapple shirts in sight: I'm wearing a black A line skirt, a white shirt with black polka dots, and a necktie. Strictly professional.

I smooth my hair back with gel into a ponytail, and push aside memories of styling my hair for my date with Michael. That seems like a long time ago now.

I click my way along the street to work in my court shoes, and it's early enough that barely any cars are in the car park. I see Michael's straight away. I ignore the jarring sensation in my stomach and head straight for my classroom. I've got a rainforest's worth of handouts to print – mental note, need to raise the paperless issue again with the eco committee – and I want to be first in line with the photocopier.

Once my laptop has finally whirred into life, and I've sent all the documents to the printer, I grab my ID card and make my way to the copy room. I start the first batch running, then hurry to the kitchen for my first fix of caffeine. As I burst through the door, I see Michael and stop dead. He turns around, interrupted from messing with his coffee machine.

'Jen,' he says. His voice sounds quiet and sad. It makes me want to cry but that would make my eyeliner run so I march over to start making my tea. I'm so cross with him that I pinch someone else's mug and tea bags, because I'm too angry to walk over to the staff room cupboard to get my own. Plus it would be the mug from *him*. I want to hear what he has to say, if he has anything to say at all.

'How are you?' he tries. I ignore him.

'Are you mad at me?'

Well done Sherlock.

'Say something.'

'I'm too cross to speak to you,' I slam the fridge door.

'Look, maybe when this is all over, we can talk properly…'

'Do you mean when this inspection is over, or the interviews?'

He looks confused.

'Both.'

'So you just want to press pause on everything, go through the next *week*, and then we can have a conversation? You must be really emotionally barren if you're actually suggesting that.'

And I thought he might have been a Heathcliff. How wrong I was.

'I know it's not ideal…'

'Ha!' I snort, clanging my spoon around my cup.

'Look, Jen, this is hard for me too,' he lowers his voice, even though no one else is around. 'I miss you.'

'Well I'm here in front of you,' I say, grabbing my mug with as much dignity as I can muster. 'If you don't want to do anything about it, then I'm afraid that's your problem.'

He opens his mouth but no words come out. I don't know why everything's changed. I feel the choking sensation of tears at the back of my throat and I swallow hard and walk back to the copy room.

When I get there, the machine's red light is flashing.

'Oh no!'

Michael rushes in after me.

'What's the matter?'

I read the screen.

'It's a paper misfeed.' I throw my hands up in despair. Everyone knows they're a nightmare. You have to follow the step by step instruction diagrams which are as helpful as IKEA's wordless pictures. I get it wrong every time.

'Don't worry, I'll sort it.'

Michael bustles about at the machine, opening it up and turning levers I didn't know existed. I stand there sipping my tea, still feeling in a huff, but if he manages to fix this then I ought to be grateful.

He pulls out a crumpled sheet, then the red light goes off.

'There you go.'

'Thank you,' I say begrudgingly.

I think he's going to say something else, but then Geoff comes in.

'Ah, I've been looking for you two,' he says, seemingly oblivious to our awkward looks. 'Inspection week! I'm calling a briefing meeting with some details to pass on to you. My room in ten minutes.'

As I sit with my tea, my notepad open in front of me, I reflect that this is the most prepared I have ever been for the lessons immediately after a half term. I have my lesson plans, my seating plans, my handouts all sorted. My room is reasonably tidy. All in all, things could be worse. My timetable for today is actually quite good. No Tyler and I've got top set Year 9 and my mentor group.

'The Head wanted me to remind you that you could be observed at any point,' Geoff says. 'Although I am aware that he has a meeting at ten so he will not be available for second lesson.'

'That doesn't mean that the visitors from Inspire won't still be coming round,' Michael points out.

'True,' Geoff says. 'They may be likely to conduct 'learning walks', where they only attend for fifteen minutes of a lesson.'

Judy rolls her eyes.

'Please don't be stressed,' Geoff says.

Hmmm, really?

'What are they going to do: fire me?' Judy jokes as we gather our things ready for registration. 'I'll be retired soon anyway.'

The thought makes me more glum. Geoff syphoned off into Senior Management, Liz fallen down a black hole (never thought

I'd mourn the loss of her), Judy probably off to the Bahamas and just me and Michael left to try and scrape enough C grades to lift Whidlock County out of the extinction zone.

The bell sounds, and it's time to begin.

My Year 9 class is an absolute joy. They are just what every class should be like: keen, motivated, able to work together with focus. We are annotating a Wilfred Owen poem and it lifts me up out of the anxiety of the inspection, hearing their ideas and interpretations. No one comes in, which is disappointing, but I know that they all enjoy the lesson and I sit down afterwards in satisfaction.

My mentor group is also lovely, in such a different way. The pace is a lot slower, and they need a lot more support, but as I watch them try their hardest at each task, I feel my heart swell up with pride for how far they've come since last year, where every sentence was a struggle. Now they are reading out loud to each other, which they would never have done six months ago. Again, no one comes in, but it's so good to be totally absorbed and not to have to think about Michael.

By the time it's lunch, I have almost forgotten about him being completely emotionally incompetent, and a jerk, and I sit next to Steph ready to tuck into my healthy wrap and carrot sticks. Eat better, feel better. That's Katie's mantra anyway.

'So come on, then,' Steph says in a confidential tone, expectantly.

'What?' I take a huge bite.

'What's going on with you and robot-guy?'

'Oh,' I chew for a moment to buy time.

'End of term drinks, you arrived together. Then you snuck out and got a bus home. Then he picked you up… I lost track of what was happening.'

'You were also drinking cocktails.'

'True,' Steph admits. 'So, are you two… together?'

I sigh.

'I thought so, but I don't think so now.'

I tell her that he wants us to 'have space' while the mini inspection and interviews take place.

'You're both still going for the same promotion?' she asks, eyebrows raised.

'Do you think I should pull out?'

She doesn't answer with an immediate 'no', which surprises me.

'Jen, do you actually want the job?'

I stare at her.

'That's a stupid question.'

'No, it's not. Do you really want to be Head of English?'

I feel like I've been tackled by one of my own team.

'Why are you asking me that?' I ask, trying to buy time.

'It's just… You came back in September, you'd been writing, you were all excited about it… You were happy with your job as it was. Since Michael came on the scene, you've been in some kind of war with him and it feels like this promotion is all wrapped up with that.'

'You don't think I can do it? You don't think I'm good enough?'

It's like a touchpaper to all my old insecurities.

'I never said that. I just wanted to ask if you want to be a HoD, because if you do get it, you're not going to have much time for the things you care about, like your writing.'

'My writing is a hobby; it's never earned me any money,' I remind her. 'I can't pass up this opportunity to move up the ladder, up the pay scale. Plus, I can use the extra money to fund my book and get it out into the world.'

Although as I say it, I think back to David's offer of the ALNCo position. That would involve a pay rise too. But I don't even know if that offer still stands. Or if it would be ethical to take him up on it.

'What's the point in getting more money if you never have time to spend it?' Steph points out, stirring her yoghurt with a teaspoon.

Before I can reply with something smart about saving to buy my own place, Michael strides in and stands at the other end of the table. He looks at me but doesn't say anything for a moment. Then he inclines his head towards the kitchen.

'Can I have a word?'

He sounds like a Head of Year, hauling a naughty kid out of a lesson. I look at Steph who shrugs, then reluctantly leave my lunchbox and follow him into the kitchen. Thankfully no one else is in there.

We stand a few feet apart, waiting for the other to close the distance. Neither of us does.

'How are you?' he asks.

The competing, the games, the theatre trip and the time away together swirl between us like a tornado.

'I'm sorry,' he says. He knows it's not enough.

Done with staring him out, I look for a distraction and put the kettle on. I set about making a cup of tea. Sue comes in and retrieves her lunchbox from the fridge, and thankfully doesn't try to do small talk. Once she's gone, I try to reach past Michael to get the milk, and he takes hold of my arm.

'Don't try and manipulate me, Michael,' I shake him off.

'I'm just trying to be there for you.'

'Be there for me?' I scoff as I slam the fridge door. Why do we always argue in this narrow kitchen with a wonky drawer full of missing cutlery and dirty plates that never make it back to the canteen? 'I was waiting for you to be there for me last week, but you never came back from golf with David, and then you signed up for a Duke of Edinburgh expedition!'

'I'm sorry,' he says, but he looks away.

'You're not sorry,' I say, measuring his expression. 'You'd do it again today if you had to.'

His eyes move to meet mine. He doesn't deny it.

'You said yourself that we wouldn't be able to… be together, in school. I don't think we really thought through what would happen,' he speaks in an annoyingly measured tone.

'I didn't want the whole school to know about us,' I begin, 'but I didn't think you would just stop talking to me and then suddenly I don't know where I am with you anymore.'

'I'm trying to do what's best for you.'

That's the most infuriating thing anyone can say.

'How does it benefit me for you to stay away from me and stop talking to me with no explanation?'

'When all this is over, I'll be able to explain…'

'Why you got the job and I didn't,' I interrupt.

'Don't be like that, Jen.'

His eyes are searching mine, pleading with me to understand. But I'm tired of being buffeted about.

'I don't have time for this,' I say, then head back to sit with Steph.

'He looks miserable,' she comments.

'He seems pretty good at engineering his own misery,' I comment acidly, biting at my carrot sticks and trying to look as though they taste better than cardboard.

'Aren't you going to make it up with him?' she asks.

I shake my head.

'He just wants me to withdraw from applying for the job, so he can get it uncontested. And I'm not doing it.'

'Are you sure this is about the job?'

'What else can it possibly be about?'

Steph sighs.

'I said it before, Jen, but I hope you know what you're doing.'

26

Being mad at Michael seems to help fuel my frenzied pace in this crazy week. By lunch time on Tuesday I've still not been observed by anyone, and now it's starting to annoy me. It's not that these lessons are wasted, but it's so hard maintaining that level of energy all the time. I feel so cross that all of this is down to a whim of David Clark's. In my mind David and Michael are now so closely in league with each other that they are almost the same person. I strongly dislike them both.

Janet Patchell emails me a formal invitation to be interviewed for the HoD position, and includes some instructions. I will need to prepare a 30 minute lesson, analyse some data, and be questioned by the panel. Geoff catches me in the corridor to check I received it.

'How many people are being interviewed?' I ask. It's basically a way of asking if it's just me vs Michael.

'Two,' he says.

Head to head then.

Michael enters my room and hovers annoyingly by the door, the draught chilling the air.

'Did you get the email?' he asks.

'Yes,' I answer, then look at him expectantly. Now's the time, Michael. Now's the time to stop being my rival and start acting like a boyfriend.

'Um,' he stalls, and I raise my eyebrows. 'The rugby team is playing Prestfield after school. Would you be free to drive the bus?'

'Why can't Steve and Gareth do it?'

'They want to take an extra team, and they've hired another minibus, but then Gareth's daughter was sick in school and he's had a phone call to go and collect her. I said I'd ask you.'

I sigh.

'It's probably the worst possible week for me to be chauffeuring the school rugby team. And you criticised my driving.'

'Prestfield is only fifteen minutes' drive,' Michael pleads. He actually is pleading with me. 'And I thought I could come along and… we could spend some time together.'

I facepalm. It's the only possible reaction.

'So, Michael, instead of just *asking me out on a date*, you've signed me up to drive a minibus and are suggesting we can have some quality time on the sidelines of the rugby pitch with the P.E. department?'

'Look, when you say it like that, it sounds bad…'

'Correct.'

'But we don't have to *watch* the rugby. We can go for a coffee or something.'

'You are possibly the worst boyfriend I've ever had. And that's saying something.'

'How many boyfriends have you had?'

'A few.'

'What is that, like one or two, or ten?'

'Three. Now stop interrogating me.'

'So I'll just tell Steve to cancel the minibus and the B team game, then.'

I groan.

'You. Are. Manipulating. Me.'

'It's fine, they can rearrange… They'll probably be able to fit it in next year sometime.'

'I'll do it Michael,' I explode. 'Now leave me alone.'

'Thanks Jen, I knew I could count on you.'

My afternoon lesson with Year 8 flies past with no visitors. At the end of the day, Michael escorts me to the yard and gives me the keys to the hired minibus– presumably so I can't run off and abscond.

'Thanks, Jen, you're a star,' Steve shouts to me from the other bus.

I give a reluctant wave and then start the bus. It's a sign of how desperate Michael is that he's volunteered me to drive it again.

Prestfield is our main rival school. It's on the other side of the city, and it was built at around the same time as Whidlock: again, a masterpiece of 1960s architecture. But it does have a lot more field space than us, because whereas our school is in the middle of a residential area, their site backs on to countryside.

The drive is –mercifully– short, and the hired bus is much newer than our own, so the ride feels smoother. Michael even lets go of the dashboard.

The rugby team piles out and heads towards the pitch.

'Shall we go to get a drink?' Michael asks.

'Okay, I saw a snack van in the layby back there,' I hop down from the driver's side.

'A snack van?' Michael repeats.

'Yes. You can buy me a bacon roll and a cup of tea.'

The sky is shrouded in grey cloud, with weak sun rays breaking through. I've got my winter coat, hat, scarf and gloves, and Michael's got a coat over his usual suit. We sit on the wobbly, stainless steel chairs as traffic zooms past, steam from the drinks rising under our noses.

'You know, you ate a ham roll at lunch, so maybe you ought to vary your diet a bit more?' he comments, as I bite into the bacon roll.

'I don't care.'

This is his big chance to apologise, to make it up to me, and he decides to berate my choice of snack van food?

'What kind of school is Prestfield?'

I give a sardonic laugh.

'It's a lot worse than Whidlock, if that's what you mean.'

'Why?'

'Four heads in four years. Poor results. Challenging catchment area. The list goes on.'

'Right.'

He seems deep in thought. It's clearly not on his radar that we might need to talk. I sigh and drink my tea.

'Shall we head back to the game?' he asks.

That was it? That was our quality time?

We walk back to Prestfield in silence. I've finished my roll and I'm savouring the dregs of my tea. The last thing I want to do is stand on a muddy field and be a bystander to the banter of the P.E. boys.

'I'm going to stay in the bus and get a few things done,' I announce.

'Oh, right,' he looks torn. 'I probably should go and see Steve…'

'Yes,' I reply. 'Yes, you should.'

My anger at Michael is possibly only surpassed by Katie's. We rant down the phone to each other and I don't reply to his text: Are you okay? No, Michael, I am not okay, and if you can't work out why, then you are severely lacking in emotional intelligence.

I break my silence on the WC chat too. He's gone too far.

Me: I have a date now for the job interview. And Michael is being very frustrating so I am not really speaking to him.

Clare: What's he doing? And when's the interview?

Me: Next week. He dropped me off at Dad's after our time away, then barely contacted me for the rest of the week.

Deena: Is he ghosting you?

Me: No. He tried to speak to me today. But he doesn't get it. I want someone who's going to be there for me, not disappear.

Clare: Has he got cold feet or is he just busy?

Me: He's always busy. But you make time for people you care about, don't you?

Deena: Of course!

Clare: Some guys don't, though. They compartmentalise.

Me: Well, he signed me up to drive the rugby bus so we could 'spend some time together'.

The ensuing barrage of emojis say it all.

I need to stay focused for this inspection. Throughout Wednesday morning, I still have no visitors… including Michael. With Year 9, I'm well into the lesson when I notice a scrap of paper on my desk. Picking it up, I see my address scrawled on it in untidy handwriting: Flat 2b, Harcourt Way. That's it: no message. I look around at my class.

'Did anyone leave a note on my desk?' I ask.

They all look confused and shake their heads.

'Are you okay, Miss?' Victoria, a girl sitting at the front of the class, asks.

'Fine,' I say automatically. 'Carry on, everyone.'

I finish the lesson and put the note in my bag. I put on my coat – I need a walk to clear my head. As I head towards the school gates, I pass Tyler and his crew, playing basketball.

'Hi Miss,' Tyler says, too loud to be polite and with an insolent grin. 'I'm going to Harcourt Way tonight, have you ever been there?'

I quicken my pace. I don't want him to think he's scared me, so I wave my hand in the air dismissively.

'Not now Tyler, I've got things to do.'

It was him. But what does it mean? Is the note a threat? What should I do?

My head foggier than before, I step out of the school gates and follow the footpath. The trees are looking bare and the air is cold, but it's dry. I can smell the pine trees. Stupidly, it reminds me of Michael's after-shave.

I breathe in and wish that things were different. I miss him like a deep soul ache, and it hurts so much that he doesn't seem to feel the same.

I walk a quick circuit but I can't unwind. There's too many questions buzzing in my head, and I have no idea what to do about Tyler. As I approach the gates again, I spot two of my mentor group girls. One of them is crying.

'Maizie, what's wrong?'

Maizie is definitely a memorable pupil. She's a girl who looks a lot younger than she is, like she should still be in primary school. She's a little overweight and always out of breath. She has bright ginger curls that bounce as she speaks, and her front teeth protrude not unlike a rabbit's.

'Mith Baker,' she stutters with a lisp. 'A boy's being nathty to me and stole my bag, and he's hidden it and I don't know where he's put it.'

'He said he should have been given Maizie's place on the trip,' Emily, the other girl, tells me.

It must be Tyler.

'Right.' I march towards the yard.

Tyler is bouncing a basketball with Ollie and Sam, looking complacent. Here he is, this entitled child, and he's picking on a girl from my mentor group who's clearly got enough problems in life without him making it worse for her.

'Where is Maizie's bag?' I demand.

Tyler shrugs and grins at Ollie.

'I haven't got time to waste here,' I speak sharply. 'Last chance Tyler, before I go to your Head of Year.'

'I don't know what you're talking about,' he says, avoiding my gaze and continuing to pass the basketball.

'Your choice then,' I snap, and head to the staff room.

Eventually, I find the Head of Year, Matt Myers, who's a stocky rugby player and incurs instant fear in the boys, and Maizie's bag is retrieved. The bell rings, and I realise I now have to teach Tyler's class. I rush back to the classroom, and an inspector is waiting for me.

'So sorry, I got held up in an incident,' I explain breathlessly as I hastily show her a seat, log back onto my computer, and welcome in the boys who are waiting.

Tyler is nowhere to be seen.

Inwardly railing at the appalling luck of being observed for the one lesson where I am late, I try to sail ahead anyway with the topic.

'Today we're looking at the features of a newspaper article.'

I've placed some broadsheets out on the desks. The boys who are present – and there's still a few missing– start looking through and making a list of features. I take the register and wonder if I should make a call to the office about the missing students. Just as I am about to lift up the phone, Tyler saunters in with his friends. The inspector scribbles down a note, and I can feel her looking expectantly at me to deal with this appropriately.

'You're late, boys,' I say, trying to keep my tone friendly, but the hard edge seeps through.

'Mr Myers was speaking to us,' Tyler's eyes flash with anger, blaming me.

'It might be good to leave other students' bags alone then,' I retort. 'Sit down then, boys, and join in our activity.'

As I feel my anger simmering, I move away from Tyler to speak to some of the more responsive boys, who are actually doing the task. But I can see Tyler is deliberately taking a very long time to sit down, moving his chair and then swapping it for another (identical) one, then keeping his coat on and zipped up, and I can see him chatting to the boys on his desk without even opening his exercise book.

'Coats off, please.' I project my voice as airily as possible. Don't mention his name. Don't turn it into a confrontation. 'Ollie, what have you found out about newspaper features?'

Before he can open his mouth, I hear Tyler say something that sounds like 'Don't answer.' Ollie gives a grin and says,

'I don't know.'

'OK, Spencer, then.'

Spencer makes eye contact with Tyler, who shakes his head slightly.

'I don't know either,' he says.

'Well, you've all been looking at a newspaper so you must have noticed something,' I say, trying not to get cross but failing.

'I lost interest when I saw there was no page 3,' Tyler mutters, loud enough so everyone can hear, and the boys start sniggering.

I feel my cheeks turning red. This means war.

'Tyler, what do we call the main title on the front of the newspaper?'

'I don't know, Miss.'

'It's a headline,' I say, knowing that he knows this and determined to make a point. 'Say it again for me, what is the main title called?'

'Sorry, Miss, I don't think I heard you the first time.'

He mocks a yawn. The boys snigger more loudly.

I have to just move on, and get through the lesson. At every possible point, if Tyler can make it difficult for me, he does. When they come to a writing task, he puts his hand up.

'Yes, Tyler?'

'I don't have a pen.'

'Would you like to ask me if you can borrow one?'

'Can I have a pen?' he asks in an equally rude, abrupt manner.

I open my drawer, find a pen, and walk right up to his desk.

'I'm giving you a warning now, Tyler,' I say in a low tone. 'You need to think carefully about your behaviour.'

'You need to think about yours too, Miss,' he mutters in a biting tone.

I hesitate. Ordinarily I would send him to work in another room at this point. But I have an inspector in the class and I don't want to send him to Michael. I swallow my anger and move on to another desk.

My goal for the rest of the lesson is not to cry in front of the class.

Somehow, I limp through the rest of it and the bell finally goes. Although then, I'm facing the inspector, and I'm dreading it like an axe about to fall.

She's about Janet's age, smartly dressed in a pinstripe suit. She looks at me with concern in her eyes once the last pupil has gone.

'Are you all right?' she begins, and it's so unexpected, and I'm so exhausted, that I burst into tears.

'I'm sorry,' I say, brushing tears away awkwardly. 'This is not very professional.'

'Please sit down,' she takes my arm and guides me into a chair.

She waits for me as I cough and sniffle.

'You prepared a good lesson,' she says. 'You are dealing with some very difficult individuals in this class. Are they usually like this?'

I nod, still brushing tears with the back of my hand.

'There was an incident at lunch,' I manage to say. 'He got into trouble and he obviously resents me for it.'

I don't mention the note.

'I'd say there was a lot of aggression evident. In fact, I'd say that this is a form of harassment, and I'm sorry to say it ties in with a culture of misogyny that I have observed in this school.'

I'm gobsmacked to hear her say this, and all I can do is nod dumbly.

'I am going to raise this with David,' she says firmly. 'Please don't feel you have done anything wrong, but I'd like you to come with me.'

27

David's office is very… corporate. He's sitting behind a desk and indicates for us to sit at a board table with large chairs around it. His suit is a sharp cut, charcoal grey, and his hair is immaculately in place as always. I can feel him staring at me, evaluating my red eyes, though I've done my best to clean myself up and calm down.

'Jen, is something wrong?' He speaks as though he is a caring headteacher and we have these kind of conversations regularly.

'I just observed Miss Baker with the Year 11 boys' class,' the inspector says. 'I'm very concerned by what I witnessed. They are harassing her.'

He raises his eyebrows and then looks at me. 'Yes, I've heard that you've been having some problems with the boys' group.'

It's clear what he's trying to say. I'm having problems with the group; no one else is. Therefore the problem is me.

'This group is also taught by Michael Chase, one of our lead practitioners,' David addresses the inspector. 'Perhaps we can arrange some team-teaching, to offer Jen some more support.'

I glower at him.

'I have a meeting now,' the inspector stands to leave, 'but I want to see that this has been dealt with appropriately, David.'

With a pointed look at him, she walks out. David and I lock stares.

'Tyler Cots has found out where I live and is threatening to come to my flat.'

His fixed expression wavers, and he blinks. I win the stare contest.

'When did he make this threat?'

'This afternoon.'

I hand him the paper note.

'This is your address?' David asks, examining the scrap. 'How did he find it?'

'He saw me get off a bus outside my flat. He didn't see me go in, but he must have found out which one is mine.'

'When you say he threatened to come to your flat, when did he do this?'

'Earlier on, he made a comment to me in the yard.'

David asks for what he said, the exact words. I repeat it for him. He stares at the note again.

'Can you prove that he wrote this note?'

'I think it is highly likely, given the comment he made on the yard.'

'Perhaps this is just an unfortunate coincidence.' He makes a gesture as if to say 'these threats, they just seem to happen'. He'd take a different attitude if it was his address.

'I don't think so.' My tone is getting more abrupt. 'Shall I call the Police?'

David winces.

'That would be a bit difficult…'

'Why?' I press. 'You can't stop me calling them.'

'No,' he concedes. 'Maybe I should speak to Matt Myers…'

'Am I meant to go home and wait for Tyler to turn up on my doorstep? What do I do then?' my voice is rising and I can feel my eyes burning again. Don't cry. Don't cry.

'If he does actually turn up,' David doesn't sound convinced, 'then you can call the Police, naturally.'

I shake my head.

'I hope you can at least punish him. At the very least, a suspension.'

'This isn't a great time for that,' David looks annoyed.

'Don't you understand how stressful this is for me?' Dammit, my voice cracks. I'm hoping my anger will make my tears evaporate. My face is hot enough to emit steam anyway.

'Maybe you should take a few days off to recover, then.'

David has a glint in his eye. I know what he's saying. If I take a few days off, I'll miss the HoD interviews.

He pretends to look away at his screen with an air of nonchalance. Typical: he blanks me when I arrive because I remind him of an inconvenient moment in his career when he was just starting out and not at the top of the tree. He makes inappropriate comments to me, just to unsettle me, along with his thinly veiled threats and manipulations. He wants Michael at his beck and call, so he tries to split us up. Now that I need him to do something, he's playing it cool, as though he has nothing to lose.

'I'm not backing out of the job application,' I say with gritted teeth.

David shrugs.

'Hopefully you're not too traumatised then,' he leans back in his chair. 'But then again, perhaps you want Michael to give you the sympathy card so that he does exactly what you want.'

Blinded by tears, I stumble out into the corridor, nearly bumping into someone.

'Jen, what's wrong?'

It's Michael.

'Just coming to give your daily report, were you?' I sneer, my usual sharp delivery somewhat ruined by my snotty nose.

He reaches out to me but I draw back, stepping away.

'Don't!' I'm fuelled by a new wave of pure rage. 'Just because I'm crying, you're here to rescue me again? It feels like you want me to be an emotional wreck, so that you can be the strong one.'

I am barely thinking what I am saying, but as the words ring in the air, I realise they have landed. Michael looks like I've just punched him in the gut.

'I don't need you,' I enunciate venomously. 'Stay away from me.'

It's a killing blow, but as I walk out, my victory feels hollow.

In my flat later, I'm trying to focus on my lesson plan and interview notes. But I've read the same sentence six times and I'm not taking anything in. The reality is, I'm sitting tensely on my sofa, looking at the clock every five minutes, waiting for Tyler, and possibly a few drug dealers, to turn up.

Michael tried to call. I didn't answer.

Katie sends a 'good luck for tomorrow' text. I reply:

Tyler knows my address. I think he may come here tonight.

It takes about thirty seconds before my phone starts ringing.

'Hi Katie.'

'What the Thomas Jefferson are you doing?'

'Just waiting to see if Tyler turns up. I told David and he wouldn't do anything. He's just going to use this against me in the interview tomorrow.'

'You're not playing Poirot, Jen,' she says crossly. 'Why don't you just call the Police?'

'That's what I'm going to do, *if* he turns up.'

The sound of voices in the street carries over and I stand at the edge of the window, peeking through the curtain.

'Looks like a fight is starting.'

I can see a tall boy in his late teens, with two other boys with him, shouting at someone.

'Told you not to live near the shops.'

Suddenly, the tall boy grabs him and pulls him up roughly, twisting him to the side. I can see the kid's face clearly under the orange glow of the lamp post.

'Miss Baker!' he shouts. He's calling me for help.

'It's Tyler,' I blurt to Katie. 'Gotta go.'

I hang up and my fingers tremble as I call the Police.

After I've made the call, I hear Tyler call my name again. The fear and pain in his voice cuts my heart; I can't sit here while he gets attacked. He needs me.

I run out into the street.

'Stop!' I shout.

Two of the boys run off, leaving two holding Tyler.

'You're not *our* teacher,' one of them scoffs.

'I just want to speak to Tyler.'

I'm so aware of how precarious this situation is, but I need to keep him safe. I can see Tyler's face. He looks so young and fragile; it makes it almost funny to think I was sitting in my flat, scared of him turning up.

'Come on, Tyler, let's go inside the chip shop,' I say, ignoring the other boys.

'Go!' someone shouts from behind me.

The two boys drop Tyler and sprint off. He steadies himself and avoids my gaze.

'Come on,' I say. 'Let's go into the chip shop.'

I've never been so glad of the bright strip lighting and Sam's presence. The shop has a queue of customers so I usher Tyler to sit in the waiting area. I just want him to look at me so we can have a proper conversation.

'Tyler.'

He looks resigned to whatever I'm going to say.

'Are you in trouble with those boys?'

His eyes shift and he doesn't say anything for a moment.

'If you tell me, I might be able to help.'

He shakes his head.

'Did you leave a note on my desk?'

He finally looks at me.

'I wanted to warn you–'

At that moment, two Police officers step into the chip shop. Tyler jumps up.

'You called them!' he accuses.

'You looked like you were in trouble.'

'We'd just like to speak to you for a moment,' one officer says.

'Is there a back room we could use?' the other officer asks Sam.

They escort Tyler through the side door behind the counter. For a painful moment, I remember Michael's enthusiasm when we were away to dive into restraining a criminal. If he was here, he would be trying to involve himself as much as possible. Before I can linger on the mix of emotions this provokes, another two officers arrive. I turn and walk towards the door, but I don't want to leave Tyler.

'I made the call,' I tell them.

'Do you want to take us to your flat?' the officer asks.

As I lead them, my mind races to reinterpret the scenario.

'I think I got this all wrong,' I say. 'He said he was trying to warn me.'

'Warn you? About what?'

'I don't know. I don't think he's done anything wrong.'

Then I stop in my tracks. The door to my flat is open.

The officers enter first and beckon me in after doing a quick sweep. I step inside tentatively, looking all around the room for any signs of movement, but everything is quiet and still.

'It doesn't look disturbed,' the officer comments.

I assess the room, and it's as we left it. Except for one thing.

'My laptop's gone.'

My interview is tomorrow and I have no laptop.

I sink onto a chair. I'm numb and I can vaguely hear the officer asking,

'Is there someone you can call?'

It's that moment when I think of Michael that I start to cry. I'm single again, the one item of value in my slummy flat has been stolen, and this is not how I wanted my life to be.

'Jen!'

My dad bursts through the door.

'What's going on?' he asks, looking from me to the Police officers.

'Are you a relation?' the officer asks.

'Yes, that's my daughter.'

My heart swells to hear these words. For the first time in years, my dad sits next to me and wraps his arms around me. All the distance, all the pain, is suddenly burnt up in this, this feeling of being held, of being someone's daughter. I didn't even know I had lost it.

'Katie rang me,' he says. 'What happened?'

I stutter through an account of the evening, while an officer takes notes. The other one sweeps the flat for fingerprints.

'Is this a security camera?' he asks.

'Yes,' I answer. At least I have something to thank Michael for.

I overhear snatches of conversation on the Police radios as the other officers feed back information from Tyler.

'They wanted your student to steal your laptop,' the female officer tells me. 'When he refused, they started beating him up to create a diversion.'

'I fell for it,' I brush my tears out of my face and blow my nose for the sixth time. 'I just wanted them to stop hurting him.'

'You did what you could,' she reassures me. 'You put yourself at risk to help him. That was brave.'

'When he called my name, I just…' the tears well up again, 'I just wanted to take him home and make sure he was safe.'

'We're going to get him home and speak to his family,' she says. 'You just need to contact your insurance and we'll keep you updated if we find your laptop. I think you will need a new one, though.'

'Thank you very much for your help,' my dad says, showing them to the door. He walks back and looks at me. 'What do you want to do now?'

It's a simple question, and I'm surprised at how clear the answer forms in my head before I speak it.

'I want to come home.'

28

An hour later, we're sitting at my dad's kitchen table with Katie present via my phone screen, propped up in the middle by the salt and pepper. I'm on my second cup of tea –Dad has made a pot, so I can keep refilling and topping up. There is also a packet of chocolate biscuits which I am steadily consuming.

'I can't believe Clark did nothing when you told him about the note,' Katie shakes her head. 'You can't let him get away with this, Jen.'

'You could take this to the governors, you know,' Dad chips in. 'At the end of the day, it's his responsibility to look after the welfare of his staff.'

'I'm supposed to be interviewed tomorrow,' I remind them. 'How am I going to tackle David about gross negligence when he's meant to be assessing my competence at potentially leading a department?'

'I'm sure if you just explain what happened…' Dad begins.

'But if I pull out of the interview, David will just give the job to Michael.'

'He can't do that,' Katie says flatly.

'He's David Clark. He'll find a way to use it as a sign of my mental instability or something like that.'

'So what, you're just going to go in and do the interview like nothing's happened?' Katie folds her arms sceptically.

'What about your laptop?' Dad asks. 'Wasn't your work on there?'

'I've got everything on my email or in the cloud.' Another thing to be thankful for.

I chew another biscuit thoughtfully. Who could help? Who would understand?

'I've got an idea,' I say.

As Dad drives me to work in the morning, I reflect that this is the Friday of the longest week of my life. But I'm feeling surprisingly chipper. As much as it sucks to have my laptop stolen, I am slightly comforted by the fact that Tyler wasn't going to slide a death threat under my door. I can't even feel angry at him, because I can still clearly see in my mind his expression when the boy was hauling him around and threatening him. I just hope he's all right.

I check my reflection in the window. I'm wearing my pineapple shirt with pride today. My make-up provides a helpful layer to cover up any lingering signs of emotional trauma from yesterday, but it was amazing how much a hot bath and a good night's sleep made me feel ready to take on the world again. I take a selfie and post it on the WC chat.

Me: Wish me luck for today!

Deena: You look AWESOME! Go get em.

Clare: Go for it, Jen! You've got this.

I read their messages and smile. I don't believe I am going to get this job, but I have decided this: David Clark is not going to ignore me anymore.

And secondly, I'm going to enjoy every minute of it.

When I walk into the building, the first place I head to is Janet Patchell's office. I'm in early, and she is sitting at her desk, sipping coffee.

'Jen,' she smiles when I stand in the open doorway. 'Are you all set for today?'

'Nearly,' I reply. 'But I do need your help. My laptop was stolen last night so I need to borrow one, if that's okay.'

'Stolen?' Janet repeats, springing up out of her chair. 'Oh no, Jen, that sounds horrendous. What happened?'

I look behind me and then shut the door.

'One of my Year 11 boys was involved,' I explain. 'He left a note to me yesterday and I showed it to David, but David didn't think it required any immediate action.'

The expression on her face changes. She understands exactly what I mean.

'I see,' she says, pursing her lips. 'Why don't you take a seat and I will make you a drink, and then you can tell me everything.'

I sit in a comfortable chair on the other side of her desk and watch as she grabs two mugs and a kettle in the corner of her room. It's a small and cosy office with a green fern by the window. I notice photographs of her family– it looks like her children are in their late teens. Janet must be in her early fifties, and today she's wearing a dove grey suit, immaculate as always. She is someone who embodies the gold standard, and I love her for it.

'I teach the boys' group once a week. Tyler Cots has been particularly challenging. I wouldn't give him the spare space on the trip to Blood Brothers, and yesterday he sabotaged my lesson when the inspector was observing me. He made comments to me about my address, and then last night, he was outside my flat. There were other kids with him. They were hitting him and he called my name for help.'

Janet hands me a mug of tea and sits down herself, her eyes wide as she hears the story.

'I went out to try and intervene. While I was outside, two other kids stole my laptop. I called the Police and they spoke to Tyler. They think I will need to claim from my insurance to buy a new laptop.'

'Don't worry about that,' Janet says immediately. 'I'll find something for you.'

'The Police said that they wanted Tyler to steal the laptop, but he wouldn't, which is why they started fighting. I'm really concerned about what he's become involved with.'

My throat chokes up, and I gulp down some hot tea.

'This is a lot to take in,' Janet comments, frowning in concern. 'Jen, I'm so sorry about what happened. It must have been very frightening.'

'It's hard because I live alone,' I explain, determined to say what I feel without holding back. 'And I feel so angry that David knew something could happen, but he brushed it off as nothing. He made me feel stupid for being afraid.'

'You're not stupid, Jen,' she says. 'He may not have been able to prevent something from happening, but he shouldn't have dismissed it. I'm so sorry.'

Just having someone who's on my side, who understands, brings a wave of relief. I drink more tea.

'Do you want me to postpone the interview?' Janet asks.

I shake my head.

'I just… don't want to give David any more ammunition against me,' my voice shakes slightly. 'And I want to get it over with. I know I'm not going to get it anyway.'

'You don't know that,' Janet corrects me. 'You can't write yourself off, Jen. You have a strong application.'

'Michael is better than me.'

It's the drumming mantra that's been in my head since the first day of term, but this is the first time I've said those words out loud.

'He's *different* to you,' Janet says. 'It's not the same thing.' She appraises me frankly. 'It's none of my business, but I thought I would ask you… Are you two seeing each other?'

I blush, feeling all the awkwardness of the situation.

'David… said we shouldn't.' I avoid giving a direct answer.

Janet sighs.

'He can't control the personal lives of his staff,' she says. 'As long as your behaviour in school remains professional, he has no reason to complain.'

I'm encouraged that she hasn't backed David's viewpoint. If only Michael was the same.

'I just want to be taken seriously,' I say. 'Why is it so hard?'

'Things are much better now than twenty years ago,' Janet says. 'Far from perfect, but we don't give up. We keep pressing forward, and we refuse to accept the status quo.'

'You're amazing, Janet,' I say. 'I want to be just like you.'

She smiles.

'Then you'd better get ready for this interview. But first, we're going to see David.'

'David?' Janet pushes the door into his office, with me directly behind her.

David looks up from his desk, more tired and lacking in composure than I've seen before.

'Janet, I'm afraid I have a meeting in just a minute–'

'Cancel it,' Janet snaps.

David reassesses his options, taking in the two of us.

'Is this about the interview?' Then his expression changes. 'Did something happen?'

Janet gives me a nod.

'Tyler was outside my flat last night,' I say, noting with satisfaction the colour draining from David's face. 'Some older boys were threatening him. I called the Police and went out to help him. While I was outside, they went into my flat and stole my laptop.'

I'm oddly strengthened by the fact that David looks worse than I do. He swears and presses one hand to his forehead.

'Luckily,' Janet says, clearly furious at his reaction, 'Jen wasn't hurt, even though this situation put her at great personal risk.'

'Yes of course,' David says quickly. 'I'm very glad that you are … unharmed.'

Probably because I can't sue him.

'The Police may want to come here today to speak to us,' Janet continues. 'It might be prudent to think about how we can move forward with Tyler, given that he knows Jen's address. We don't want this to be an ongoing situation.'

David's eyes slide from Janet to me. His expression says 'what's all the fuss about?' He says nothing.

'I think we should talk to Matt, as Tyler's Head of Year,' Janet says. 'We should also log this as a safeguarding issue.'

'Yes,' says David, but his face says 'no'. 'I can cancel your interview today; you've clearly been through a lot.'

He looks at me: a challenge.

'I want to continue with my interview,' I state.

'You look… upset,' he says. 'I wouldn't want you to be at a disadvantage.'

'I know there will be a governor present,' I watch as he sets his mouth in a thin, hard line. 'I would quite like the opportunity to discuss your response to the note on my desk yesterday, given how matters have developed.'

'Don't let this get personal,' David says, licking his lips nervously.

'Personal?' I repeat. 'It got personal when a student left a note with my address on my desk, and you did nothing about it.'

'I'm not the Police,' David tells me, like I'm an idiot.

'You're the Head of this school,' I can't help raising my voice. 'Anything to do with safeguarding, anything to do with staff welfare… Ultimately, the buck stops with you. And I think you know that.'

Janet folds her arms and nods in agreement.

'Are you threatening me?' David's voice is soft and dangerous.

'I'm telling you that you have a duty of care in this situation, whether you like it or not.'

The phone rings.

'Yes?' David snaps as he picks up the receiver. He looks at us. 'Fine. Can you find Matt and send him up here too please?'

He replaces the phone.

'The Police are here.'

I don't know how, but news travels faster than the speed of light in a school. By 9am, when I enter the staff room, Steph has heard about the Police and gives me a crushing hug.

'Jen, what happened?'

Thankfully most teachers have left for lessons by now, but I notice Michael is sitting on the other side of the room. I give Steph a brief update and he jumps up in agitation, moving towards us.

'What was that?' he says, just as Janet enters and hands me a brand-new laptop.

'Thank you,' I take it gratefully.

'Her laptop was stolen,' Steph tells him, glaring.

He looks visibly shocked. Actually, as I turn to face him, I notice that he doesn't look his usual suave self. His face is pale. Perhaps he hasn't been sleeping well.

'Now, can I just speak to you both briefly about arrangements for today?' Janet addresses Michael and me.

'I'll catch up with you later,' Steph says, leaving and making a face at Michael's back as she goes.

Janet hands us both a timetable for the day.

'We're going to start with the lesson observation. Then we'll give you a set of data which we want you to analyse and present your findings to the panel, followed by interview questions. Good luck!'

Once she's gone, it's just the two of us left in the staff room.

'Jen,' Michael says, discarding the timetable. His voice sounds raspy and hoarse. 'Are you okay? What happened to your laptop?'

'It's a long story,' I say. 'I need to get myself set up with this, ready to teach.'

'Can I help you?' He looks desperate.

'Well, there is one thing…' I say, the beginnings of a smile playing upon my lips. 'I would really love a cup of tea.'

He blinks at me for a second, then grins.

'I think I can do that.'

While Michael's in the kitchen, I set up all of my documents on the laptop ready for the imminent lesson. Breathe, Jen. It's just a lesson. You do this every day.

He brings me tea in the *Wuthering Heights* mug –which means he even knows my secret hiding place.

'Thanks,' I say.

He sits down next to me and takes a deep breath. I watch expectantly.

'You know when Heathcliff is separated from Cathy, he feels tortured, like nothing will ever be right again? That's how I feel right now. About you.'

This must be the deepest thing anyone's ever said to me. I didn't think Michael did tortured love. There's some Heathcliff in him after all.

I'm just about to open my mouth to try to frame a reply – although I have no idea what to say– when Janet enters again.

'Okay Michael, we're ready to start your lesson.'

He gives me a lingering look, and his eyes are swirling dark cloud and misty fog, spellbinding… And then he stands up to follow Janet.

'Michael,' I finally manage to speak. He looks back over his shoulder. I smile. 'Good luck.'

By the time it's my turn for the lesson, I feel a nervous, fluttering anticipation, but not in an overwhelming, I-can't-think-straight way. I've had time to look over my plan, and I'm confident in the content of the lesson. I'm playing to my strengths.

When Janet escorts me to the classroom, a hand-picked small group of Year 9 students are there waiting. They're not pupils I teach. It's only a thirty minute slot, so it's a truncated exercise, but I follow the plan and they seem really engaged.

'Everyone pick an object and you have two minutes to write imaginatively, using the object as a starting point.'

I can see them all writing and then when we have a discussion time, they share their ideas.

'Work with a partner now to discuss where your story could go next.'

Geoff is writing notes at the back. I'm buzzing with energy: I know what I'm teaching, I know it works, and I know what the students are going to learn from it.

'Now I want you to use highlighters to start to edit your work. Find words that you think you need to improve; see if you can spot any mistakes.'

The students pore over their own work, then they swap with a partner, and finally we're on to the plenary.

Thirty minutes has flown by. I take in the papers and thank the class, then Janet meets me at the door and walks back to the staffroom with me.

'How did it go?'

'I was really happy with it.'

'Great,' she says. 'I'm going to take you up to my office now, so you can look at the data.'

It's funny being back in Janet's office for the second time in one day.

'I'm aware that both you and Michael teach the boys' group in Year 11,' she says. 'There are many of our key marginal students in that group, on the borderline between passing and failing. This data is of their most recent assessment performance. I'd like you to identify which students need extra support because they are not progressing as they should be, and create an intervention plan for them.'

She tells me she'll be back in about an hour, and I start looking through the spreadsheet. Well, it certainly helps that I know the students. I start pulling out names of boys who are underachieving, and start scribbling notes. I wonder how Michael's getting on, and my stomach flips when I remember what he said in the staff room, but I can't let myself get distracted.

It feels like no time at all, and Janet's back.

'Are you ready, Jen?' she asks. 'It's time for your interview.'

29

David's office is bad enough with just David in it, but now there's a table full of people with folders and notepads. David, Janet, Geoff, and someone who must be a governor. I clutch my papers nervously and try not to freak out.

'Thank you for coming today, Jennifer,' David says, though his face doesn't agree. 'We'd like to start by hearing your analysis of the boys' group data.'

I explain my findings, tentatively at first, but then as I talk about these students I know, I forget this is an interview and I just share my thoughts honestly about them. Which ones are lacking motivation, which ones need genuine support, and which ones could raise their achievement to a grade C by the time they sit the exam in May.

'Tyler is a key example here,' I say. 'I think we need to contact his parents and see what his home situation is like. If we can prioritise our students' welfare and pastoral needs, this will have a direct effect on their attainment. They will see that the school doesn't just see them as another grade, but as a person, an individual who matters.'

The panel is making notes and I can see some of them nodding. The questions begin.

'Can you explain to us what you feel you would bring to this role?' David asks. I can't miss the sense of underlying sarcasm but I ignore it.

'I realise this is an important role with a heavy weight of responsibility, particularly when it comes to our achievement as a school,' I begin carefully. 'Our grades need to be the best they can be. I don't want to compromise on that. But I also believe that a good Head of Department needs personality and energy; they need to get their staff on side, and work collaboratively as a team to achieve the best results. We don't want to be an exam factory; we want to use our creativity.'

I explain my idea for the creative writing festival, and talk about the writing club and giving students space to reflect and develop their own writing, whether it's a grisly horror scene or a wildly implausible car chase through New York.

'I want students to love English as much as I do.'

It seems to be going really well. Then David starts a new question, and I can see from his face that it's not going to be an easy one.

'What do you feel are your weaknesses? For example, when you teach the boys' group… Have you ever had any issues with discipline?'

It's a cheap shot, and he knows it.

'I've certainly found the boys' group a challenge,' I say. 'It doesn't help that I teach them after lunch, in the last lesson of the day, towards the end of the week. But I don't give up with groups like that. It just takes time to win them over. I plan my lessons carefully. I have high expectations. I keep showing them that they can't get away with a lack of effort. Gradually, I'm starting to see them respond.'

'Your trip to see Blood Brothers was very successful,' Geoff chips in. 'That must have helped to build more of a relationship with that group, along with your mentor group, who are really exceeding their targets this year.'

Thank you, Geoff.

'I think that's all we've got time for,' Janet looks at her watch. 'Thank you, Jen.'

Now it's just a waiting game.

I return to the staff room, look for my lunch bag in the kitchen, then realise I forgot to bring lunch today. Ah well.

'Jen.' Michael hovers in the doorway, nervously running a hand through his dishevelled hair. His eyes dart back and forth to check we're alone. 'How did it go?'

'I think it went okay,' I nod. 'I couldn't have done any better.'

'That's great,' he says hurriedly, nodding too.

'How about you?' I ask.

I'm not used to being the one who's composed.

'Could have been better,' he says, inclining his head. 'I don't think Janet likes me very much. She kept firing awkward questions at me.'

I try to hide a smirk. Looks like Janet wasn't going to let David get away with grilling me and going easy on Michael.

'After my interview, I saw Matt Myers. He told me what happened.'

Michael's eyes are wide, appealing to me. He crosses the space between us.

'I should have been there for you. I could have helped you.'

I sigh and shake my head.

'When will you just figure it out, Michael? I don't want you to *help* me. I want you to *love* me.'

Did I just say that out loud? I clear my throat to clarify swiftly,

'Or at least, feel something for me the same way I feel about you.'

'Jen, my feelings for you haven't changed,' he moves towards me and tries to take me into his arms. This is what he always does when I am upset. I raise my hands as a barrier.

'How can you say that you like me and then not speak to me?'

'I wanted to protect you…' He trails off, reluctant to say more. I glare at him expectantly. He sighs. 'I know David doesn't want us to be together. He wants to give me the HoD job and with the situation the school's in right now, he's got to be three moves ahead of the authority.'

I stare at his shifting eyes, the flush on his cheeks.

'There's something you're not telling me.'

I keep staring. What is it? What is it, Michael?

'Did he tell you something at the golf club?' I prompt.

Michael looks at the door, then back at me.

'I'll tell you everything, on one condition.'

'What?'

'You come out for dinner with me.'

Unbelievable.

'It had better be good,' I say.

His posture sags with relief.

'I haven't lost you forever then,' he says.

It's a joke-but-not-a-joke kind of comment. Then Janet appears in the doorway.

'Can you both come up to David's office, please?'

I try to read her expression but she's impenetrable. We follow her and she pauses outside the door.

'Michael, you go in first. Jen, wait here and he'll call you in.'

With a last look at me, Michael pushes open the door. Janet walks off and I stand there, hoping this isn't going to take ages.

Michael's got it. I always knew he'd get it. I just don't want David to be even more of an annoying idiot than usual about it.

Just then, Tyler appears. He looks startled to see me.

'Are you okay, Tyler?'

He recovers and gives a small smile.

'Yeah, thanks Miss.' He stands there for a moment. 'I'm sorry about your laptop, Miss.'

'Don't worry about it,' I reply. 'It wasn't your fault.'

He nods and shuffles off towards his Head of Year's office. At least it was a chance to break the ice.

'Jen, do you want to come in?'

Michael's appeared again at the door, and he's beckoning me in.

I step inside and David indicates for me to sit at the table, next to Michael.

'I would like to congratulate both of you. You have performed extremely well today.'

I raise my eyebrows and look sideways at Michael.

'Jen, I've offered Michael the Head of Department role. But the panel was very impressed with you. We are advertising the Additional Needs co-ordinator role and we would be very keen for you to apply. You wouldn't need to do the lesson observation again; just the interview.'

'I think I'd like to apply,' I say, looking at Michael. His jaw is set and I don't quite know what he's thinking.

David pushes some papers towards him.

'Now, if you would just sign this contract…'

'I have a few things I would like to clarify first,' Michael says, in a steely tone.

Do I really need to be here for this?

'Maybe I should leave you to discuss this.' I stand hastily.

'Please Jen,' Michael appeals to me. 'I would really like you to stay.'

Holding his gaze, I sink back into the chair.

'First of all,' Michael begins, with the air of a lawyer about to present his case in court. 'I would like you to examine this photograph.'

He produces a photo and places it on the desk. I peer at it: it's me with some friends, in Sixth Form, packing up some Christmas hampers. A younger David Clark is standing next to us.

'Kevin dug this out,' he says in explanation. He's a senior teacher. 'I don't know if you remember this, David?'

David looks at it, and his jaw moves slightly. He looks at me.

'Perhaps I do,' he says.

'Then maybe you were mistaken when you said you didn't remember teaching Jen.'

I gape at Michael. He's supposed to be signing his contract and cracking open the champagne, not going at loggerheads with David.

'I'm sorry,' David says finally, holding out his hands.

'And when you showed Jen that text on your phone in the nightclub, that wasn't about her, was it? It was actually about Liz,' Michael says. 'You've been trying to keep us apart.'

'I was merely concerned…'

'No,' Michael cuts him off. 'We have given you no cause for concern in our conduct whatsoever. If you try to interfere in our personal lives again, I'm going to the governors.'

'All right, you've made your point,' David says sulkily.

Michael picks up the contract.

'I'm taking this away to examine the terms, and I'll see you first thing Monday morning to let you know if I accept.'

Now David and I are both gaping at him.

'Are you ready to leave, Jen?' he speaks softly to me.

All I can do is nod. I'm still speechless as Michael takes my hand and leads me to the staffroom.

'Do you want to collect your things, then we can go?' he says.

I look at my watch: two- thirty.

'We can't leave,' I protest. 'The bell hasn't even gone yet.'

'The interview is finished and our classes are covered,' Michael shrugs. 'Why do we need to stay?'

I open my mouth to protest about staff policies, but it's been the week to end all weeks so why not? I grab my new laptop and my bag.

'Let's go then.'

We head outside to Michael's car, the staff car park full up with vehicles. Joseph Vermont is donning a high-vis jacket for bus duty. I flash him a (slightly guilty) smile and enjoy his look of surprise at me climbing into Michael's car. And I realise: I don't really care.

'Have a nice day, Vermont,' I drawl, even though he can't hear me.

Michael laughs and starts the engine. I message Dad, Katie and the girls: I didn't get the job, but they want me to apply for a different role. Just going out for dinner with Michael. I lean back and catch him smiling at me. His eyes are warm now, smouldering and smoky grey...

Even though he's been a complete idiot, I still like him.

'Where do you want to go?' he asks.

'The Three Blackbirds.'

It's tucked away, on the edge of the countryside, and it's straightforward. I can't deal with anything complicated right now. I'm going to order lasagne and a lemonade, and then I'm going to figure out exactly what's going on between me and Michael.

'You were playing hard ball back there with David,' I say.

'I realised you were right about him,' he replies. 'I should have listened to you from the beginning. I'm sorry.'

'Tell me what happened at the golf club.'

He nods.

'Whidlock had a building inspection last month. There's several serious issues and David thinks something might blow up any minute.'

'What do you mean?'

It's an old building, but surely it's not that bad.

'There are a ton of health and safety hazards all across the site,' Michael continues. 'David's worried that if something happens, he could be personally liable.'

'Well, it might do him good to get sued.'

'He is getting sued.'

I sit up in surprise.

'What?'

'A teacher from our previous school is suing him for unfair dismissal.'

'Let me guess: it's a woman.'

'Yes.'

'That's why the inspector said to me about a culture of misogyny then,' I muse. It's all starting to make sense.

'What was that?' he asks.

'The inspector came to observe me with Tyler's class. They were… particularly challenging that day. She told me that she felt the boys' behaviour was part of a wider picture of misogyny in the whole school.'

'I bet that went down well with David,' Michael raises an eyebrow.

'He tried to punish me by not doing anything about Tyler when I showed him the note he left on my desk.'

'Wait, what are you talking about?' Michael swerves the car slightly as he looks intently at me.

'Focus on the road please!' I joke. It's like me driving the minibus all over again. 'I thought you knew the full story.'

'Tell me,' he says.

When I explain about the note and what happened with David, his knuckles turn white.

'I'm pulling over,' he says, driving into the same layby, appropriately, that has the snack van by Prestfield school. I'd comment but he doesn't look as though he'd appreciate it right now. He turns the engine off and runs his hand through his hair.

'You're telling me that Tyler had your address, made comments that he was going to turn up at your flat, and you told David but he did *nothing?*'

His voice is pure, blind fury.

'I thought you knew,' I repeat.

'I don't know how I'm going to see him again without killing him.'

'Michael,' I lay my hand on his arm. 'The school is aware of the situation now. I'm okay.'

'But what if something had happened–' as he looks at me, his voice breaks off. His eyes are glazed with… tears? Is Michael Chase *crying?* 'Jen, if anything happened to you…'

I feel my own eyes well up.

'I'm a bit obsessed with you,' he says.

I reach up and brush a tear from his cheek.

'I'm a bit obsessed with you too.'

We both laugh.

'But Michael,' I clear my throat. 'Why did you freeze me out? It felt like I meant nothing to you.'

'Sorry, I'm not doing a very good job of explaining,' he says. 'So Whidlock had bad news from the building inspection, and the authority told David their plan. They want to merge Whidlock with Prestfield. On Prestfield's site.'

Ironically, we are within viewing distance of Prestfield's ugly block buildings. The kids are streaming out of the gates now, a Friday afternoon unstoppable tidal wave.

Suddenly our little visit to Prestfield for the rugby fixture makes sense. He obviously wanted to suss it out. I wish he'd just told me why.

'The authority will sell the Whidlock site for development…' he continues.

'And give the kids a shiny new uniform and say they're 'raising standards',' I roll my eyes cynically.

'And there will be redundancies,' Michael says. This is it, the bombshell he's been hiding.

'How many?'

'I don't know. They'll offer early retirement packages, that sort of thing. But Jen, I knew that David had no idea what an amazing teacher you are. He told me if we continued to see each other, he would be putting you first in line for the chop. I just wanted to take a step back, give him nothing to hold against you, and let you show him how fantastic you are in this whole interview process, and then he'll never be able to justify letting you go.'

He takes hold of my hands in his own.

'I thought I could wait for a week or two, and it wouldn't be that hard. But I was stuck up a mountain in the rain the night after the golf club and all I could think about was you. I can never justify letting you go, either. When we were back in school, I wanted to tell you everything, and I wanted to be there for you, but I felt that I was putting your job on the line and that it would be selfish to do that. I could see I was hurting you but I couldn't see a way out.'

He squeezes my hands tightly.

'I wished I had known about that note so I could have been there with you last night, then you wouldn't have been alone.'

'What would you have done, joined in the punch-up?' I joke. 'Listen, Michael. If this,' I go back to using the gestures that he used right on the first evening we spent together, 'is going to be a relationship, then it can't be based on you being the rescuer. I'm sorry but I want to be your equal. I want to be friends. I don't want to feel that I'm only interesting when you get to bail me out.'

'You're interesting to me every day,' he says, brushing my cheek. 'Whether it's a pineapple day, or a trip day, or a job interview day… And I'd say 'interesting' is a rather weak adjective to describe my feelings for you.'

'Here you go again, always have to go one better.'

'Captivating, maybe. Scintillating.'

I pull him down to kiss me before he says anything else.

The kiss is long and sweet, like summer and rain both at the same time.

'You know, Jen, this was never about me rescuing you,' he murmurs. 'It was always about you rescuing me.'

30

In a cosy corner of the quiet pub, our drinks arrive and I take a long sip of lemonade, enjoying the cool fizz on my tongue.

I love Fridays.

I love Friday dates with Michael Chase. May this be the second of many. I hold up my glass to toast him.

'Congratulations on your promotion.'

He looks unsure as he chinks his glass with mine.

'I'm sorry you didn't get it,' he says apologetically.

'Michael, I *knew* you were going to get it,' I laugh. 'It's not your fault that you're practical, efficient, data-focused, and marvellous at Excel.'

'Don't joke about it, Jen,' he takes my hand. 'You must care a lot about it.'

I look into his guilt-ridden eyes. I think back to my conversation with Steph. I think over this whole 'inspection' week.

'I care about doing my job well,' I say. 'I care about not being overlooked or pushed around. But to be honest, my main motivation for going for the HoD role was so that you didn't get it uncontested. Now that I know you a bit better, I don't think I would hate being in your department as much as I thought I would before.'

Michael blinks.

'So… the main reason you applied for this job was because you don't like me?'

'That pretty much sums it up.'

'I'm not sure what to say to that,' he sips his drink.

'I don't dislike you now… as much.' I raise an eyebrow.

'That feels a slight regression from you being obsessed with me.'

'Love and hate are on the same scale,' I shrug. 'Anyway, at least I got to work on my novel while you were AWOL.'

'Really?' he looks at me with interest. 'Can I read some more then?'

'If you like.'

'Was your story backed up then?'

'It's in the cloud,' I wave my hand to gesture. 'I should also tell you that I'm moving back in with my dad. He said he'd put me on his car insurance so I can drive again.'

'I thought it was for society's benefit that you didn't drive too often,' Michael says, wincing. 'Anyway, I've booked that County certificate test so next time we run a trip, *I* will be driving.'

'I can't believe with all this going on you've still managed to organise that.'

'If I'm stressed, I do admin. Though I have to admit, I don't want to look at my laptop this weekend. At all.'

'I'll drink to that,' I say.

'What did the Police say about your laptop?' he asks.

'The chances of getting it back are slim,' I reply. 'If those guys were stealing it to buy drugs, or something, it's probably miles away by now.'

'Do you think they'll catch them?'

'I hope so, more for Tyler's sake than mine.'

'Are you going to keep teaching the boys' group?' He must still feel guilty about that.

'Yes,' I smile. 'Tyler doesn't scare me any more.'

'I think he should be very grateful that you've been so gracious to him.'

'He's just a kid.' I think about him with sadness. I really hope as a school we can help him. 'What are your plans for the weekend?'

'I don't really have any,' he answers. 'All I want to do is see you.'

I smile. Now that's more like it.

The weekend passes in a happy blur. Michael takes me home and meets my dad. Later on, I video call Deena and Clare to fill them in— it's way too complicated to text. They're still cautious, but they're coming round to the idea that Michael's not so bad after all. On Saturday, Katie gets the train home and we all clear my flat, taking bags and bags of junk to the tip. Michael's machine-like efficiency proves very useful sometimes, when channelled correctly.

When the flat is bare, I expect to feel a sense of sadness… but actually I just feel relief. I needed *mental* headspace from Dad, not physical distance, but I was too stressed to see the difference.

'You won't miss this place, surely?' Michael jokes, examining my wistful expression.

'No,' I sigh. 'I think I moved here because I found it hard to live at home… being reminded of my mum all the time. But the grief follows you. There's no quick fix for it.'

He crosses the room to put his arms around me.

'Makes sense.'

'Group hug!' Katie shouts, barrelling into both of us.

I catch Michael's eye and smile. I love my sister.

Later, we enjoy a take-away all together, and I would never have expected this three months ago. As I look at Michael squabbling with Katie about the correct way to use chopsticks, and Dad more lively in conversation than he has been for years, it feels like the hole in our family is finally healing. I can't erase Mum, and I don't want to. I want to make the most of the people I'm privileged to have in my life.

That includes school, too.

My first priority on Monday is to find Steph and fill her in.

'I didn't get the job, and you were right: I didn't actually want it,' I tell her. 'Thank you for being honest with me, even though I didn't listen to you.'

'Don't be silly, Jen.' She gives me a standard Steph-hug: obliterating the oxygen capacity of my lungs. 'Now tell me what's going on with…'

She looks towards Michael, who is hovering at the kitchen door, waiting for me.

'We're back together,' I say in a low tone, smiling. 'He's apologised for ignoring me. Plus I think he dislikes David as much as I do now.'

'He's finally seen the light,' she says. 'I'm happy for you.'

Michael brandishes my mug and I nod.

'Just going to make tea,' I say.

I think the kitchen may be my favourite place in the whole school now. Michael and I make our drinks side by side, just like we've done so many times before, but this time, we're not trying to kill each other. In unison, we grab our mugs and head for my classroom.

'Which classes have you got today?' he asks, looking at my timetable on the wall. Colour coded, of course.

'Year 7, Year 8… Oh and I'm meant to be starting the writing club today.'

I remembered to bring cake, and at lunch I have a small group of 5 students for the club. As we sit, eat cake, and do some short bursts of two-minute creative writing, I am freshly reminded that I love my job. I'm not going to let passive-aggressive headteachers or local drug dealers take that away from me.

'Right, time's up everyone,' I say. 'Let's hear what you've written.'

They're all really shy but one or two of them share, and then the bell goes so they gather their things to leave. Beatrice hovers at my desk.

'Are you okay?' I ask.

She holds out a piece of paper.

'I just wanted to show you.'

I take it and read:

The clock ticks. I know that sound well. It's always five minutes fast on your mantelpiece.

I love the smell of your velvet curtains, and the musty tinge of your living room.

Now that you're gone, your clock is on my bedroom shelf. It keeps ticking.

I look up and her eyes are filled with tears.

'This is beautiful,' I say.

'It's about my grandad.'

The rawness of grief shoots to my heart and my eyes swim too. It's like it goes straight to the wound of losing my mum. The arrow never fails to reach the same spot.

'I think he would be very proud of you.'

I give her the page back.

'Miss, can we come in?' My mentor group is waiting at the door.

'Yes,' I call, and give Beatrice a smile. 'Sorry I can't talk for longer. But you have real talent. Thank you for sharing what you wrote.'

'I've never written about that before,' she says. 'Thank you, Miss.'

As she leaves, I wipe my eyes absently as the mentor group rolls in and bustle about getting their books.

'What are we doing today, Miss?' Connor asks.

'Please say something fun,' Lacey adds.

I sigh.

'How about some story writing?'

31

The pub has a roaring fire and wooden beams running along the walls and the ceiling. I'm sitting at the table with Michael, Dad and Katie, enjoying the best Sunday lunch I've ever eaten, celebrating my appointment as the new Additional Learning Needs co-ordinator.

No one else applied for the role. The more I looked into what the job description entailed, the more I felt convinced that it was the right next step for me. It wasn't nearly so much of a struggle to write my application (plus I had Michael at my shoulder reminding me of different examples of where I helped or supported students, and also adjusting my wording).

'You should be an editor,' I comment, then have a brainwave. 'You could help edit my book!'

'Sure,' he agreed.

While I went through another week of preparing for an interview, he was working through my story document at lightning pace. I would expect nothing less from him by now. On the day of my interview, when I was waiting nervously in the staff room to hear the outcome from the panel, he kept me distracted by discussing Alice's character arc and whether a dagger in the boot was a more effective weapon than seizing a sword from an unwitting soldier.

When Janet called me back into the interview room, she gave me a reassuring smile. David cleared his throat.

'We would be delighted to offer you the position, Jen,' he said.

'Thank you,' I said calmly. 'I would be happy to accept it.'

It was only outside the room that I gave a silent cheer, fist-pumping the air. Before I could launch into my victory dance, complete with invisible maracas, Michael scooped me up into his arms.

'I knew you'd be amazing. Well done.'

Janet emerged from the room and cleared her throat to get our attention.

'Congratulations, Jen,' she said, extending her hand to me.

I took it and then hugged her suddenly, before I over-thought it.

'Thanks for everything, Janet,' I said, pulling back.

'I'm so proud of you,' she replied, her eyes misty.

That was a sweet moment.

I smile at the memory, look around the table at my family, and conclude that my faith has been restored in humanity. Take that, David Clark.

'I can't eat another bite!' Katie groans, pushing her chair back. 'Can you get promoted every week?'

'I don't intend to go for any more promotions any time soon,' I smile at Michael. 'I think it would finish me off.'

'How's your story coming along?' she asks.

'Getting there,' I reply. 'Michael just finished going through it this morning.'

'It's brilliant,' Michael says, giving me one of his warm smiles. 'Wonderland will never be the same for me again. I'll always be looking for silent assassins.'

'I'm hoping to pick up some tips from Judy's writer friend when she comes in for the Writing Festival,' I say. I'm proud that it's going ahead.

'I hate to break it to you, but Jen's been using your room as a writing space,' Dad tells Katie.

'Oh, I see,' she says in mock-annoyance. 'Well, just as long as you clear out when I come to stay.'

'It'll be Christmas before you know it,' Dad says, and we all groan.

'I can't even think about next week, let alone December,' I say, although Deena and Clare are already planning how they can meet Michael when they're staying in Whidlock over Christmas, so we've already booked an obligatory meet up.

'Well, now that you two are together,' Katie waves her hand between Michael and me, 'I expect you to actually have more of a social life. That includes you, Michael. I think you're both workaholics and you need some kind of therapy to help you through.'

'Thanks for the life lessons, little sis,' I poke her in the ribs. 'I'll bear that in mind.'

'A toast,' Katie says, raising her glass. 'To Sunday lunch, and not working too hard.'

We clink our glasses.

'I'll drink to that,' I grin.

Later, Michael takes me outside Whidlock, to a hill looking down on the town. Wrapped up in my stole with Sylvia's sheepskin gloves, the night air feels cold but not sharp. We climb to the viewpoint, guided by Michael's torch, and look down at the sprawling suburbs. A few fireworks shoot bright colours into the sky from one of the estates.

'Bit late for Bonfire Night,' Michael comments.

'This is probably the first dry night we've had all week,' I remind him. 'Anyway, it's romantic.'

'I thought we might try and see some stars,' he says, looking up into the sky.

It's not as clear as when we were in Sylvia's garden, but as I keep looking, more and more tiny pinpricks of light become visible.

'They were there all along,' I say, tucking my hand under Michael's arm. 'I just didn't stop and give enough time to notice them.'

We stand, enjoying the richness of the quiet and the feeling of a billion possibilities stretched out over our heads.

'You know, I've been thinking about *Wuthering Heights*,' Michael says.

'Random,' I reply.

'That quote on the mug I bought you: "Whatever our souls are made of–"'

'"His and mine are the same,"' I finish.

'I don't know if I would apply that to you and me.'

'I don't know if I would apply any of *Wuthering Heights* to you and me.'

'Ah yes, what was it? The "unflinching portrayal of a destructive obsession"?'

'Sometimes I think you have a photographic memory.'

'It was something you said, not something I read.'

'Michael!'

'Sorry,' he grins. 'What I mean to say is that I feel like we're very different, not the same at all, but I wouldn't have it any other way.'

He pulls me closer and our lips meet, and it's the arguments, the banter, the quips, the cat ornament hide and seek, the theatre, the minibus, the nose injury, the date, the car park all coming together to lead us to this moment, right now, when everything is all right. I won't say perfect because it's a little too cold for that, and I'll probably fall over on our way back to the car. But it's *us*.

'Are you still a little bit obsessed with me?' I ask.

'More than a little,' Michael says, kissing me again. 'I'd say a LOT.'

'You know, saying you are "a lot" obsessed with me is really poor grammar,' I point out.

'I actually don't care,' Michael replies. 'Shall we go back to the car? I'm freezing.'

Who wants perfect anyway? What I've got is way better than that.

"Lastly, she pictured to herself… how she would keep, through all her riper years, the simple and loving heart of her childhood: and how she would… find a pleasure in all their simple joys"

Lewis Carroll, *Alice in Wonderland*

ACKNOWLEDGEMENTS

Huge thanks to Andy. Despite being bemused at my agonised sobbing when we watched La La Land ("I thought teaching was your dream!"), he has encouraged me to tell my stories. Thank you for reading many versions, advising me on What a Man Would Do so I can at least try to avoid female wish fulfilment, and for being my soulmate. Thank you as well for my amazing cover design!

Thanks to Megan and Joshua for being the best kids ever. I am so grateful to God for you. Thanks to Megs for all her help with marketing and book promo!

Thanks to my Mum, Rachael, the Orrs and Lindsay for being my first readers. Your help, patience and encouragement are second to none.

Thanks to Sandra, Krista, Danielle, Charlene, Allendra, Kathleen, Jessica, Janae, Patricia, Thimgan and any other writers from the Romance clan I've missed. Your feedback and smiley emojis helped me so much.

Thanks to my sensitivity readers, Kelsea and Stephanie. Your comments were so valuable. Thanks also to Anna, for mentoring me back in 2020, and for your input and positivity.

Thanks to my team of ARC readers, Bookstagrammers, and bloggers. You make such a huge difference to getting this book out into the world. Thank you!

Thanks to my colleagues. In each school I've worked at, I've been blessed with so many hilarious, kind and inspiring people surrounding me. Plus some wise and firm shoulders to cry on! Teaching is a tough gig, but we love it, and I hope you feel I have represented our profession accurately in this story.

Finally, I want to thank God for being the ultimate Creator and Author of all things. Your work is always perfect. Thank You for Jesus, the Word made flesh who dwelt among us, full of grace and truth. (John 1:14)

About the Author

Sophie Toovey is an English teacher and writer. She loves Jane Austen, and a good romcom by Mhairi McFarlane, Lindsey Kelk or Rachel Lynn Solomon.

Connect with Sophie
Sign up for news of future releases at sophietoovey.com
Listen to audio chapters for free on Youtube
Instagram @Sophie_Toovey
Twitter @SophieToovey
Tiktok @sophietoovey

Wedding Bell Time

When your marathon clashes with your marriage

When the Head introduces a no-dating policy for staff, Michael thinks he's found the perfect solution. He loves the beautiful and creative Jen, so cue an elaborate proposal with a castle, Pachelbel's Canon, and a treasure hunt with Jane Austen quotes. Three months is enough to plan a wedding, right? But when he realises that he's also supposed to be running a marathon to raise money for a student with cancer on the same day, even Michael begins to worry that he's taken on too much this time.

The plan:
Run the marathon
Get married
Make sure Jen never finds out

What could possibly go wrong?

Due for release in November 2023
Read on for a free excerpt

1

'It makes sense for me to drive; I'm the one who knows where we're going.' My girlfriend Jen jangles the keys of her dad's car and strides off towards the Ford Fiesta in the staff car park.

It makes sense for *me* to drive so that we arrive without injury or accident… But I don't say that out loud.

Instead, I sigh and follow Jen, and climb into the passenger seat. At least she's not driving a bus this time.

Jen adjusts the mirror slightly, starts the engine, and the radio blares out an inane autotuned song. I buckle up my seatbelt.

As the car pulls out of the school gates, narrowly missing a bollard on the left side, Jen revs and flies over a speed bump, whilst humming along to the song.

'Michael,' she says, cutting out of her humming, 'you don't have to hold the dashboard.'

I didn't even realise I was doing it. Survival instinct, I guess.

'Sorry.'

Jen drives in the way she generally approaches life: without much forward planning. She relishes the twists and turns that seem to crop up unexpectedly, although she insists she's driven this way a hundred times before. She isn't fazed by the multiple hazards: cyclist, cat, traffic lights, busy junction.

'You should sit back and enjoy the ride,' she says, jerking the car around a tight corner. My stomach lurches.

I like to be in control. A smooth, well-planned drive, arriving early to the destination. As Jen points out when we park in front of a brightly-coloured Primary school building, we are only two minutes late. Because we zoomed over several mini-roundabouts and took liberties with the red light.

'It was amber,' Jen argues.

It was red.

The first thing that strikes me is how small the school is compared to ours. Primaries are generally smaller than secondaries, and at Whidlock County, the high school where Jen and I work, we have almost a thousand students. This school probably holds four hundred five to eleven year-olds. I suppress a shudder.

'Jen, it's great to see you,' the receptionist smiles. It's the usual reaction to Jen. Her hair fizzes with dark curls, her eyes are like warm chocolate, and her skin is coffee-coloured silk. Today she's wearing a scarlet sweater and a black skirt that flares over her knees. I wish I could put her arm around her waist, but it wouldn't be professional.

'Hi Clare.' Jen knows everyone in this county. She grew up here, lived at home while she studied for her degree, and got her first teaching job in the school that she went to as a pupil. 'This is Michael.'

'Nice to meet you,' I nod.

As we sign in, I'm scanning every wall and trying to fight the rise of panic. It's all smiley faces, handprints, 'Working together, having fun' kind of motto. My worst nightmare.

'Sally's waiting for you, if you want to go on down,' the receptionist says.

Jen beckons me through the door with a giant tree painted over it. As I reach it, I see that each apple on the tree has a word like 'kindness' written on it.

Apparently, Jen has been running this Shakespeare project for a few years now. She goes into a local primary and helps them to put on a mini-Shakespeare play. We're both English teachers, and now that I'm Head of Department, I felt that I ought to see how this project worked. And I also agreed to come in a rash moment when Jen challenged me to get involved a few months ago.

I started at Whidlock in September, and in some ways it feels like a lifetime ago. Life before Jen, anyway. I met her on my first day, putting up a hideous cat poster in her bright orange classroom, and I had no idea what to make of her. The more time I spent with her, the more I wanted to get to know her. I've never been bored when I'm around Jen. That's good, because I'm a very boring person. I like my plain suits, my shirt-and-tie combos, and my black organiser. Neat, organised, but boring.

Somehow Jen agreed to be my girlfriend, and every day when we meet in the kitchen at work I half-expect her to break up with me.

It's November, and soon we will have been together for a month.

I've never had a girlfriend before. This is major.

Before I can reflect too much upon this milestone in my twenty-nine year-old life, Jen opens a classroom door and I am shocked at the sight of thirty ten-year-olds acting out a silent slow-mo sword fight with eerie synth music rippling through the air.

I almost grab Jen's arm. I'm not sure I can do this.

2

Michael looks as though he's going to bolt.

I give him what I hope is a firm but encouraging smile, and motion for him to step forward and lead the way to the front of the room. My friend Sally waves enthusiastically, as the two students in front of her try to execute one another with imaginary swords. The soundtrack is perfect, the strings building to a dramatic climax, and by this point many of the students are now lying on the floor, clutching injuries or dying a prolonged agonising death.

Sally stops the music and the students come back to life and face us.

'Fantastic work, everyone!' She claps her hands. 'Bradley, I really liked the way you reacted as Sam drove his sword into your side. Melody, try to slow down your movement as you fall to the ground. Maybe stretch out your hand, like you're trying to hold on to your last moments.'

She extends her arm with a desperate expression.

'Like that.'

I catch a glimpse of Michael's face. Still in shock.

'I'm so excited that Miss Baker and Mr Chase have joined us today!' Sally continues. 'I can't wait to show them what you've been working on.'

It's the battle at the end of Julius Caesar. At the front, Brutus, Cassius, Octavius and Antony take centre stage, with the rest of the class as soldiers behind them. They show us their whole performance from the beginning, an enthusiastic, if a little Samurai-inspired, rendition of the war. At the end, I clap and grin, and nudge Michael when he continues to stand there, open-mouthed.

'Break time,' Sally calls.

The class disperse, with one boy lingering behind.

'Do you want to see a trick?' he says to Michael.

Without waiting for an answer, he pulls out some cards and fans them in front of Michael, then flips one over to reveal an Ace, then makes it disappear again.

'That's fantastic!' I say, when it becomes apparent that Michael doesn't know how to respond.

'I'll just go and grab some drinks,' Sally says, leaving Michael and I alone in the classroom.

'Are you okay?' I ask, nudging him to break his trance.

'I don't know if I can do this,' he says.

'Of course you can,' I say. 'Just go with it! They're kids. They want to tell you things and show you stuff. It's cute. By the time they get to us, life has kicked that out of them.'

'I'm an English teacher,' Michael huffs. 'I don't do slow motion sword fights to synth music or card tricks.'

'Maybe you should,' I grin.

'It makes sense of why their literacy is so poor when they start Year 7,' Michael says gloomily, pointing to a board of 'key words'. 'Fiery is spelled wrong. All this 'two stars and a wish' feedback, and no one has highlighted any of the errors in these pieces of writing.'

'English isn't Sally's specialism,' I admit. 'But she does a great job of getting the kids excited about Shakespeare. She uses drama and music to engage their interest.'

Michael sighs.

'It's going to be a long day.'

Most teachers would enjoy the opportunity to be off timetable to visit a feeder primary school and help develop a play as a fun extra-curricular project. Michael, however, would prefer to teach the rules of direct speech to our Year 11 boys' group, who are challenging to say the least.

He perks up when we look at some of the famous speeches of the play with the group, and do more analytical activities on how to speak the lines, which words to emphasise. This is more familiar ground. But then it's time for a final run-through with the battle scene. By the time we are back in my car, ready to return, Michael leans back in the seat and closes his eyes. He doesn't even have the energy to hold the dashboard.

I smile to myself, enjoying a moment to stare at his clean-shaven face, his dark hair slightly ruffled and out of place over his pale forehead. My stomach gives a little skip. Michael doesn't know how attractive he is. I remember watching him teach for the first time, how magnetic he was at the front of the classroom.

He was definitely out of his comfort zone today.

At one point, I went to the bathroom and came back to discover him, back pressed against the wall, shrinking away from two students duelling. I snigger as I turn the key in the ignition, and the car comes to life. Maybe I should suggest an impromptu dinner date tonight, to help him recover from the trauma.

Then he opens his mouth and I quickly change my mind.

3

'What a waste of a day,' I groan, sinking my head back against the firm headrest, a headache blazing behind my left eye. 'I've got so much to do tonight.'

A few minutes pass before I register that Jen hasn't replied. I glance across at her, and her mouth is set in a firm line. She's looking straight ahead at the road.

'Is something wrong?'

Her eyes flick angrily to mine, her eyebrow raised slightly, and then she returns her attention to driving. It's the silent treatment again.

'What have I done wrong?' I ask in resignation. There is no figuring out in this situation.

'You haven't *done* anything,' Jen snaps. 'In fact, I'd say you had a pretty easy ride today.'

I blink.

'Today was many things, but it was *not* easy.'

'So, a very difficult waste of time then?'

Oh.

'I didn't mean it like that,' I sigh, rubbing my temples. I wish that actually worked in improving headaches.

'So what did you mean, then?'

The silence rings in the air, along with the pulsing thud in my head.

'Okay, it wasn't life-transforming. We didn't achieve any top grades or win accolades from the Royal Shakespeare Company. But just because something doesn't churn out data, doesn't make it a waste of time,' Jen says angrily, her cheeks beginning to flush.

I really don't feel up for an argument right now.

'I'm sorry,' I say, as genuinely as I can. 'It's not my strength, working with younger kids.'

'In a few years' time, those children will be sitting in front of you, and you will be trying to help them understand 'Romeo and Juliet'.' Jen violently strikes on the indicator and changes gear. 'Maybe they might remember putting on Julius Caesar in primary school, and think that Shakespeare might not be so bad after all.'

We swerve around a roundabout, gaining speed.

'The impact of this project may be hard to *quantify*,' she continues, as the car flings off the roundabout and into a side street. 'I believe it forms an important component of our transition work and builds a relationship with these pupils, which makes it easier for them when they move up to our school.'

'I'd rather they didn't remember me as the one who taught them to mime a battle with trippy music in the background.'

'They'll probably remember you as the uptight one who kept checking his watch and didn't want to be there.'

She seems to lose some of her rage at this point, sighing and thankfully taking her foot off the accelerator.

'It worries me, Michael,' she says, more carefully this time, 'that you're so obsessed with numbers and spreadsheets that you miss the bigger picture.'

Now it's my turn to raise my eyebrows.

'How is a bunch of primary kids acting out Julius Caesar in a way that is, at best, mediocre, the bigger picture?'

'That's exactly what I mean.' She pulls the car back through our school gates. 'You don't value it, because it's not a number.'

I don't know why she is so against numbers all of a sudden. Nice, predictable spreadsheets. You never have to argue with them.

The car rolls into a parking space and she switches off the engine. We sit there awkwardly for a moment.

'I was going to ask if you wanted to have dinner tonight,' she says, looking down at her hands in her lap. 'But it sounds like you're busy.'

My stomach twists. Yes, on the one hand, I love the idea of seeing her. Any time with Jen sparkles with excitement, even if it's just cooking spaghetti. But it makes everything so… complicated.

'I thought we agreed that we should only see each other at weekends,' I remind her.

Well, it was my idea. She did agree to it – perhaps a little reluctantly.

'Since we went away at half term, I've barely had any time alone with you,' Jen says. 'We've had some dates, and they've been lovely, but I was moving out of my flat and back into Dad's, then we were celebrating my promotion with my family, and now this weekend, you said you wanted us to meet up with your friends.'

My 'lawyer friends', as Jen refers to them. She's still slightly baffled that I studied Law as well as English at uni.

'I can cancel that if you want,' I say, a little too hopefully. I'm slightly dreading introducing Jen to them, because I know they will love her. If I mess things up –which is looking very likely right now– then I'll never hear the end of it.

'I'm not suggesting that,' she says, shaking her head. 'You barely have a social life as it is. I just mean, if we could see each other in the week as well, then it gives us more time together.'

'We do see each other every day in school,' I point out.

'Yes, but it's not exactly quality time, is it?'

As if to prove the point, the bell rings in the distance, and students start streaming past the car, talking loudly and some of them waving and shouting, 'Hi Sir!'

'I've stayed at yours before,' she says, continuing her argument, 'so why can't I just stay over again and come with you to school in the morning?'

'You know David's funny about it.'

Our Headteacher, David Clark, has made it clear that he doesn't want us to be in a relationship. If he hadn't promoted us both recently, I think we would be in a tenuous position, but he's being sued at the moment and has got bigger fish to fry than to plug the draining bath tub that is my love life.

The fact is, when Jen stayed at my house, it was an emergency. We weren't really *together* then. And, well, things have changed since then. If she wants to stay over, I don't think she means the guest room.

When I mentioned my love life, you might think the phrasing ironic, because I've never had sex before. And I'm not sure I'm ready to tell Jen the reason why.